Knights Club

The Alliance of Dragons

SHUKY · WALTCH · NOVY

QUIRK BOOKS
PHILADELPHIA

Originally published in France as
Chevaliers: Princesse Gargea in 2014 by Makaka Éditions.
Copyright © 2020 MAKAKA.
All rights reserved.

First published in the United States in 2020
by Quirk Productions, Inc.

Translation copyright © 2020 by Quirk Productions, Inc.

Library of Congress Cataloging in Publication Number:
2020901737

ISBN: 978-1-68369-195-2

Printed in China
Translated by Carol Klio Burrell
Cover design by Elissa Flanigan
Typeset in Sketchnote
Production management by John J. McGurk

Quirk Books
215 Church Street
Philadelphia, PA 19106
quirkbooks.com

10 9 8 7 6 5 4 3 2 1

ħalt!

THIS ISN'T A REGULAR COMIC BOOK!

In this comic book, you don't read straight through from first page to the last. Instead, you'll begin at the beginning and soon be off on a quest where you choose which panel to read next. You'll go on an adventure, answer riddles, solve puzzles, and face down mighty foes—because YOU are the main character!

It's easy to get the hang of it once you see it in action. Turn the page for an example of how this comic book plays like a game!

HOW TO PLAY COMIC QUESTS

1 Pick where you want to go—doors, paths, signs, and objects can all have numbers, so keep your eyes peeled!

100.
235
27

235.
157
219

2 Flip to the panel with the matching number.

219.
48
←235
49

3 Continue reading from there, making more choices as you go to complete the quest!

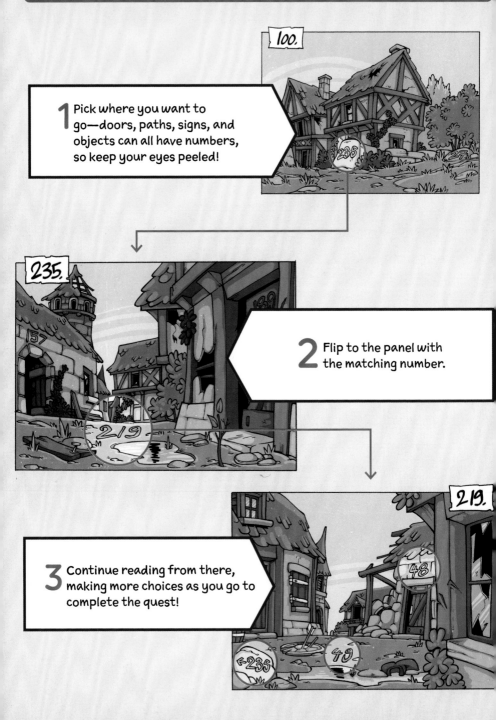

HOW TO PLAY COMIC QUESTS

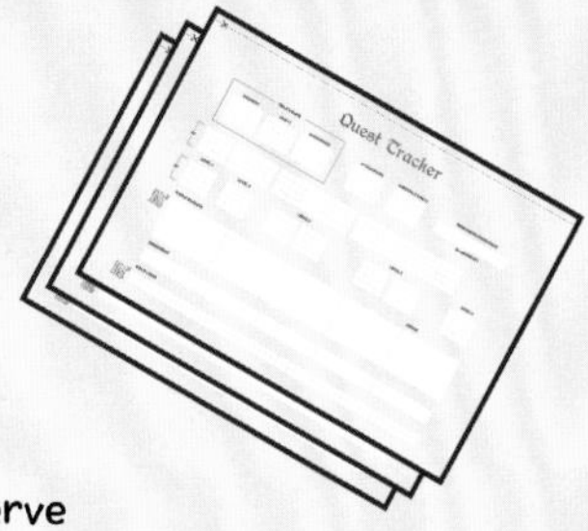
Quest Tracker

As you go, use the handy Quest Tracker sheets on the next few pages to log your progress. Use a pencil so you can erase. (You can also use a notebook and pencil, or download extra sheets at comicquests.com.)

THE RULES OF KNIGHTHOOD

While playing the game, be sure to follow these rules to preserve your honor.

Remain vigilant: Always examine your surroundings for hidden passages, objects, and people—they may be hard to spot.

Know your attack: Your weapon or your spell will have a certain number of attack points that you can keep track of on your Quest Tracker. If you get new weapons or spells, their points will wipe out and replace the ones you have, so choose wisely.

Stay true to your strengths: You may carry only as many objects as you have strength points. However, you can unload an object whenever you need to make room for a new one. Your main weapon, jewelry, armor, and clothes don't count against your strength points. Your purse can hold up to 98 gold pieces—but no more!

Keep track of your progress: Your Quest Tracker has squares to represent your Experience points (XP) and your Strike points (SP). When you have enough XP to level up, you'll gain the corresponding amount of SP for that level, and a special ability point you can use for strength, agility, or intelligence. Only a potion or leveling up will get you back your lost SP!

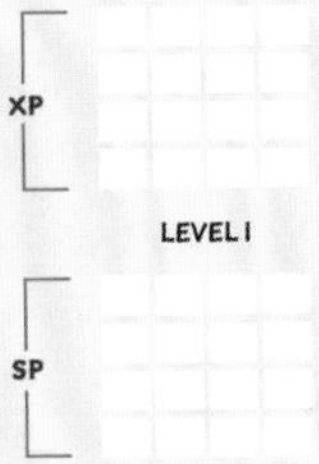
XP
LEVEL I
SP

Fight with honor: Use the combat wheel at the end of the book to fight enemies when they appear. The effectiveness of your attacks and spells will be determined by how you turn the wheel. Fight through the first battle in the beginning of the book to learn how combat works!

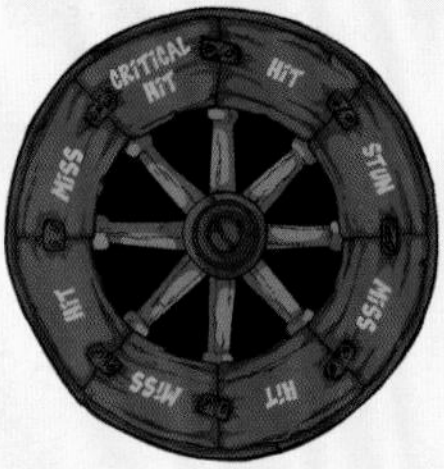
CRITICAL HIT
HIT
STUN
MISS
HIT
MISS
HIT
MISS

Collect magic cards: Throughout the kingdom are 20 types of magical cards that will give you a boost in battle. Check them off on your Quest Tracker as you acquire them.

GOOD LUCK! LET THE ADVENTURE BEGIN . . .

Quest Tracker

TRAIT POINTS

STRENGTH	AGILITY	INTELLIGENCE

ATTACK	RESISTANCE

CHARACTER NAME

(MAKE UP YOUR OWN NAME)

XP

LEVEL 1	LEVEL 2	LEVEL 3	LEVEL 4	LEVEL 5

SP

ITEMS IN YOUR PACK

NOTES

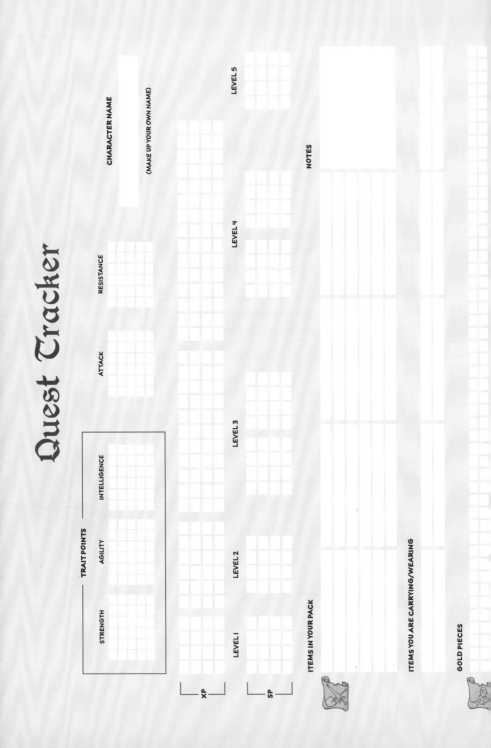

ITEMS YOU ARE CARRYING/WEARING

GOLD PIECES

Quest Tracker

TRAIT POINTS

STRENGTH	AGILITY	INTELLIGENCE	ATTACK	RESISTANCE

CHARACTER NAME

(MAKE UP YOUR OWN NAME)

XP

SP

LEVEL 1	LEVEL 2	LEVEL 3	LEVEL 4	LEVEL 5

ITEMS IN YOUR PACK

NOTES

ITEMS YOU ARE CARRYING/WEARING

GOLD PIECES

Quest Tracker

TRAIT POINTS

STRENGTH	AGILITY	INTELLIGENCE	ATTACK	RESISTANCE

CHARACTER NAME

(MAKE UP YOUR OWN NAME)

LEVEL I	LEVEL 2	LEVEL 3	LEVEL 4	LEVEL 5

XP

SP

ITEMS IN YOUR PACK

NOTES

ITEMS YOU ARE CARRYING/WEARING

GOLD PIECES

Quest Tracker

TRAIT POINTS

STRENGTH	AGILITY	INTELLIGENCE	ATTACK	RESISTANCE

CHARACTER NAME

(MAKE UP YOUR OWN NAME)

XP

SP

LEVEL 1

LEVEL 2

LEVEL 3

LEVEL 4

LEVEL 5

NOTES

ITEMS IN YOUR PACK

ITEMS YOU ARE CARRYING/WEARING

GOLD PIECES

Begin Your Quest!

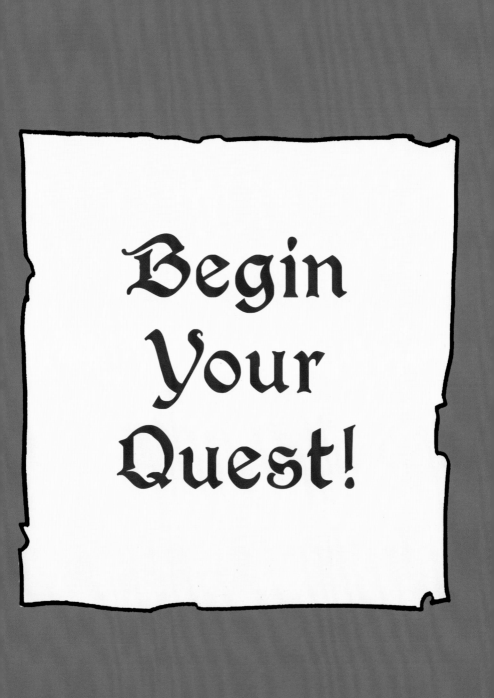

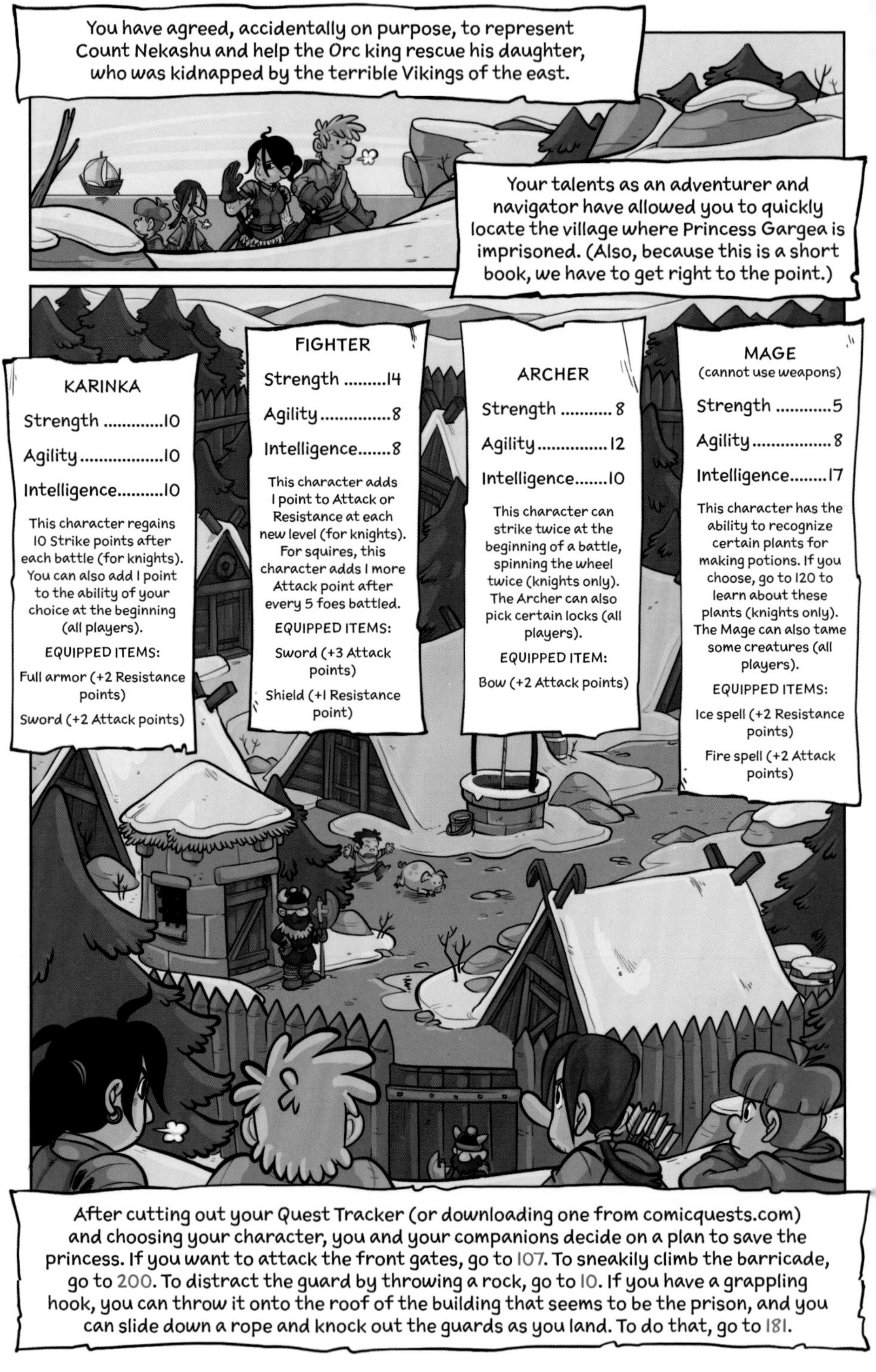
You have agreed, accidentally on purpose, to represent Count Nekashu and help the Orc king rescue his daughter, who was kidnapped by the terrible Vikings of the east.
Your talents as an adventurer and navigator have allowed you to quickly locate the village where Princess Gargea is imprisoned. (Also, because this is a short book, we have to get right to the point.)
KARINKA
Strength 10
Agility 10
Intelligence..........10
This character regains 10 Strike points after each battle (for knights). You can also add 1 point to the ability of your choice at the beginning (all players).
EQUIPPED ITEMS:
Full armor (+2 Resistance points)
Sword (+2 Attack points)
FIGHTER
Strength 14
Agility 8
Intelligence.......8
This character adds 1 point to Attack or Resistance at each new level (for knights). For squires, this character adds 1 more Attack point after every 5 foes battled.
EQUIPPED ITEMS:
Sword (+3 Attack points)
Shield (+1 Resistance point)
ARCHER
Strength 8
Agility 12
Intelligence.......10
This character can strike twice at the beginning of a battle, spinning the wheel twice (knights only). The Archer can also pick certain locks (all players).
EQUIPPED ITEM:
Bow (+2 Attack points)
MAGE
(cannot use weapons)
Strength 5
Agility 8
Intelligence........17
This character has the ability to recognize certain plants for making potions. If you choose, go to 120 to learn about these plants (knights only). The Mage can also tame some creatures (all players).
EQUIPPED ITEMS:
Ice spell (+2 Resistance points)
Fire spell (+2 Attack points)
After cutting out your Quest Tracker (or downloading one from comicquests.com) and choosing your character, you and your companions decide on a plan to save the princess. If you want to attack the front gates, go to 107. To sneakily climb the barricade, go to 200. To distract the guard by throwing a rock, go to 10. If you have a grappling hook, you can throw it onto the roof of the building that seems to be the prison, and you can slide down a rope and knock out the guards as you land. To do that, go to 181.

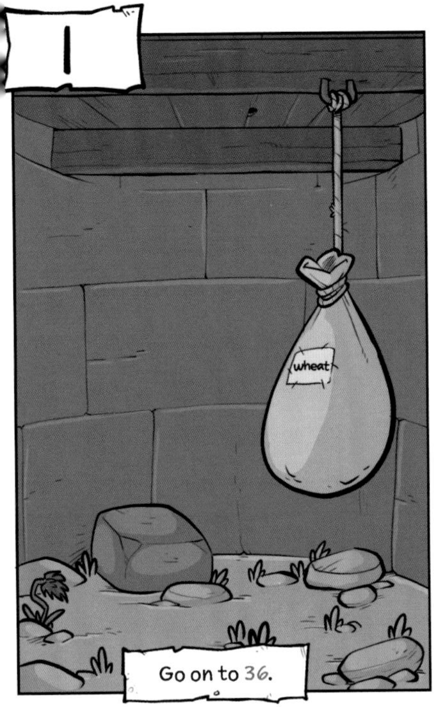
1
wheat
Go on to 36.

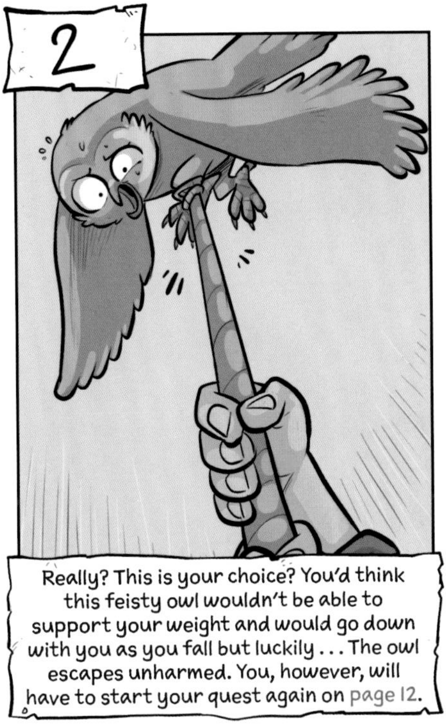
2
Really? This is your choice? You'd think this feisty owl wouldn't be able to support your weight and would go down with you as you fall but luckily . . . The owl escapes unharmed. You, however, will have to start your quest again on page 12.

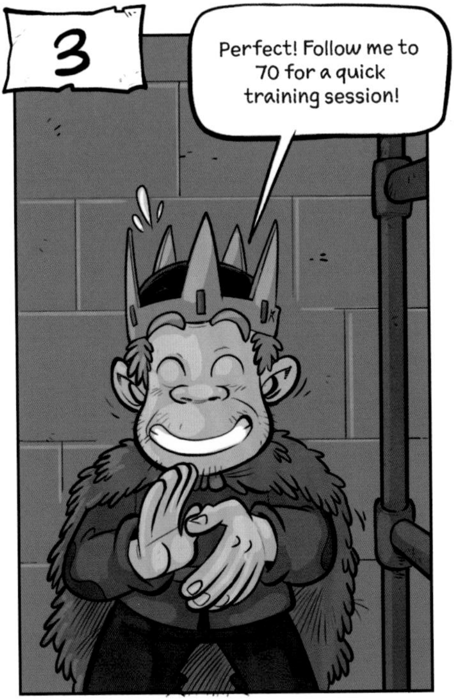
3
Perfect! Follow me to 70 for a quick training session!

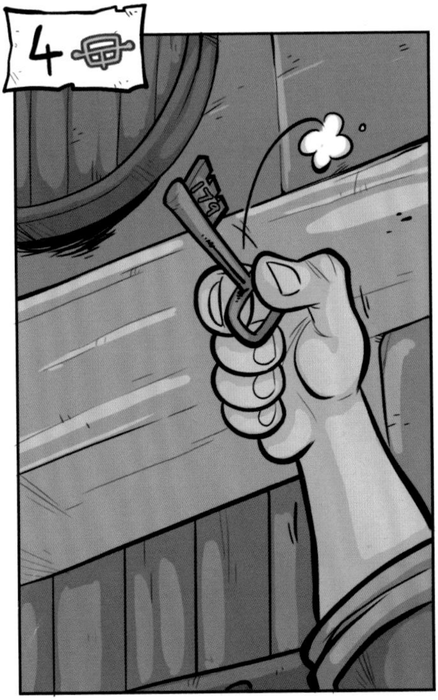
4

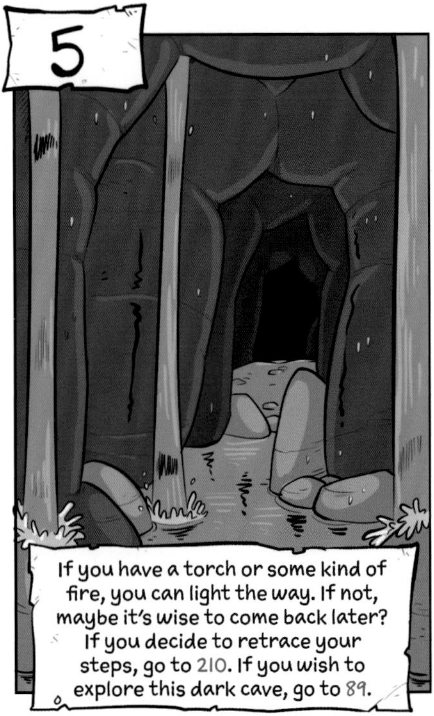
5
If you have a torch or some kind of fire, you can light the way. If not, maybe it's wise to come back later? If you decide to retrace your steps, go to 210. If you wish to explore this dark cave, go to 89.

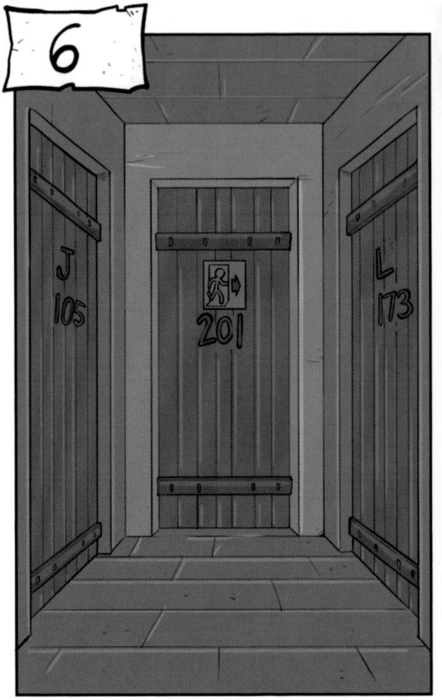
6
J
105
201
L
173

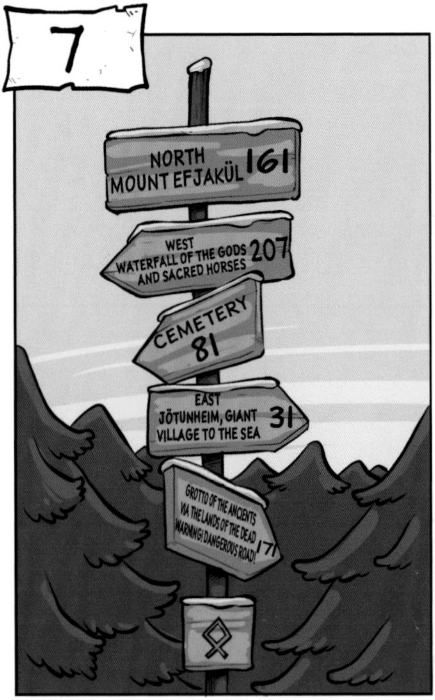
7
NORTH
MOUNT EFJAKÜL 161
WEST
WATERFALL OF THE GODS AND SACRED HORSES 207
CEMETERY
81
EAST
JÖTUNHEIM, GIANT VILLAGE TO THE SEA 31
GROTTO OF THE ANCIENTS VIA THE LANDS OF THE DEAD WARNING! DANGEROUS ROAD! 171

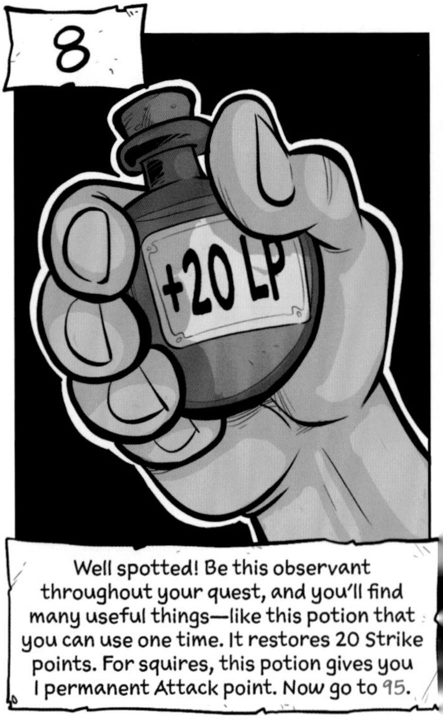
8
+20 LP
Well spotted! Be this observant throughout your quest, and you'll find many useful things—like this potion that you can use one time. It restores 20 Strike points. For squires, this potion gives you 1 permanent Attack point. Now go to 95.

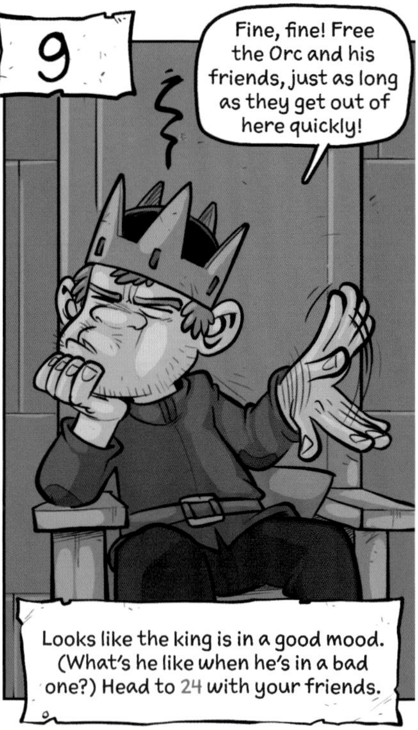
9
Fine, fine! Free the Orc and his friends, just as long as they get out of here quickly!
Looks like the king is in a good mood. (What's he like when he's in a bad one?) Head to 24 with your friends.

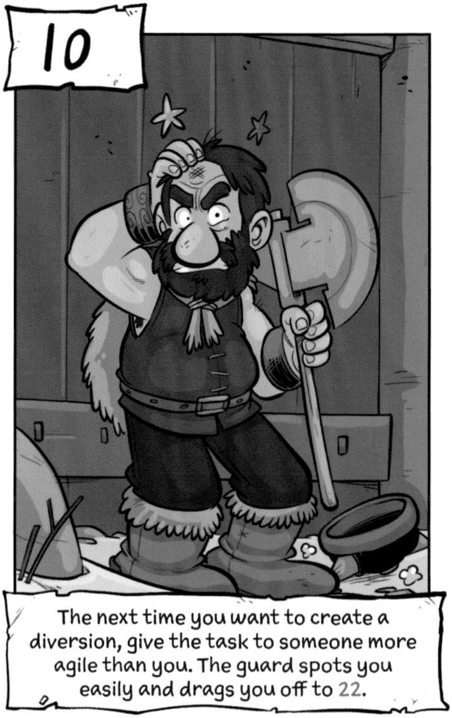
10
The next time you want to create a diversion, give the task to someone more agile than you. The guard spots you easily and drags you off to 22.

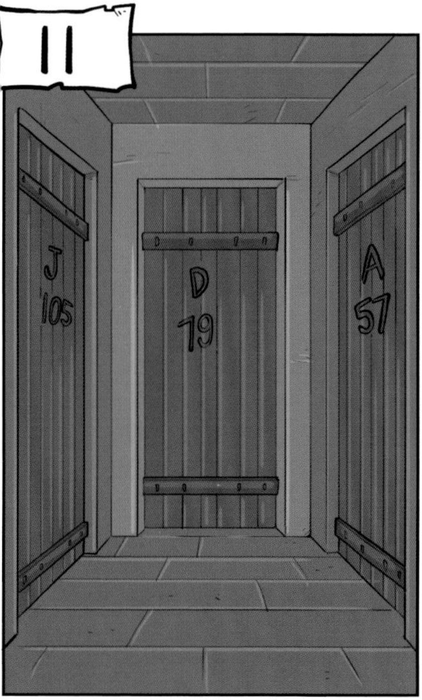
11
J
105
D
79
A
57

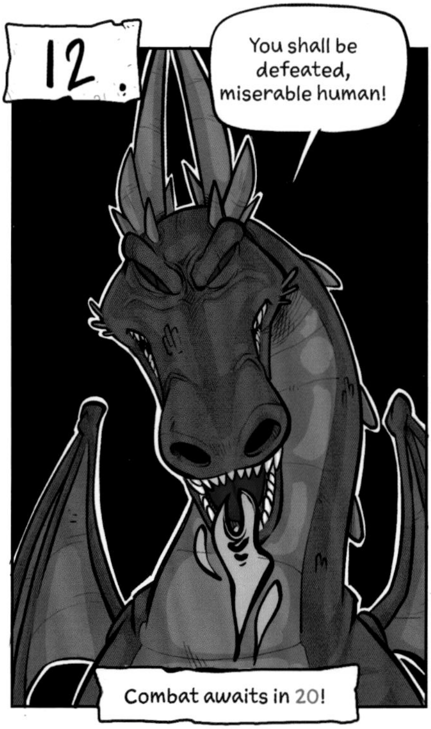
12
You shall be defeated, miserable human!
Combat awaits in 20!

13

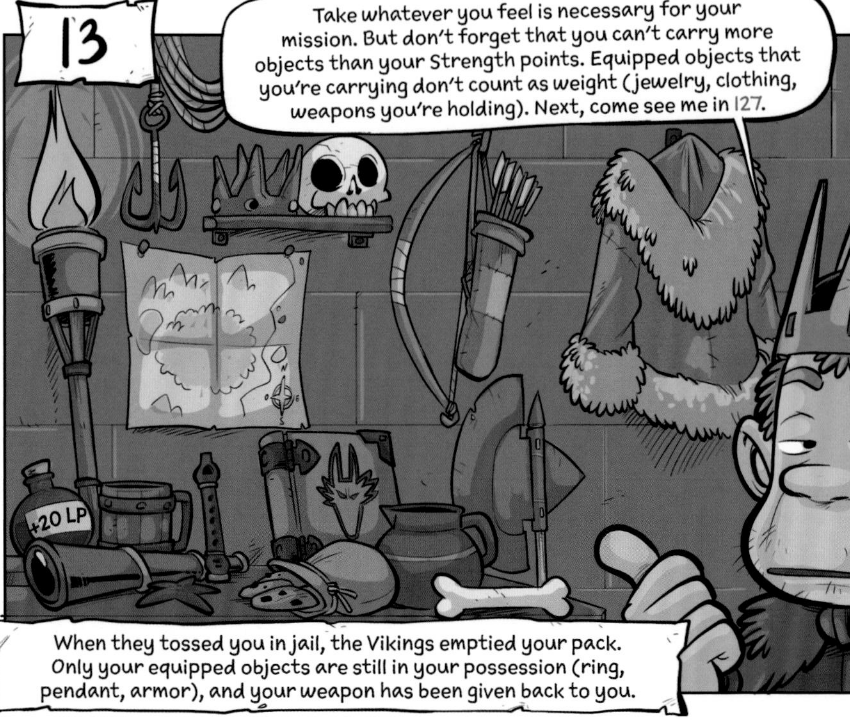
Take whatever you feel is necessary for your mission. But don't forget that you can't carry more objects than your Strength points. Equipped objects that you're carrying don't count as weight (jewelry, clothing, weapons you're holding). Next, come see me in 127.
+20 LP
When they tossed you in jail, the Vikings emptied your pack. Only your equipped objects are still in your possession (ring, pendant, armor), and your weapon has been given back to you.

14

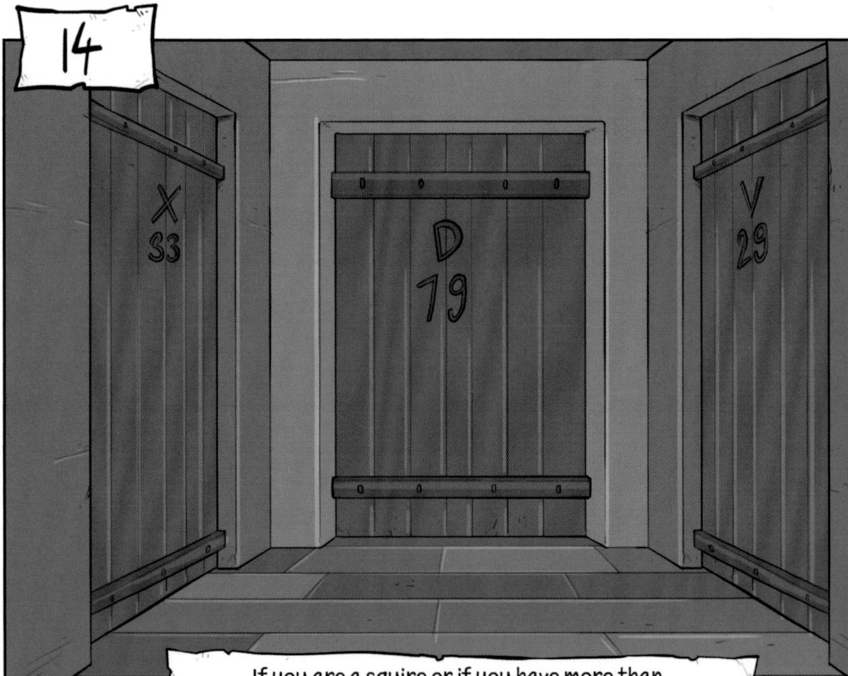
X
33
D
79
V
29
If you are a squire or if you have more than 12 Intelligence points, go to 53, then return here.

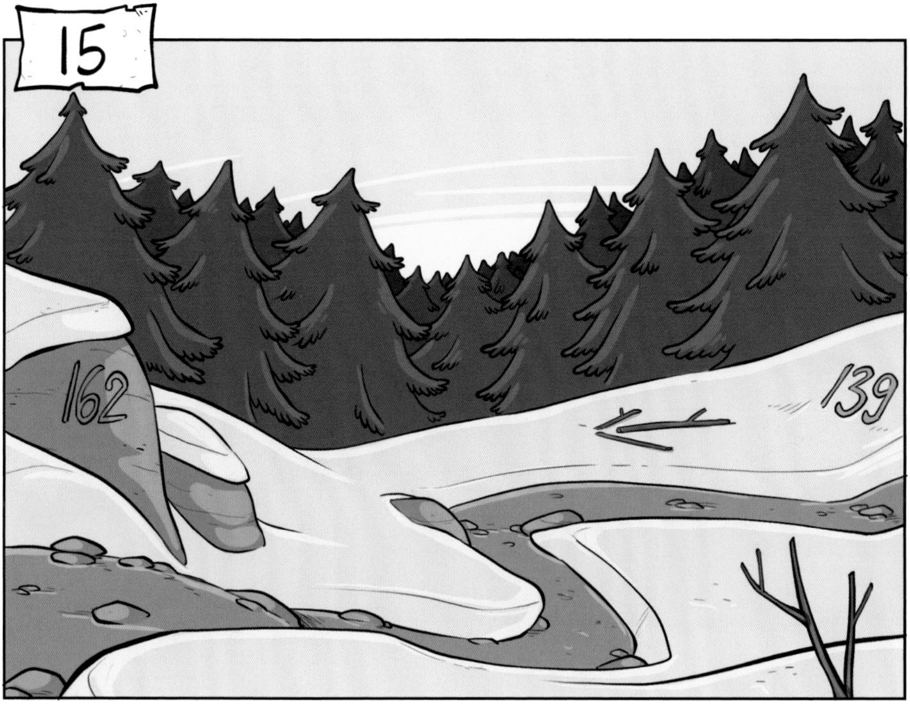
15
162
139

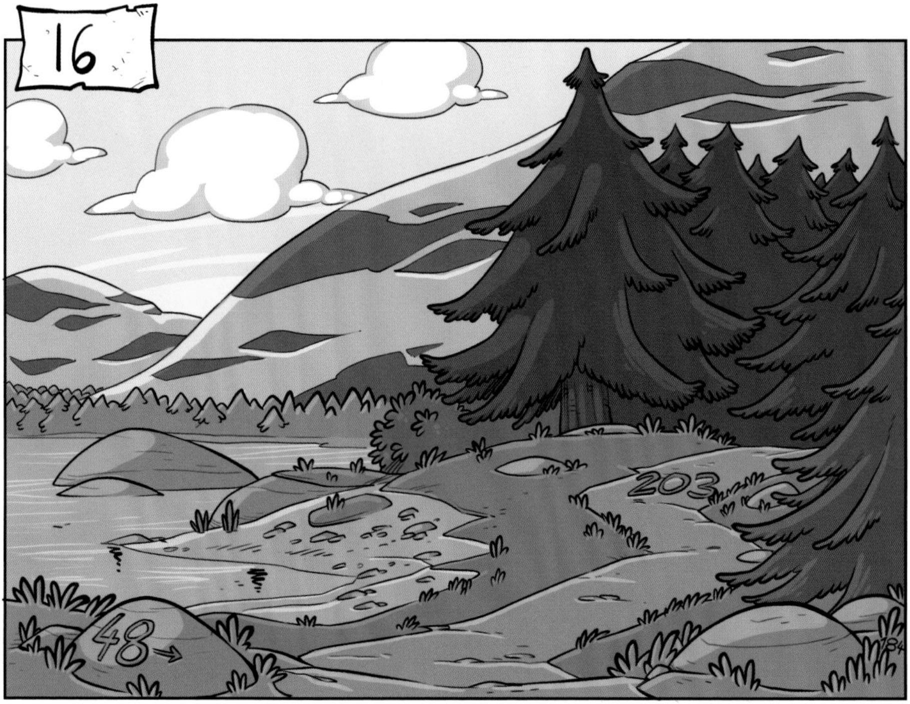
16
203
48

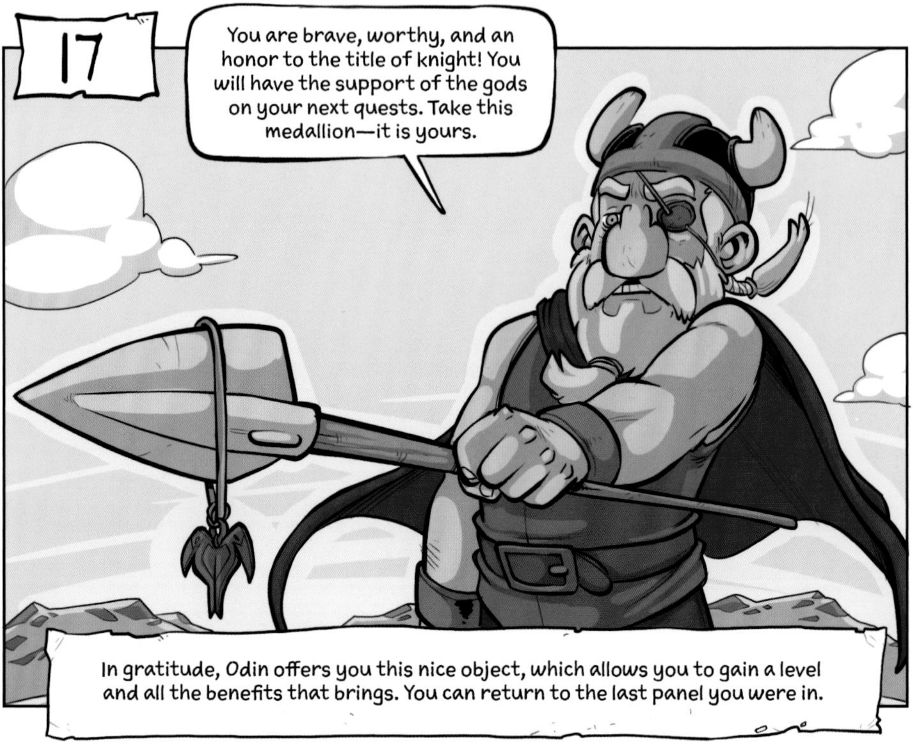
17
You are brave, worthy, and an honor to the title of knight! You will have the support of the gods on your next quests. Take this medallion—it is yours.
In gratitude, Odin offers you this nice object, which allows you to gain a level and all the benefits that brings. You can return to the last panel you were in.

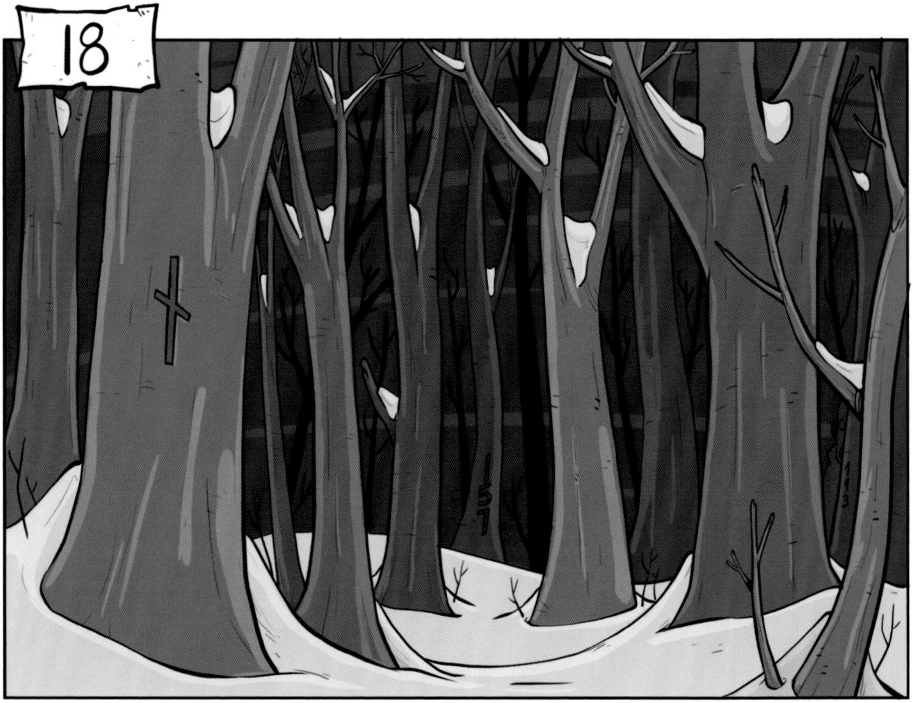
18
157
143

19

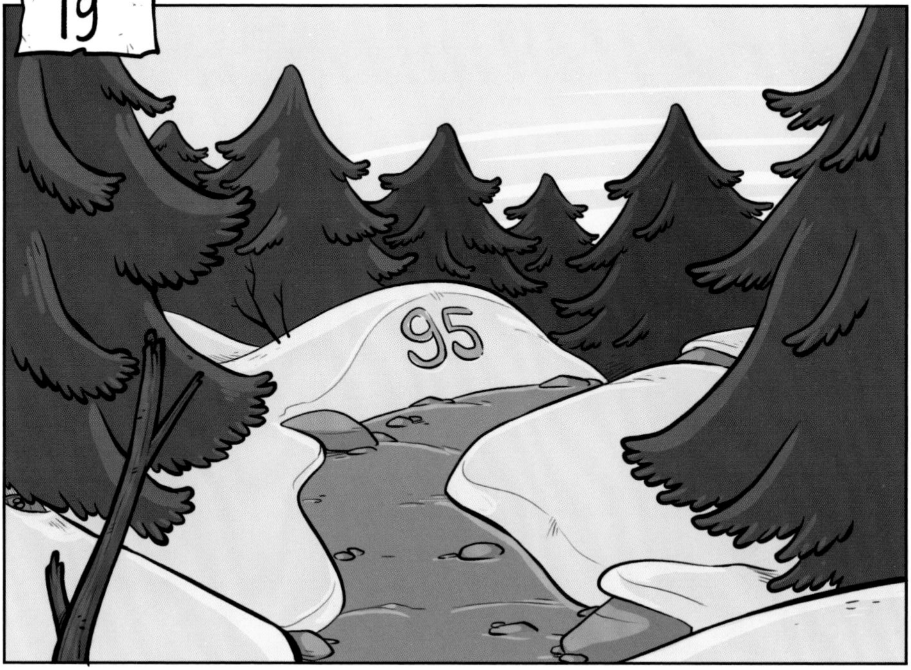
95

20

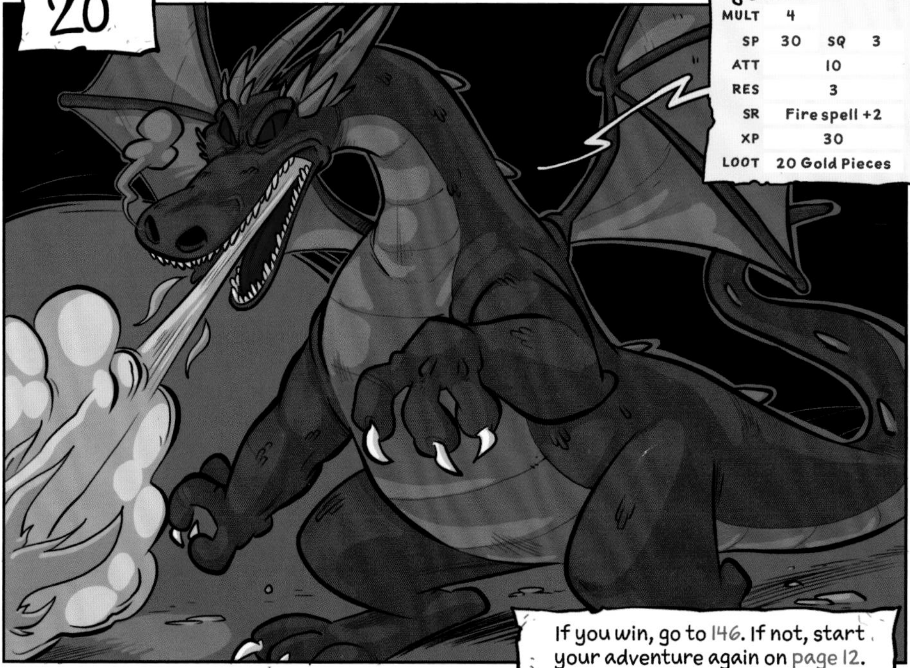

MULT	4		
SP	30	SQ	3
ATT	10		
RES	3		
SR	Fire spell +2		
XP	30		
LOOT	20 Gold Pieces		

If you win, go to 146. If not, start your adventure again on page 12.

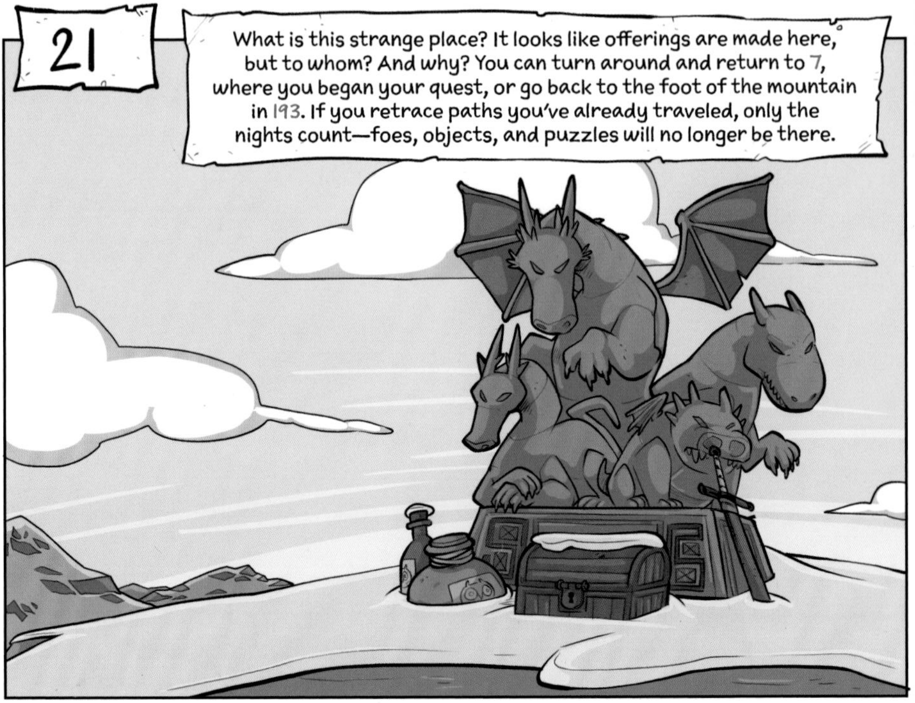
21
What is this strange place? It looks like offerings are made here, but to whom? And why? You can turn around and return to 7, where you began your quest, or go back to the foot of the mountain in 193. If you retrace paths you've already traveled, only the nights count—foes, objects, and puzzles will no longer be there.

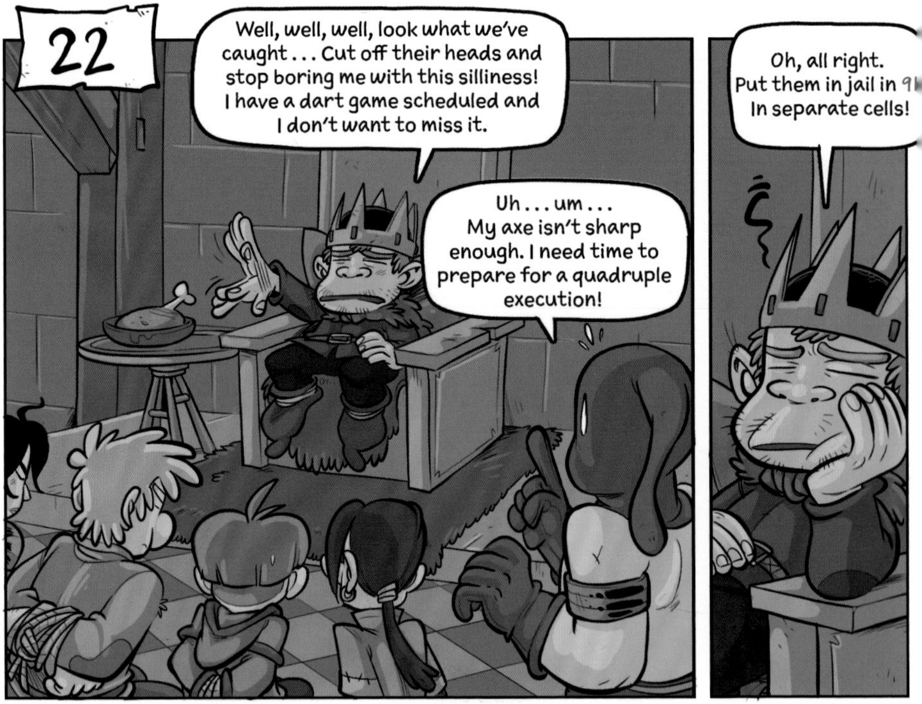
22
Well, well, well, look what we've caught . . . Cut off their heads and stop boring me with this silliness! I have a dart game scheduled and I don't want to miss it.
Uh . . . um . . . My axe isn't sharp enough. I need time to prepare for a quadruple execution!
Oh, all right. Put them in jail in 9
In separate cells!

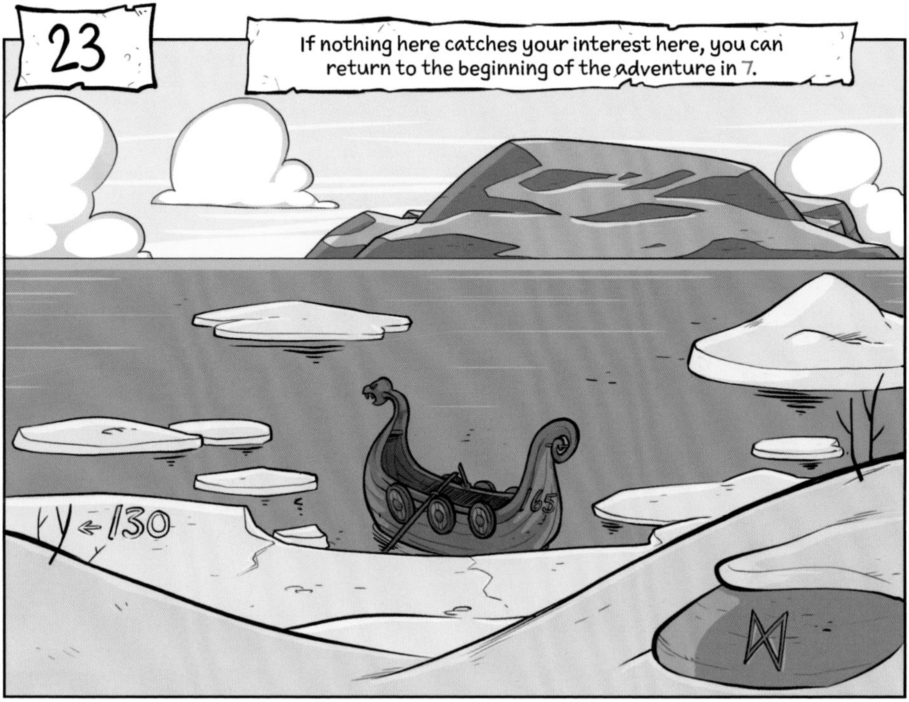
23
If nothing here catches your interest here, you can return to the beginning of the adventure in 7.
130
165

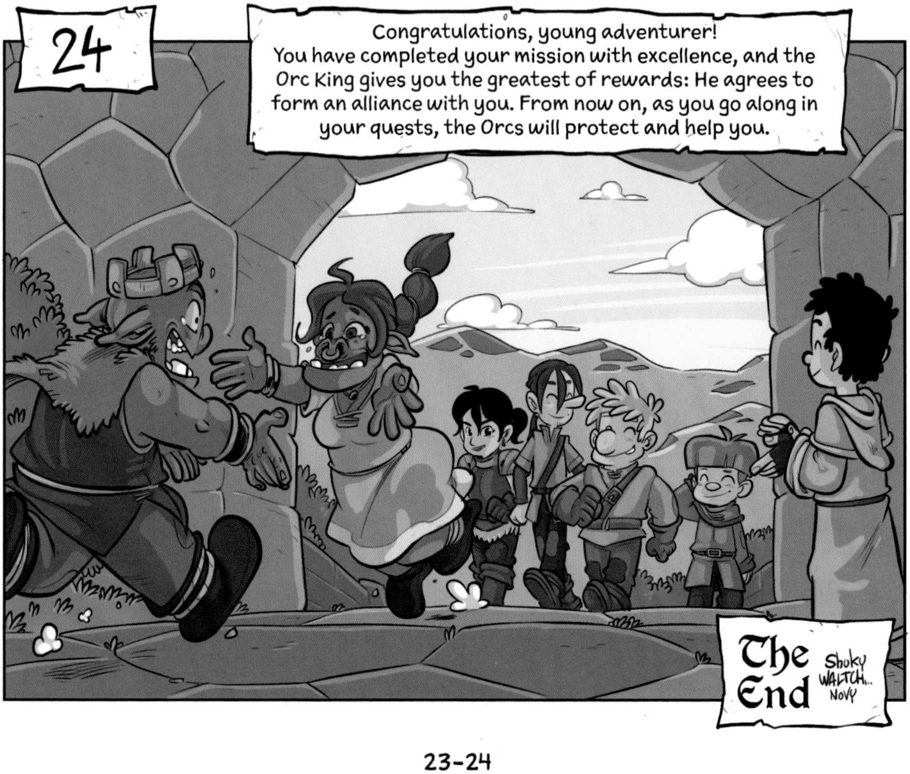
24
Congratulations, young adventurer!
You have completed your mission with excellence, and the Orc King gives you the greatest of rewards: He agrees to form an alliance with you. From now on, as you go along in your quests, the Orcs will protect and help you.
The End
Shuky
WALTCH..
Novy

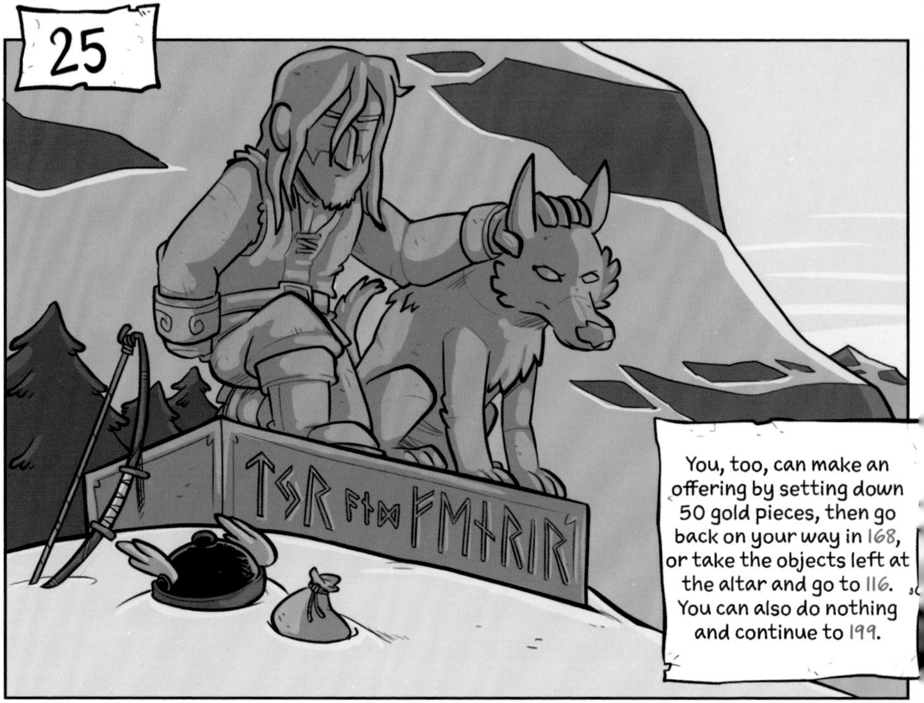
25
You, too, can make an offering by setting down 50 gold pieces, then go back on your way in 168, or take the objects left at the altar and go to 116. You can also do nothing and continue to 199.

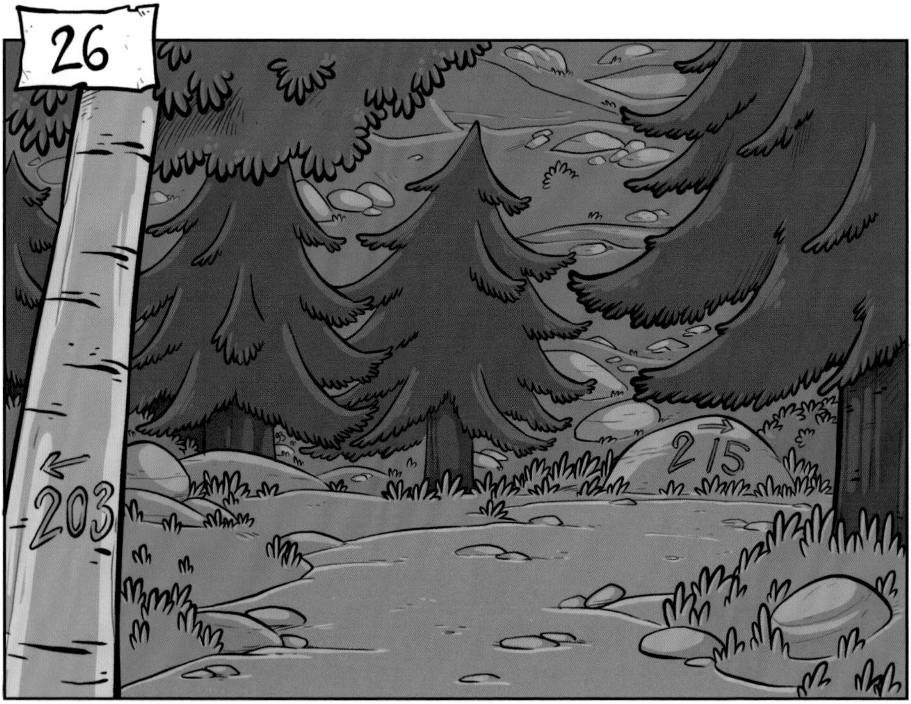
26
203
215

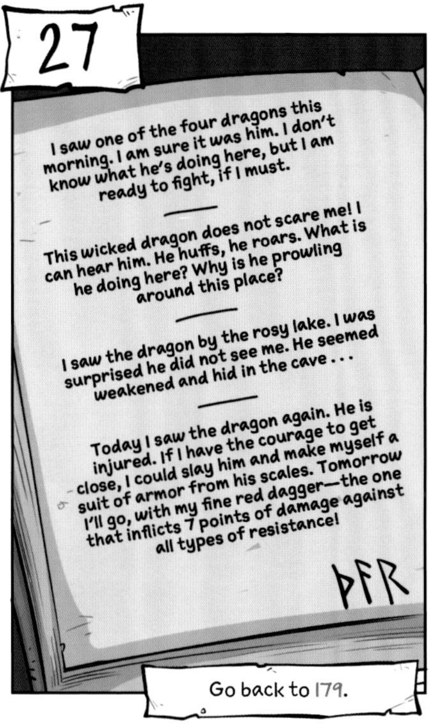
27
I saw one of the four dragons this morning. I am sure it was him. I don't know what he's doing here, but I am ready to fight, if I must.
This wicked dragon does not scare me! I can hear him. He huffs, he roars. What is he doing here? Why is he prowling around this place?
I saw the dragon by the rosy lake. I was surprised he did not see me. He seemed weakened and hid in the cave . . .
Today I saw the dragon again. He is injured. If I have the courage to get close, I could slay him and make myself a suit of armor from his scales. Tomorrow I'll go, with my fine red dagger—the one that inflicts 7 points of damage against all types of resistance!
Go back to 179.

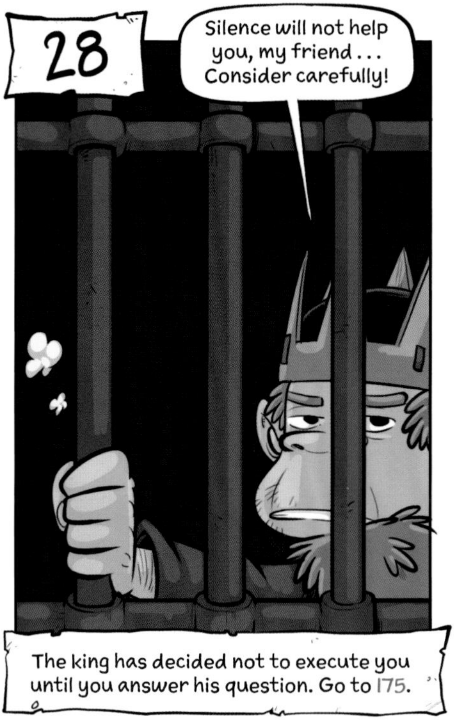
28
Silence will not help you, my friend . . . Consider carefully!
The king has decided not to execute you until you answer his question. Go to 175.

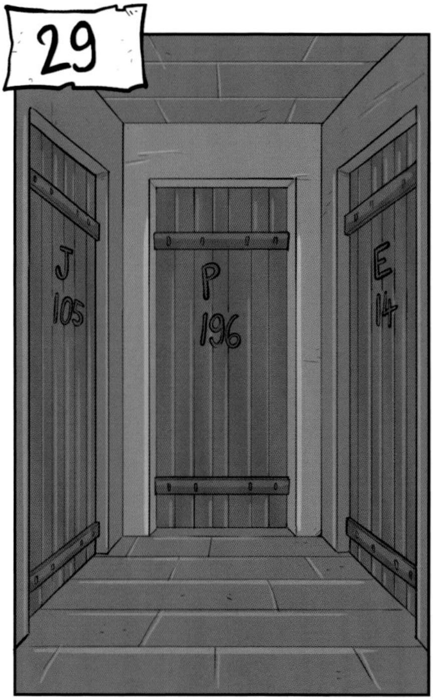
29
J
105
P
196
E
14

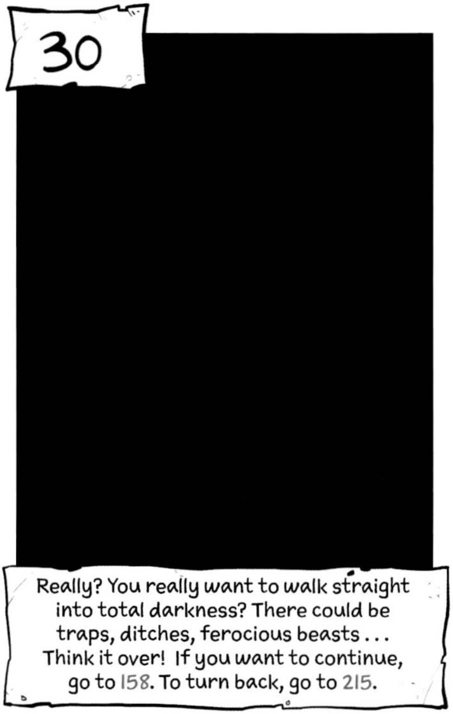
30
Really? You really want to walk straight into total darkness? There could be traps, ditches, ferocious beasts . . . Think it over! If you want to continue, go to 158. To turn back, go to 215.

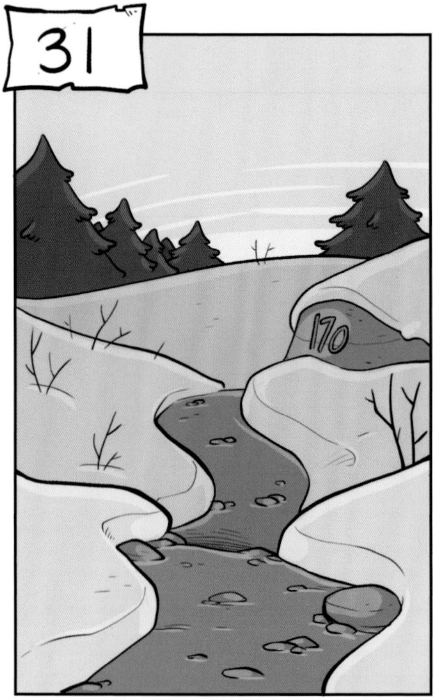
31
170

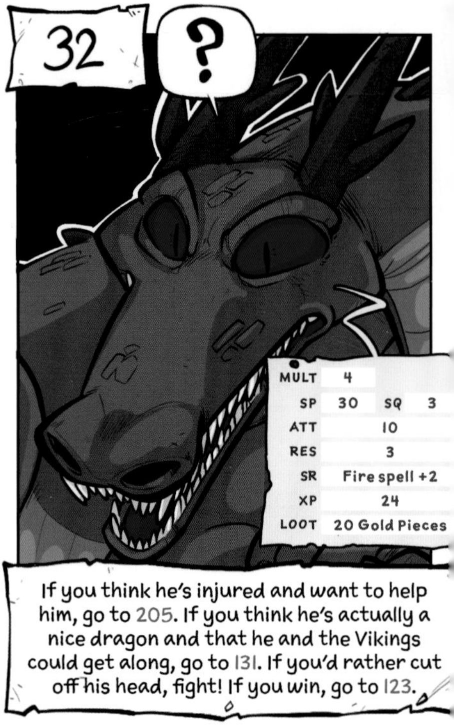
32
?

MULT	4		
SP	30	SQ	3
ATT	10		
RES	3		
SR	Fire spell +2		
XP	24		
LOOT	20 Gold Pieces		

If you think he's injured and want to help him, go to 205. If you think he's actually a nice dragon and that he and the Vikings could get along, go to 131. If you'd rather cut off his head, fight! If you win, go to 123.

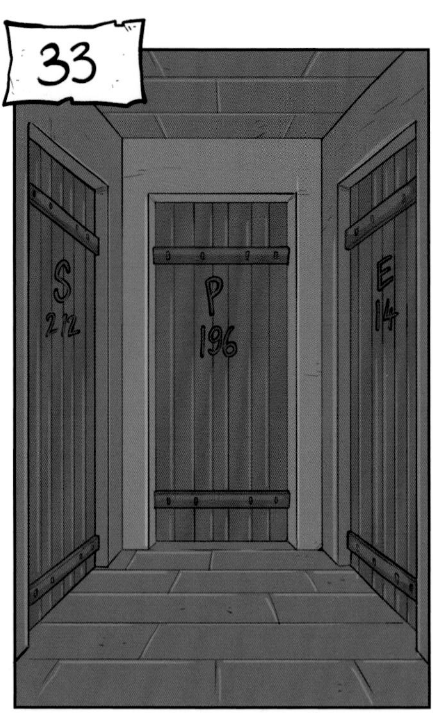
33
S
212
P
196
E
14

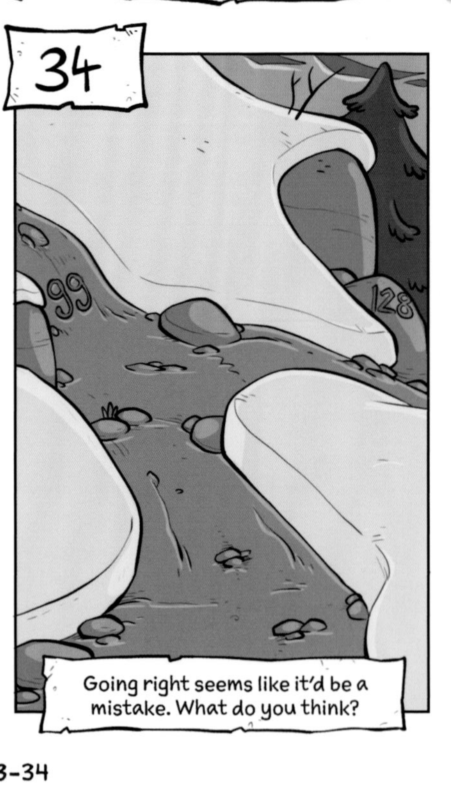
34
99
128
Going right seems like it'd be a mistake. What do you think?

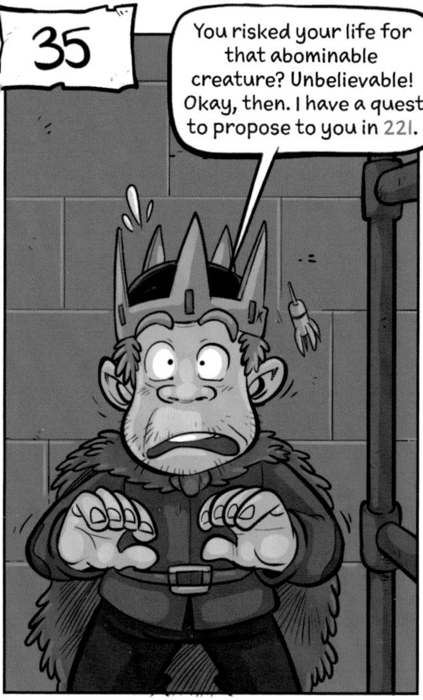
35
You risked your life for that abominable creature? Unbelievable! Okay, then. I have a quest to propose to you in 221.

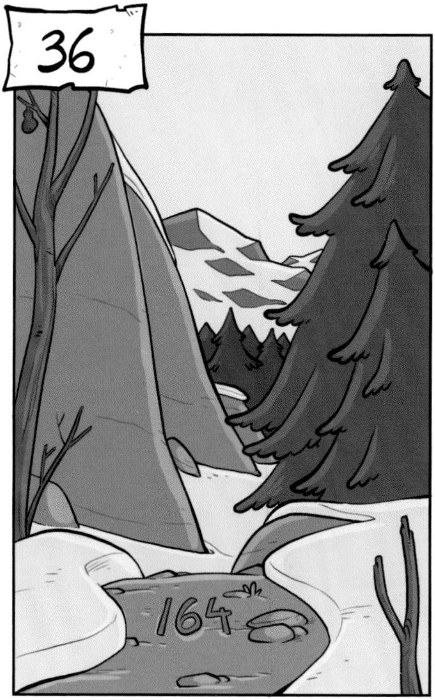
36
164

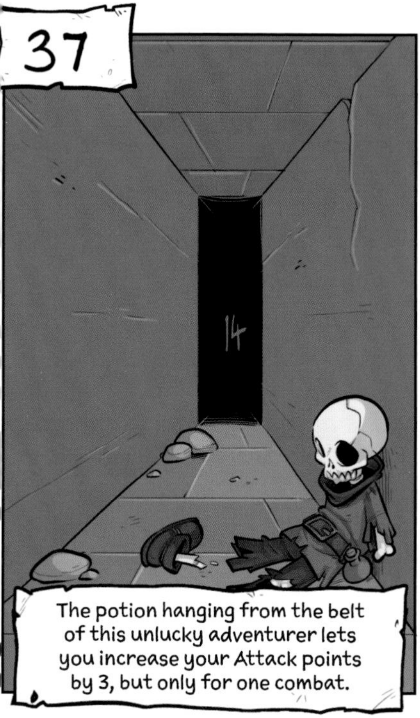
37
14
The potion hanging from the belt of this unlucky adventurer lets you increase your Attack points by 3, but only for one combat.

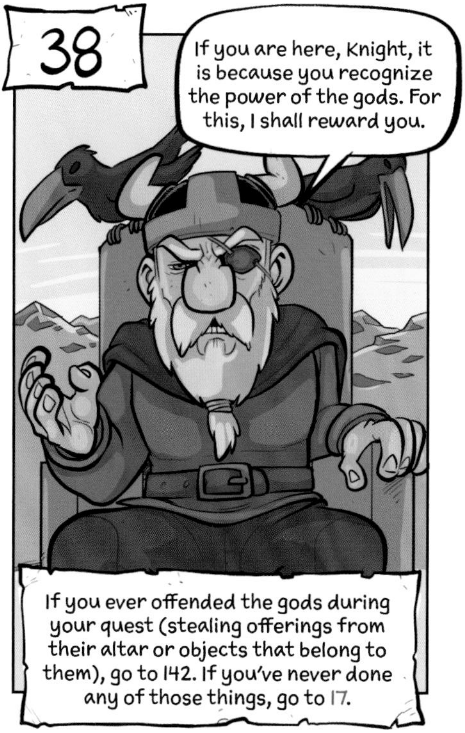
38
If you are here, Knight, it is because you recognize the power of the gods. For this, I shall reward you.
If you ever offended the gods during your quest (stealing offerings from their altar or objects that belong to them), go to 142. If you've never done any of those things, go to 17.

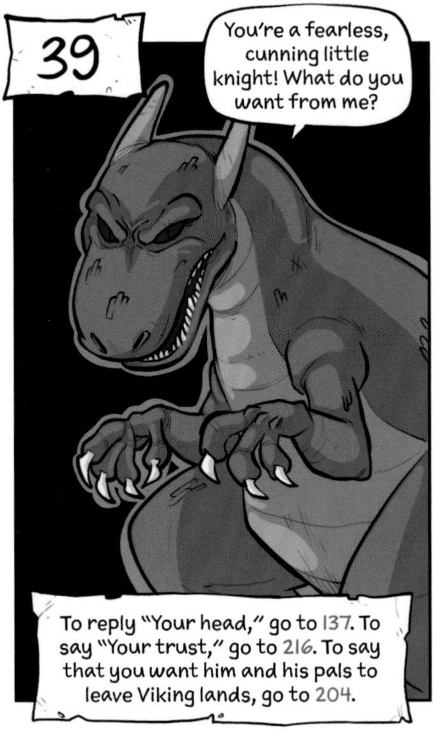
39
You're a fearless, cunning little knight! What do you want from me?
To reply "Your head," go to 137. To say "Your trust," go to 216. To say that you want him and his pals to leave Viking lands, go to 204.

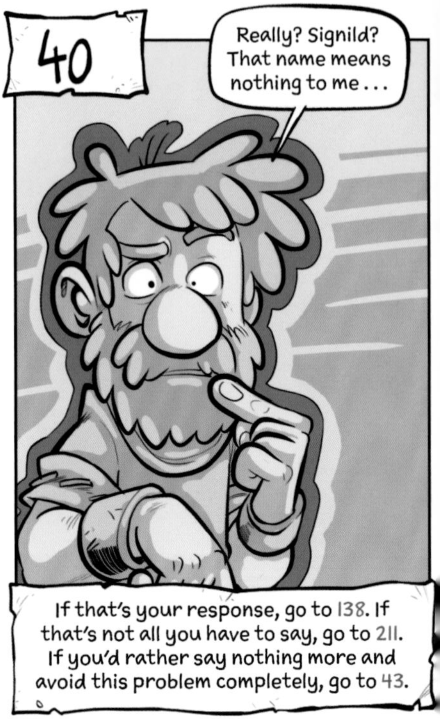
40
Really? Signild? That name means nothing to me . . .
If that's your response, go to 138. If that's not all you have to say, go to 211. If you'd rather say nothing more and avoid this problem completely, go to 43.

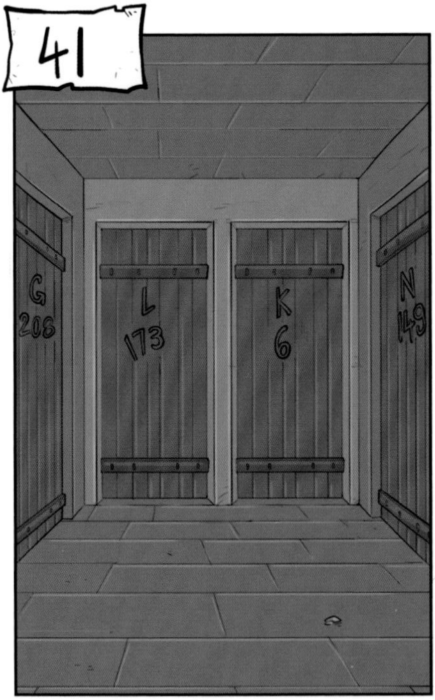
41
G
208
L
173
K
6
N
149

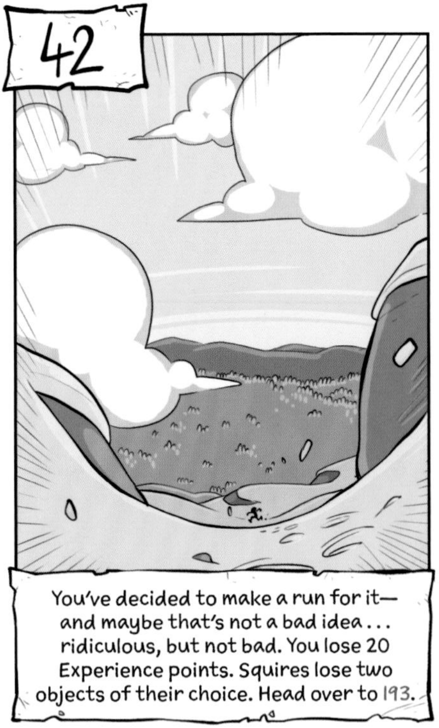
42
You've decided to make a run for it—and maybe that's not a bad idea . . . ridiculous, but not bad. You lose 20 Experience points. Squires lose two objects of their choice. Head over to 193.

43

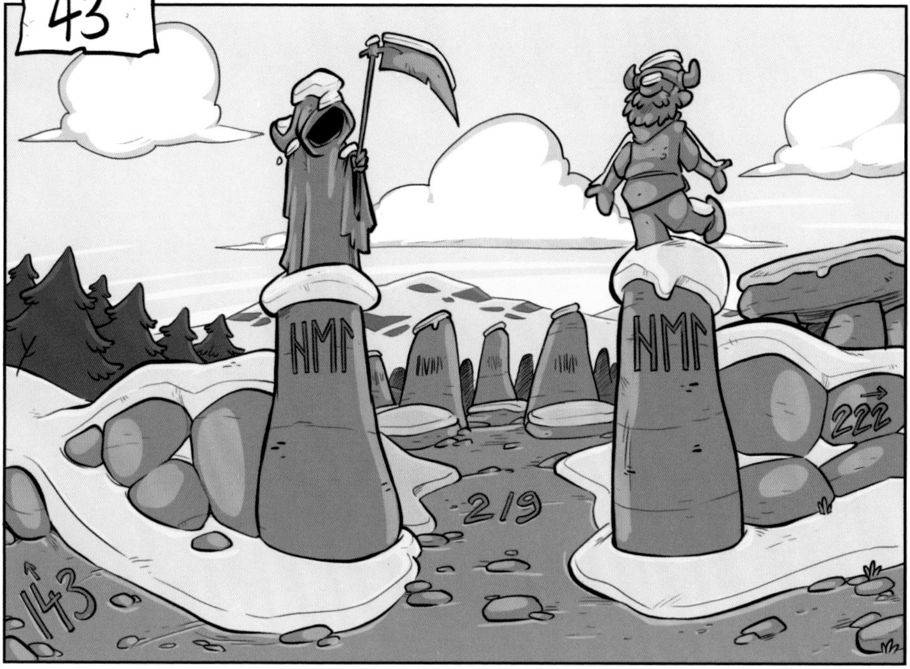

222
219
143

44

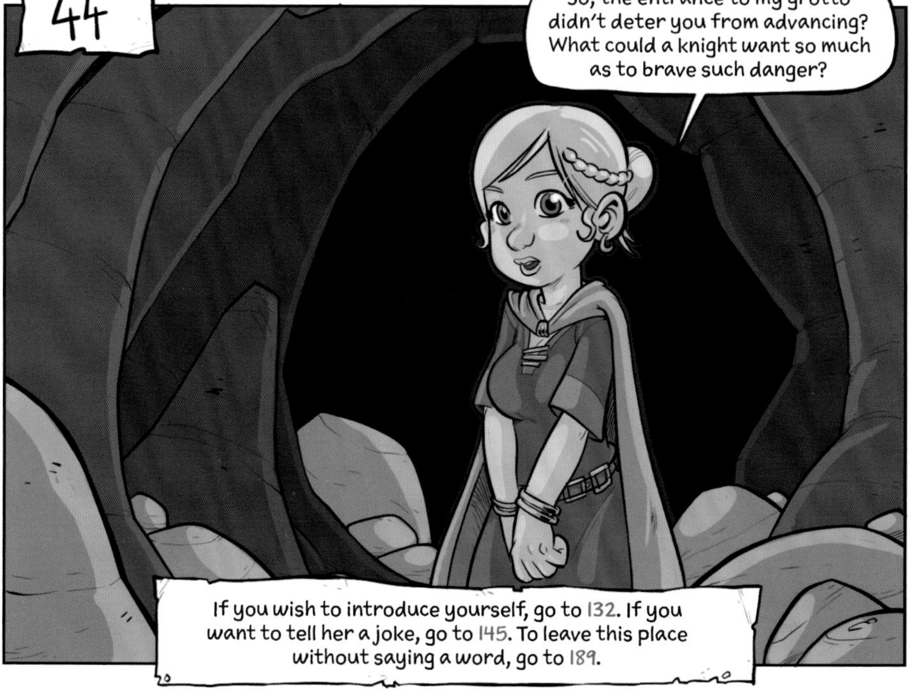

So, the entrance to my grotto didn't deter you from advancing? What could a knight want so much as to brave such danger?

If you wish to introduce yourself, go to 132. If you want to tell her a joke, go to 145. To leave this place without saying a word, go to 189.

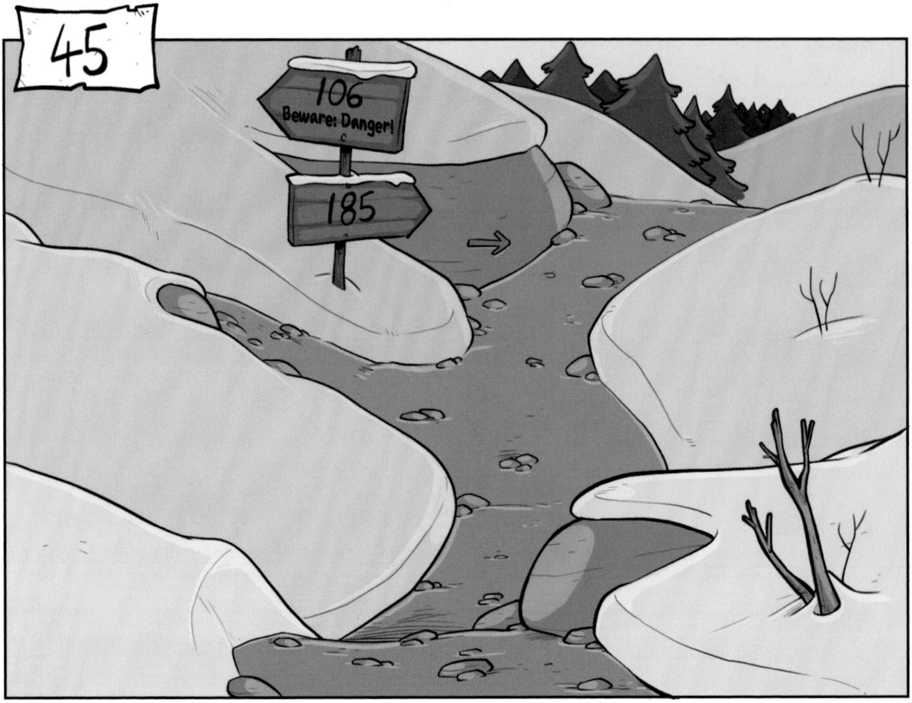
45
106
Beware: Danger!
185
→

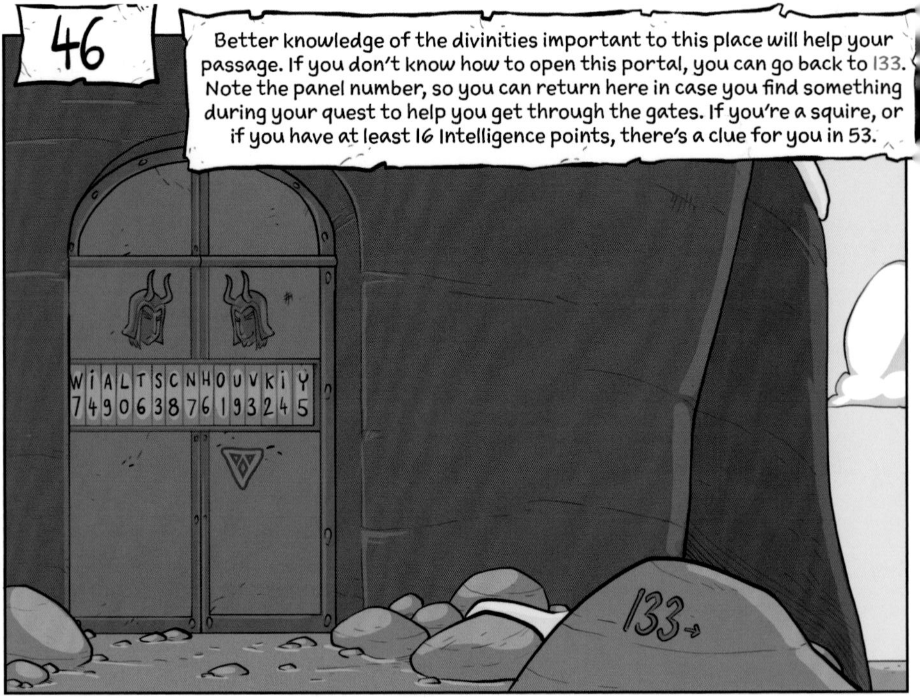
46
Better knowledge of the divinities important to this place will help your passage. If you don't know how to open this portal, you can go back to 133. Note the panel number, so you can return here in case you find something during your quest to help you get through the gates. If you're a squire, or if you have at least 16 Intelligence points, there's a clue for you in 53.
WiALTSCNHOUVKiY
749063876193245
133→

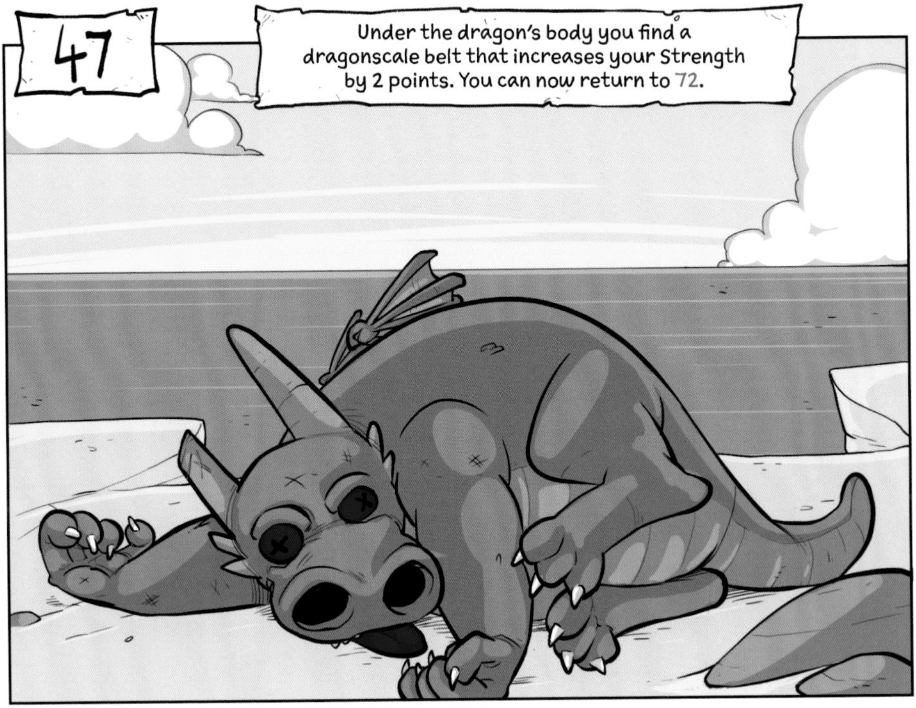
47
Under the dragon's body you find a dragonscale belt that increases your Strength by 2 points. You can now return to 72.

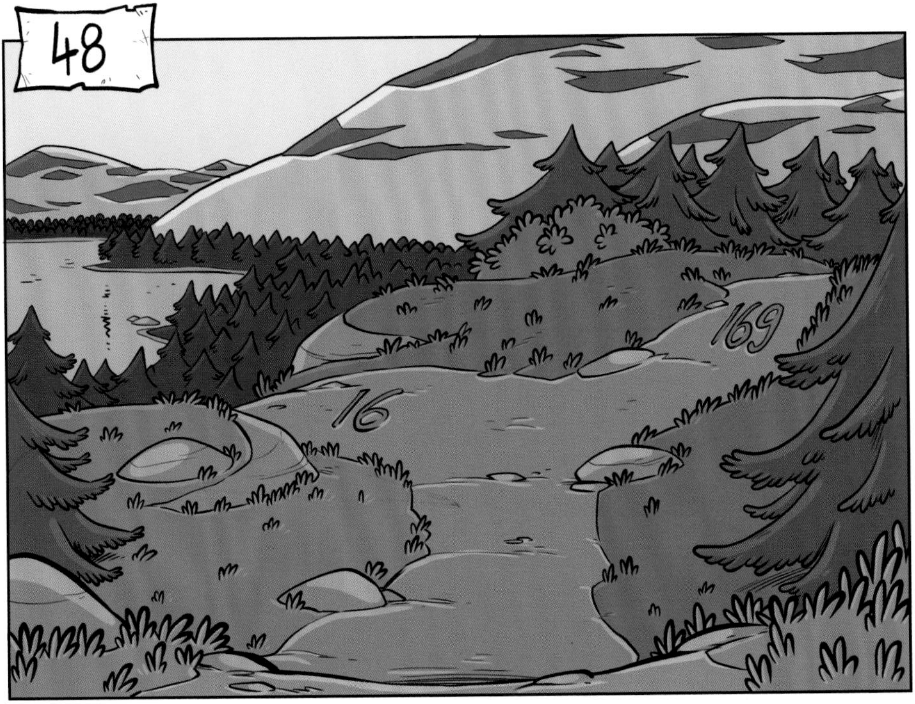
48
169
16

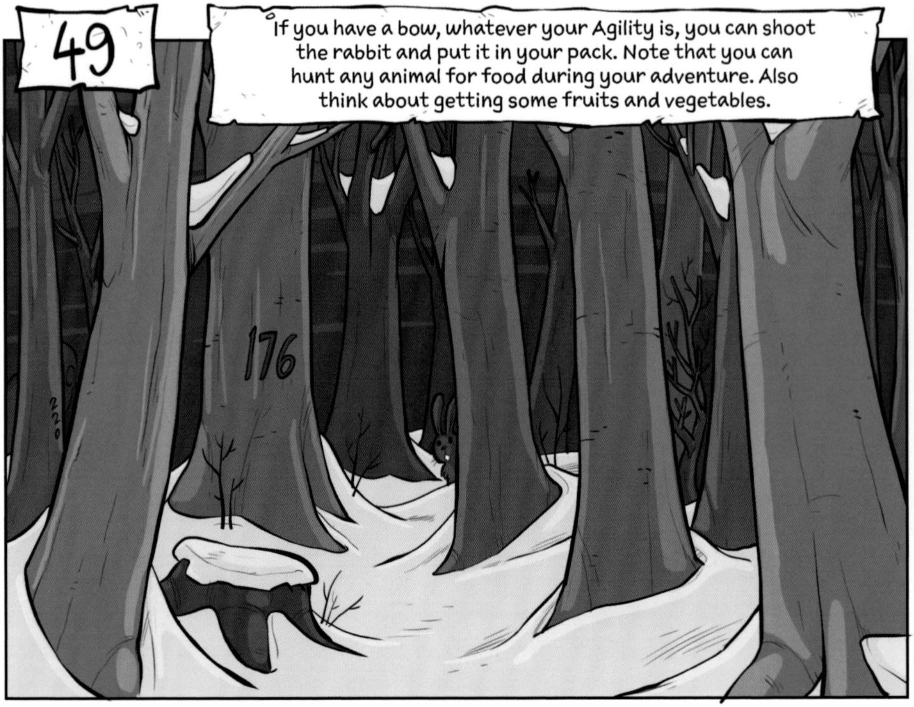
49
If you have a bow, whatever your Agility is, you can shoot the rabbit and put it in your pack. Note that you can hunt any animal for food during your adventure. Also think about getting some fruits and vegetables.
176
220

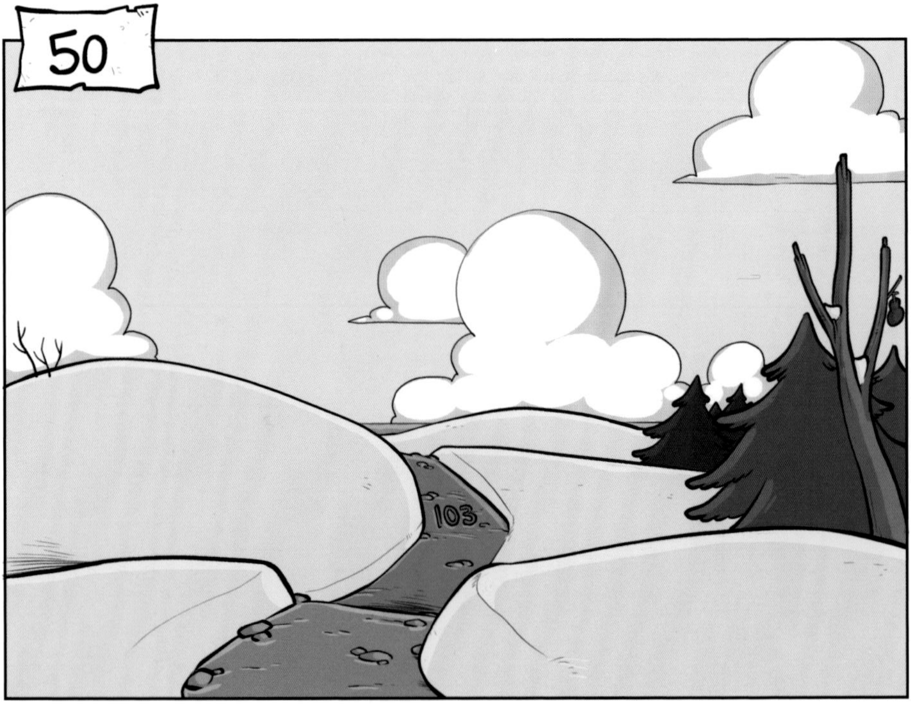
50
103

51

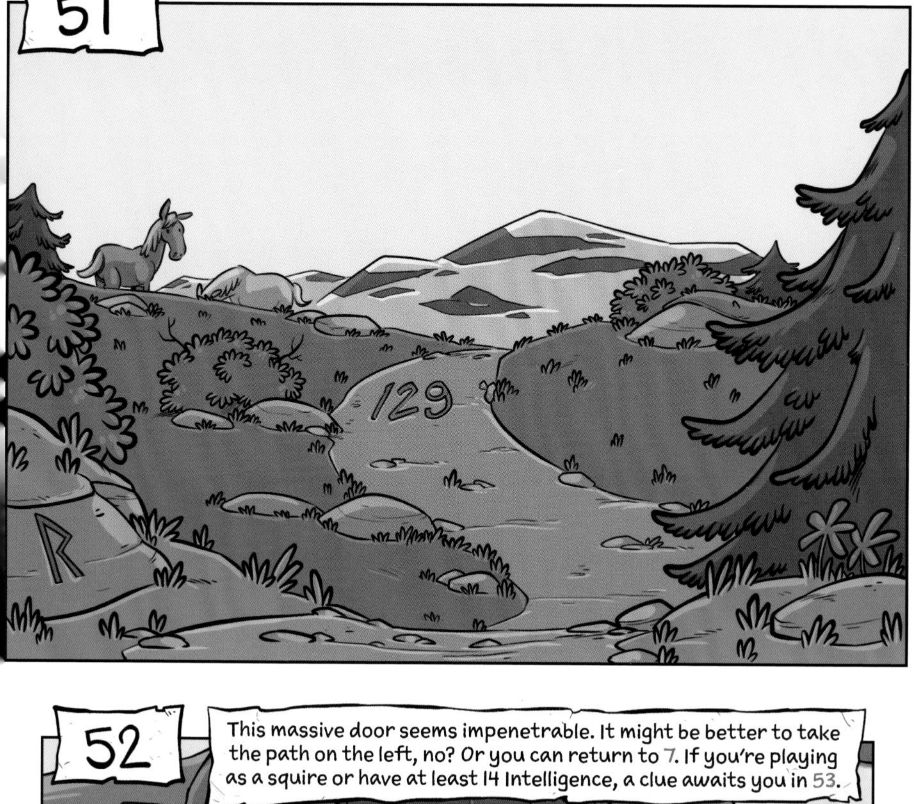
129

52

This massive door seems impenetrable. It might be better to take the path on the left, no? Or you can return to 7. If you're playing as a squire or have at least 14 Intelligence, a clue awaits you in 53.

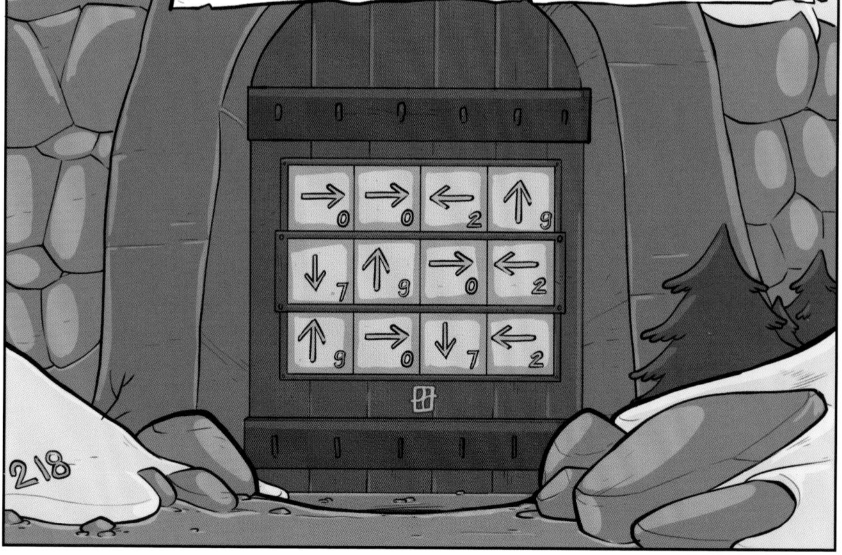
218

CLUES

ATTENTION! On this page you'll find several clues that you can collect on your quest and others that you can access through your skills. Read only the ones that apply to your character, or you'll spoil your quest!

Clue for the puzzle in panel 14:

What are you looking for?

Clue for the puzzle in panel 52:

Have you perchance seen some arrows along the road?

Clue for the puzzle in panel 46

The name of the god you're looking for has 4 letters.
But you found a number with 3 numerals. Strange, huh?

Clue for the puzzle in panel 219:

Look closely at the person you're speaking with.

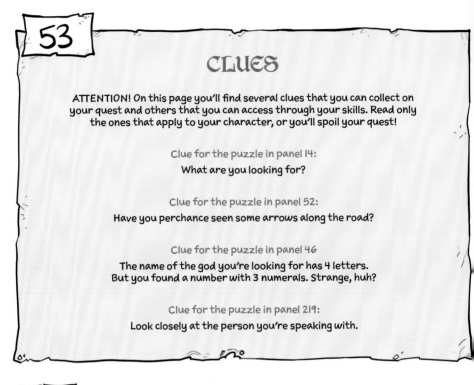

54 Knight of Shadow, you were able to help us and we have done the same for you. Join us now to find our four other brothers, and we shall make you the most powerful knight who ever lived!

And thus ends your quest! Maybe you didn't save the princess, but you've been given a new title: the Knight of Shadow. You've earned important allies, the powerful dragons . . . surely a life of adventure awaits you.

The End

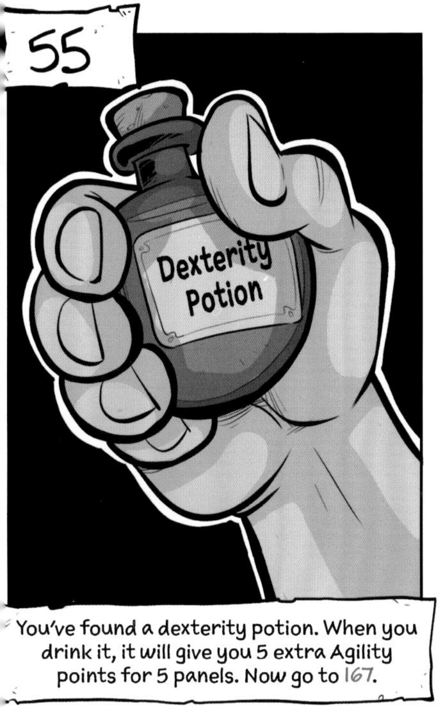
55
Dexterity Potion
You've found a dexterity potion. When you drink it, it will give you 5 extra Agility points for 5 panels. Now go to 167.

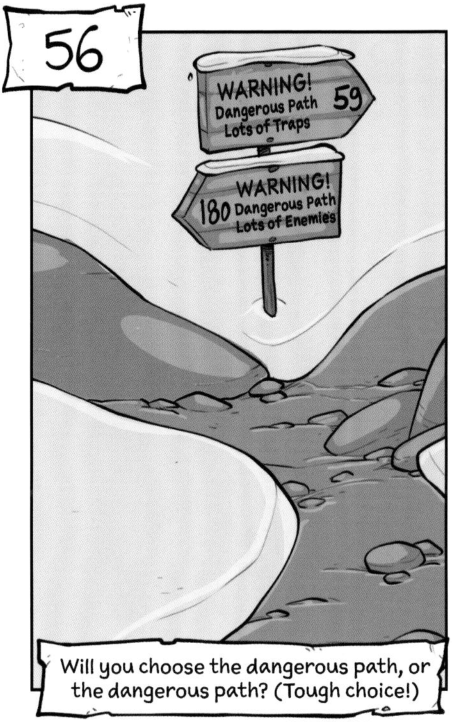
56
WARNING! Dangerous Path Lots of Traps 59
WARNING! 180 Dangerous Path Lots of Enemies
Will you choose the dangerous path, or the dangerous path? (Tough choice!)

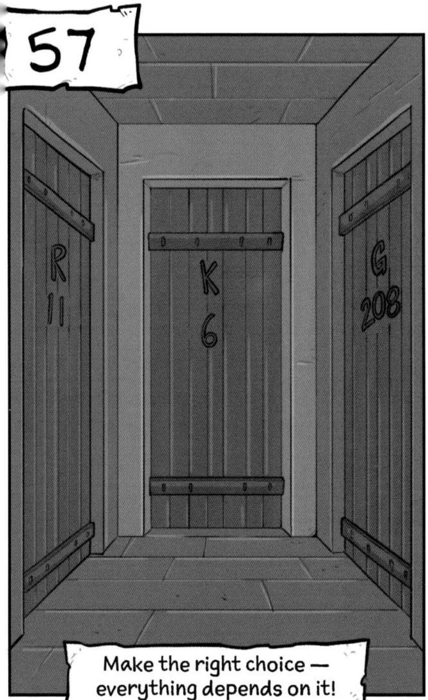
57
R 11
K 6
G 208
Make the right choice — everything depends on it!

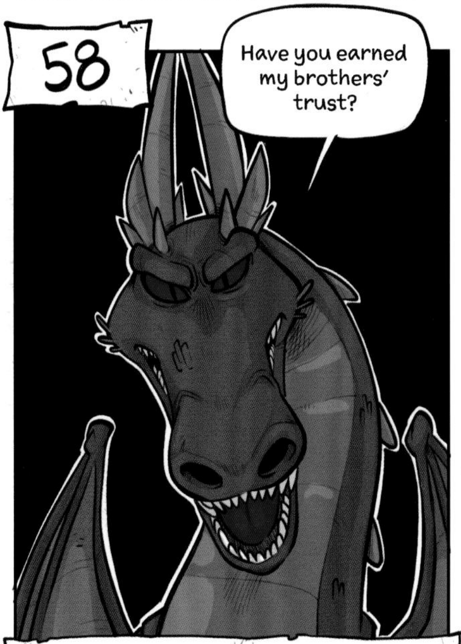
58
Have you earned my brothers' trust?
If the answer is yes, go to 109. If the answer is no, go to 78. If you've had enough of these questions and would rather cut the head right off this dragon, go to 20.

59

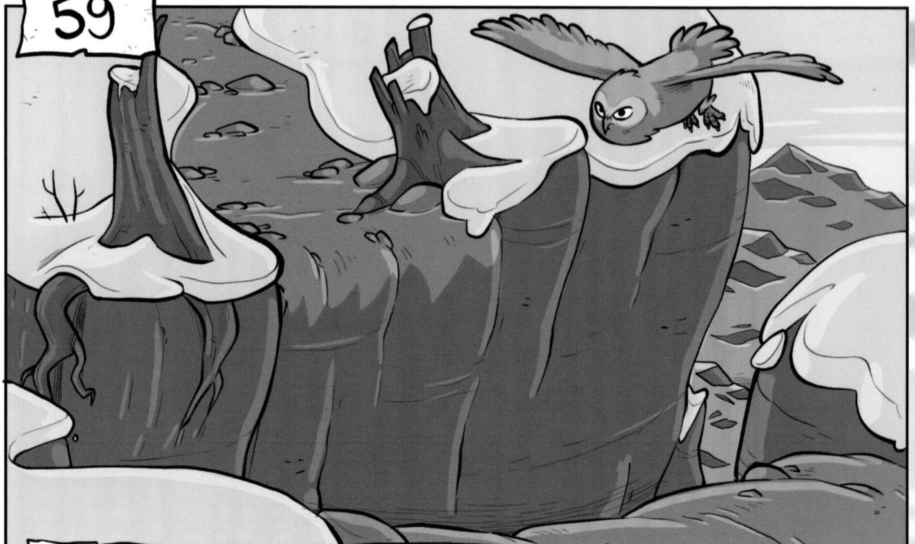

Jump to the other side if you have a minimum of 10 Agility points—and then go to 94. You can also toss your rope to the other side . . . but do you have one? If you do, go to 118 if you want to throw it around the big tree on the left. Go to 82 if you pick the little tree. Or go to 2 to catch the rope on the owl's legs. If none of that sounds good, or if you don't have a rope, go to 180.

60

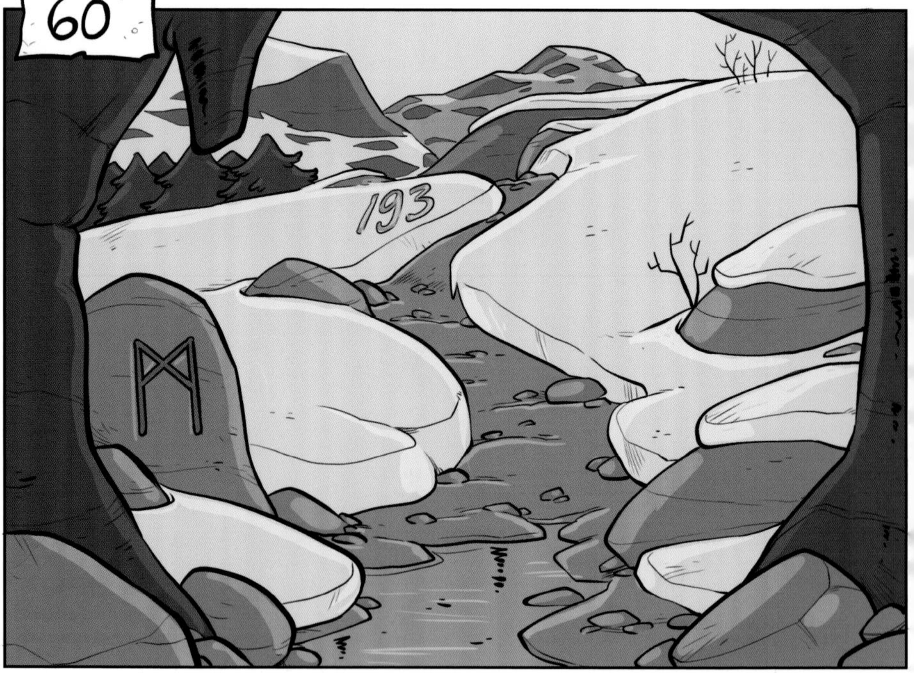
193

61

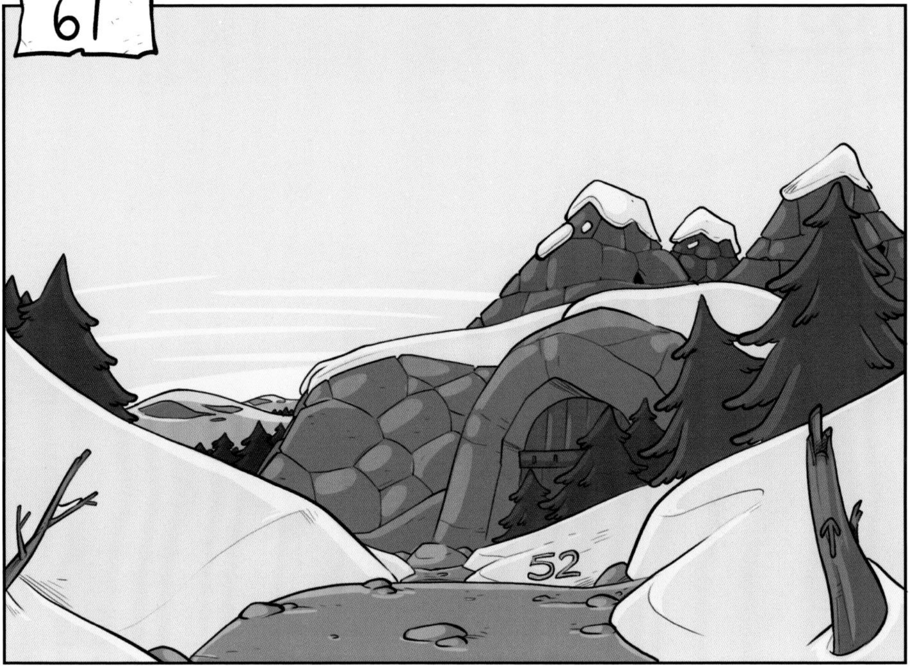
52

62

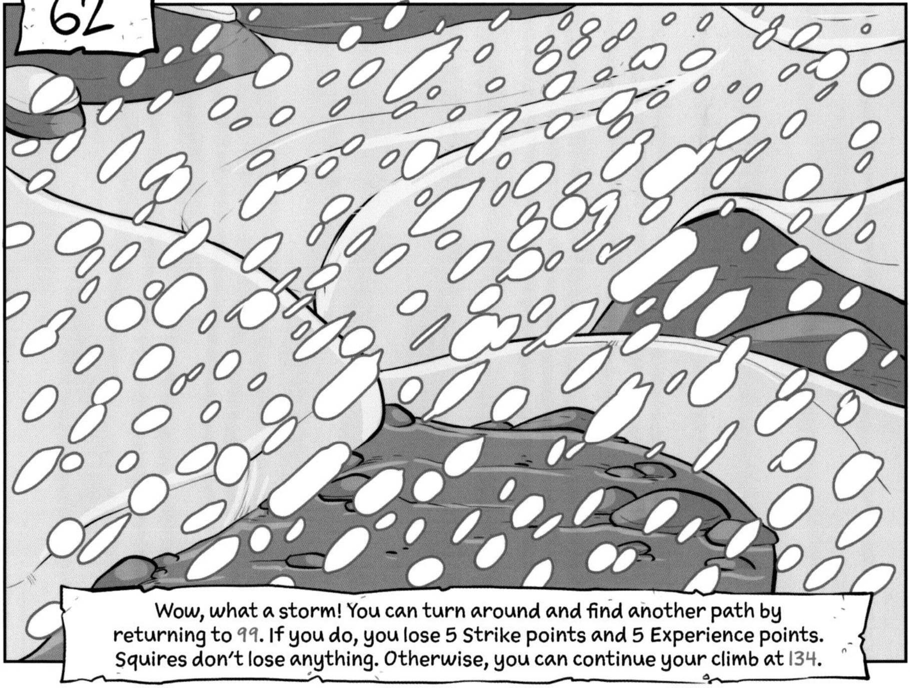
Wow, what a storm! You can turn around and find another path by returning to 99. If you do, you lose 5 Strike points and 5 Experience points. Squires don't lose anything. Otherwise, you can continue your climb at 134.

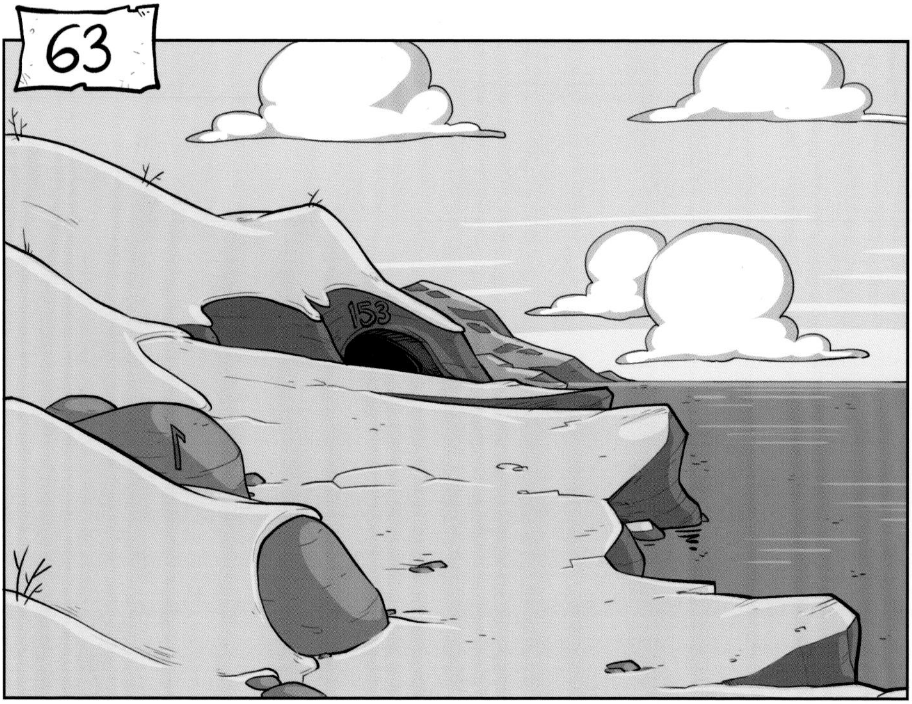
63
153

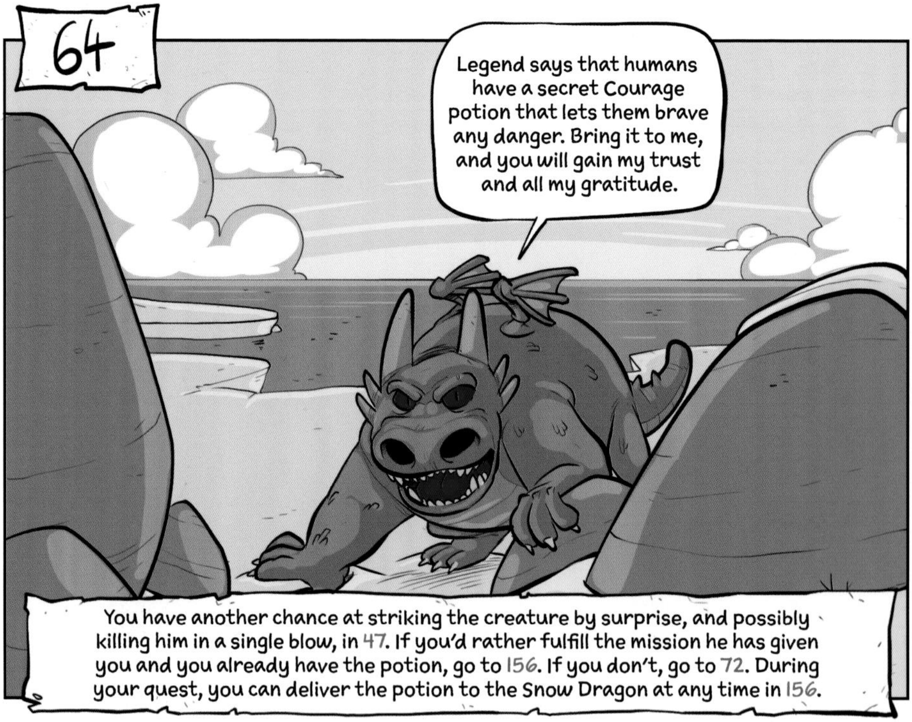
64
Legend says that humans have a secret Courage potion that lets them brave any danger. Bring it to me, and you will gain my trust and all my gratitude.
You have another chance at striking the creature by surprise, and possibly killing him in a single blow, in 47. If you'd rather fulfill the mission he has given you and you already have the potion, go to 156. If you don't, go to 72. During your quest, you can deliver the potion to the Snow Dragon at any time in 156.

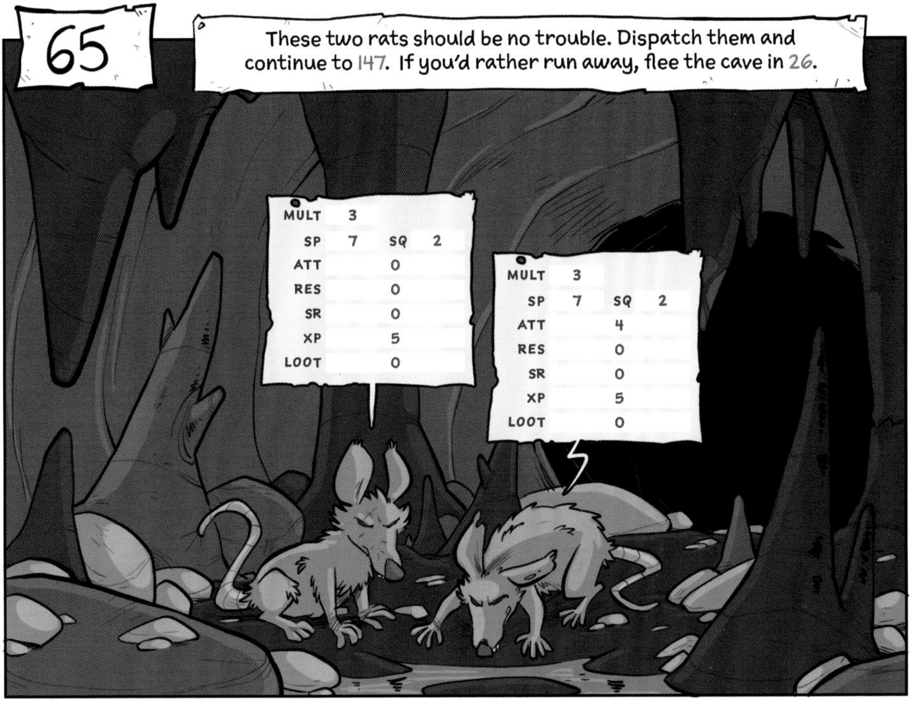
65
These two rats should be no trouble. Dispatch them and continue to 147. If you'd rather run away, flee the cave in 26.
MULT 3
SP 7 SQ 2
ATT 0
RES 0
SR 0
XP 5
LOOT 0
MULT 3
SP 7 SQ 2
ATT 4
RES 0
SR 0
XP 5
LOOT 0

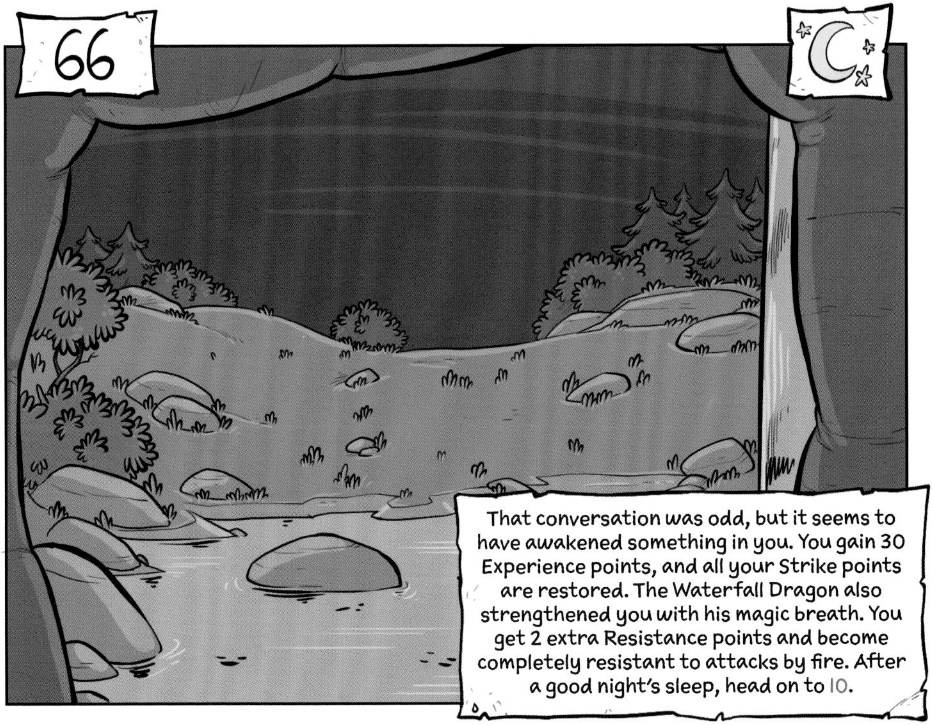
66
That conversation was odd, but it seems to have awakened something in you. You gain 30 Experience points, and all your Strike points are restored. The Waterfall Dragon also strengthened you with his magic breath. You get 2 extra Resistance points and become completely resistant to attacks by fire. After a good night's sleep, head on to 10.

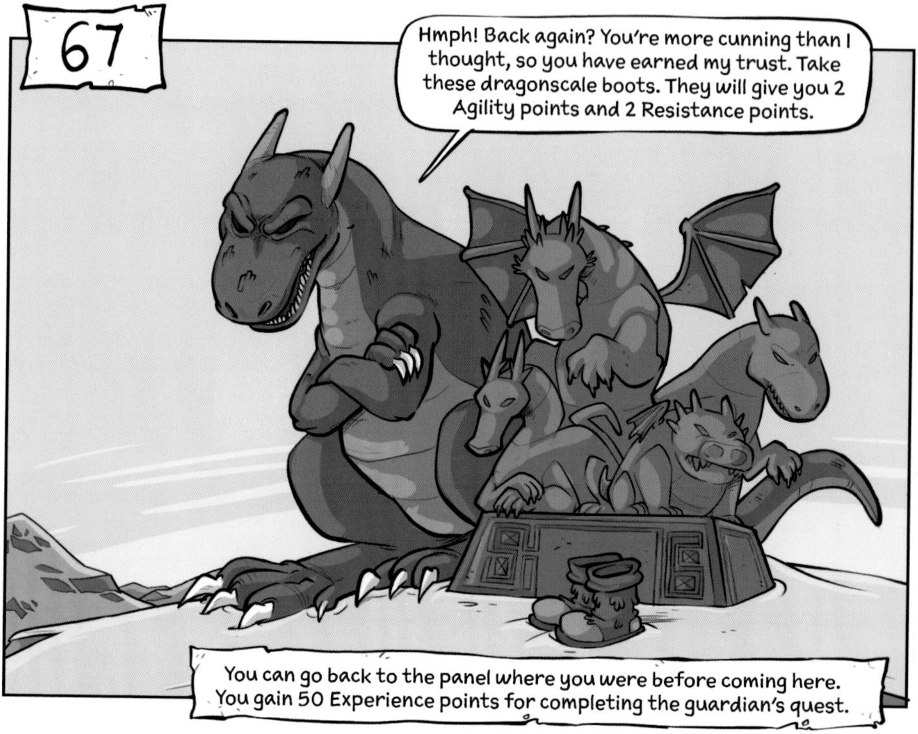
67
Hmph! Back again? You're more cunning than I thought, so you have earned my trust. Take these dragonscale boots. They will give you 2 Agility points and 2 Resistance points.
You can go back to the panel where you were before coming here. You gain 50 Experience points for completing the guardian's quest.

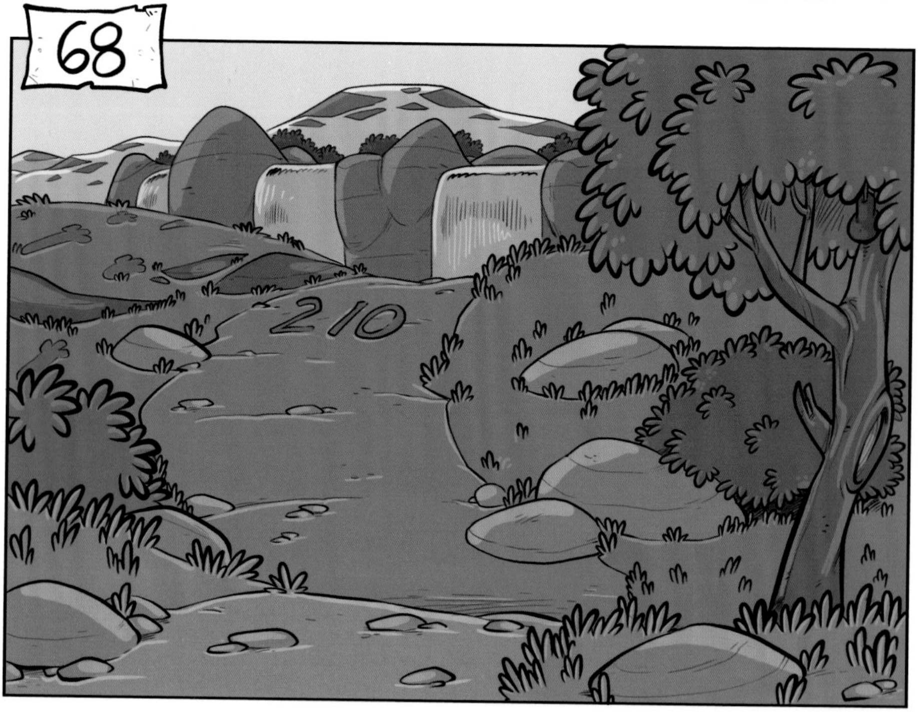
68
210

69

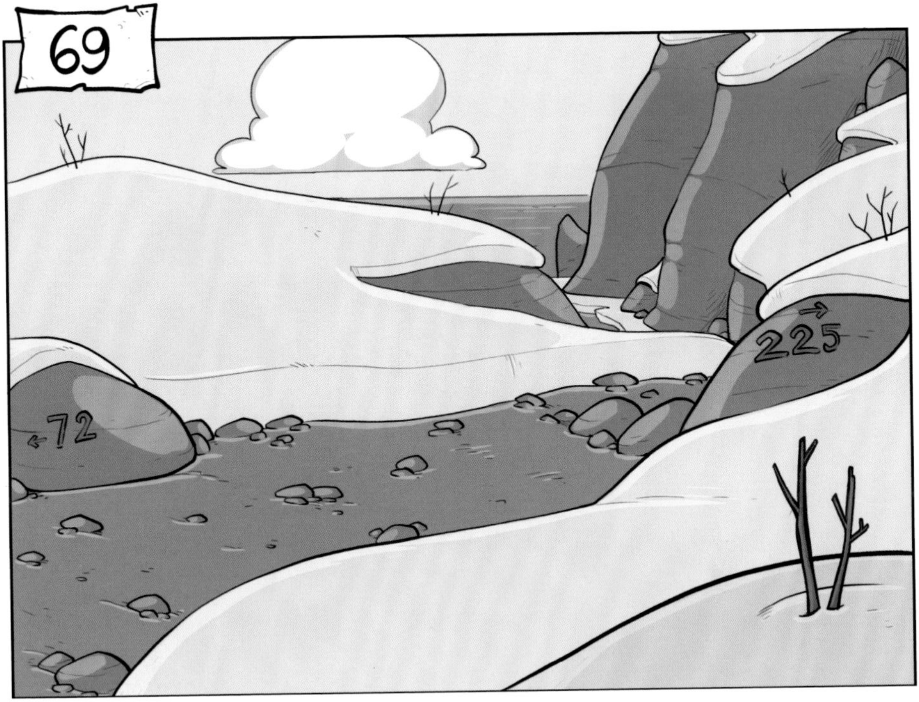

225
72

70

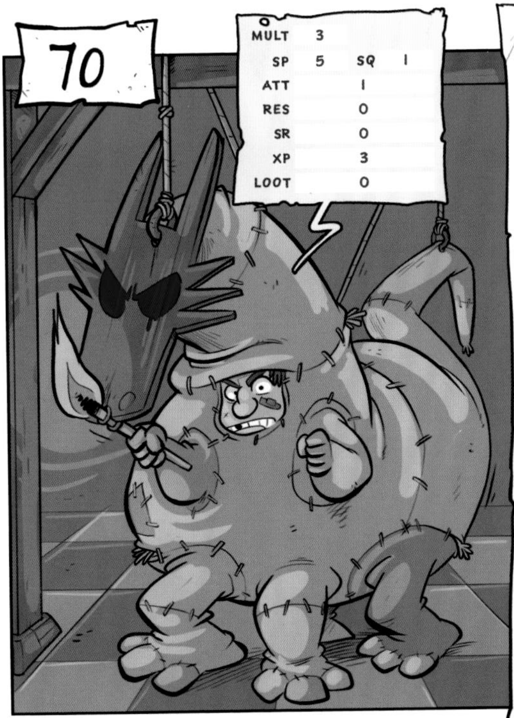

MULT	3		
SP	5	SQ	1
ATT		1	
RES		0	
SR		0	
XP		3	
LOOT		0	

Here it is—your first big fight! Remove the Combat Wheel or spin a pencil around it. Take turns spinning the wheel for yourself and for your foe.

If you're a squire, only the EP number matters. And you don't need to use the Combat Wheel. Your Attack points just need to be equal to or more than that number. If they aren't, run away!

You can always choose to run away—even in the middle of a battle. You'll find out what you've lost in the next panel. If it doesn't say, then you escaped without losing anything other than the points you lost during the fight.

If you win, you get 3 Experience points, which you should note on your Quest Tracker. If you're a squire, you win 3 pieces of gold.

ATTENTION! If you start on this quest using a character from a previous "Knights Club" adventure the Multiplier is 3. So your enemy has 15 Strike points and 3 Attack points. The experience and loot you win stay the same. The Multiplier changes with each enemy, so keep an eye on it.

After you've practiced, go to 217.

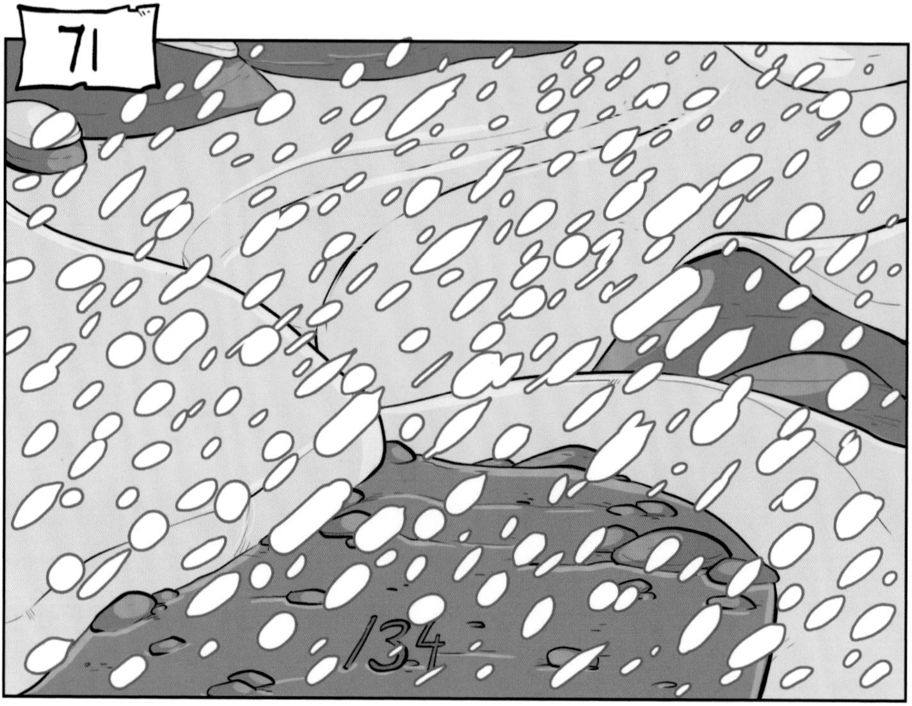
71
134

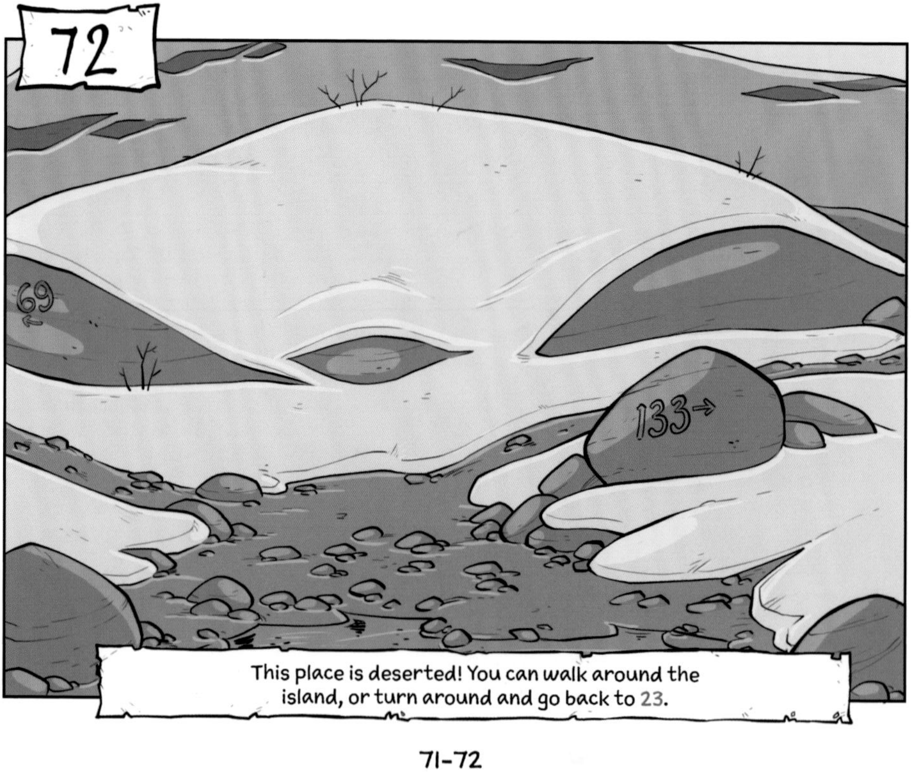
72
69
133
This place is deserted! You can walk around the island, or turn around and go back to 23.

73

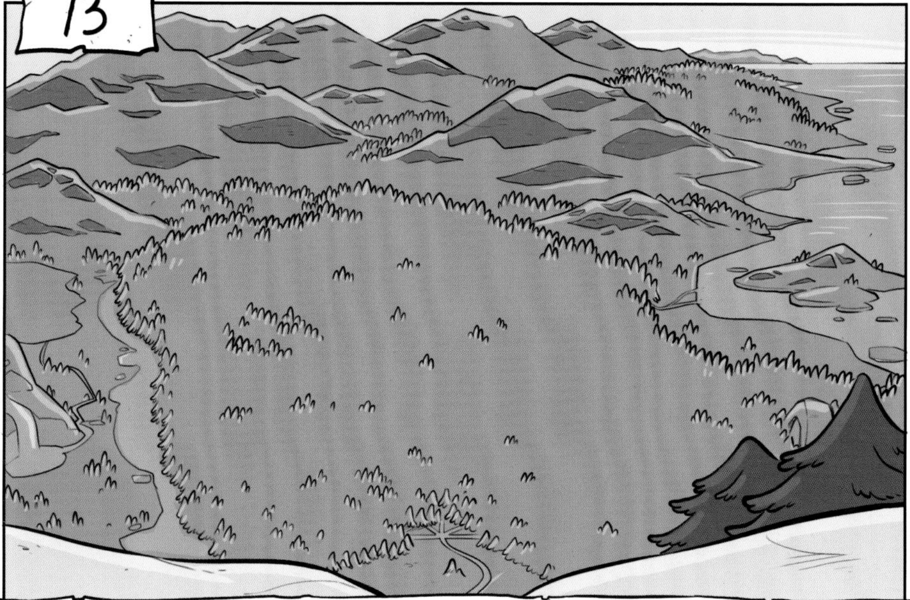

You know what would be useful on a quest: a map! If you were paying attention and took take one from the treasure room, go look at it in 102, then go to 7. If you don't have the map, go directly to 7.

74

Taking the path with the traps would have been a better idea, don't you think? Go to 84, weapon in hand, and get ready to deal with this 30-foot-tall giant.

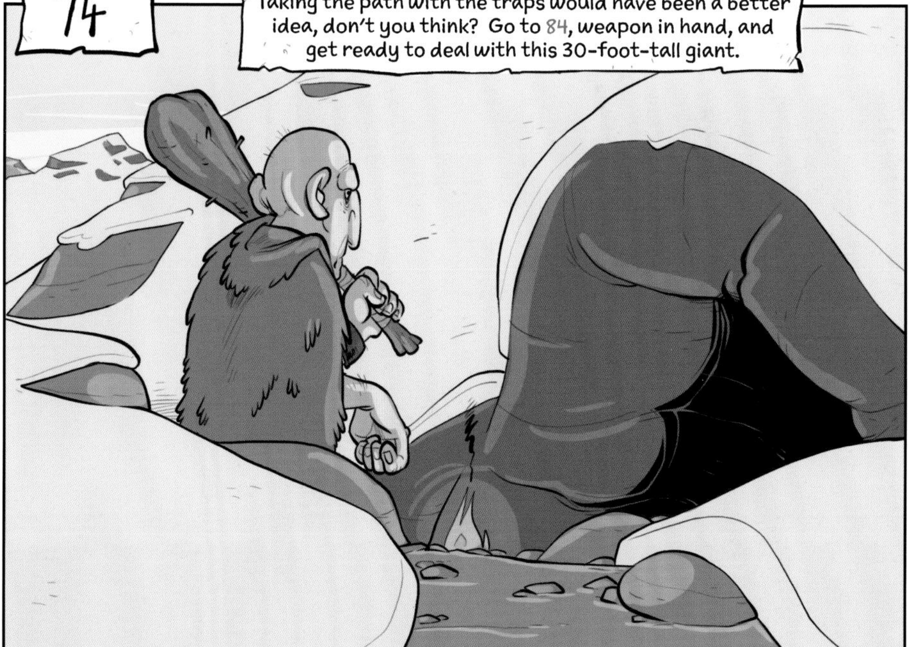

75

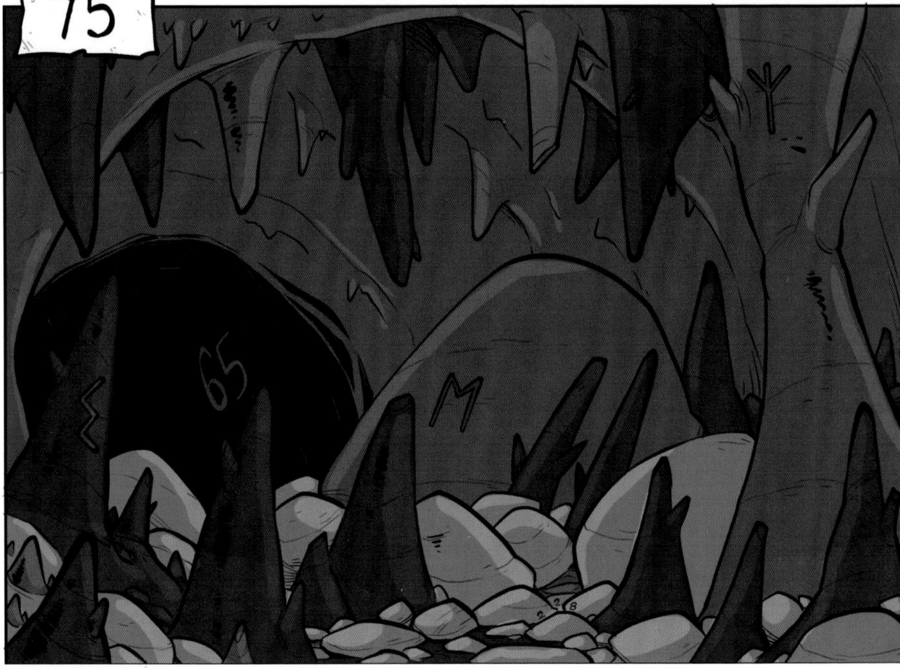

76

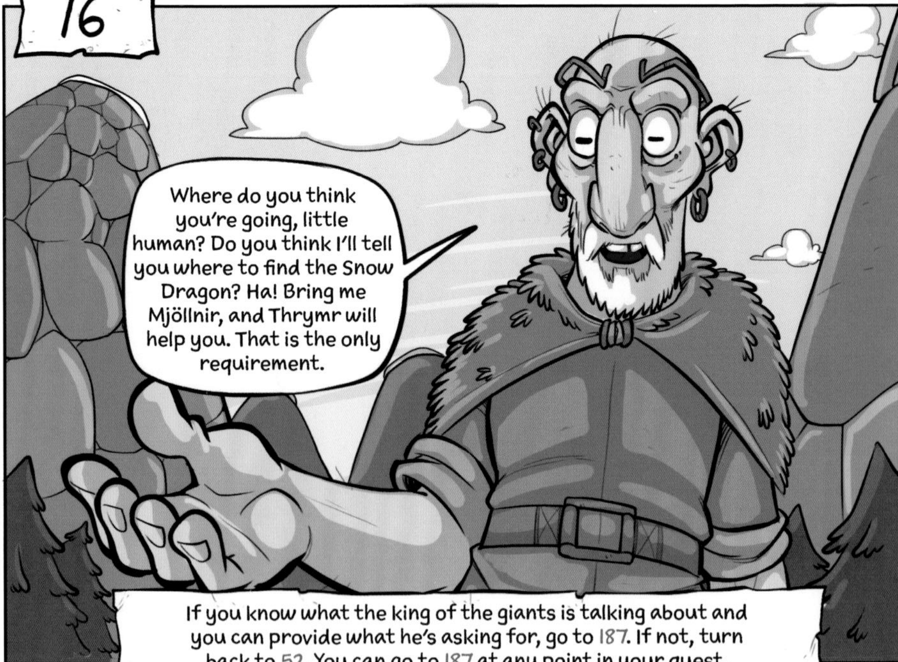

Where do you think you're going, little human? Do you think I'll tell you where to find the Snow Dragon? Ha! Bring me Mjöllnir, and Thrymr will help you. That is the only requirement.

If you know what the king of the giants is talking about and you can provide what he's asking for, go to 187. If not, turn back to 52. You can go to 187 at any point in your quest.

77

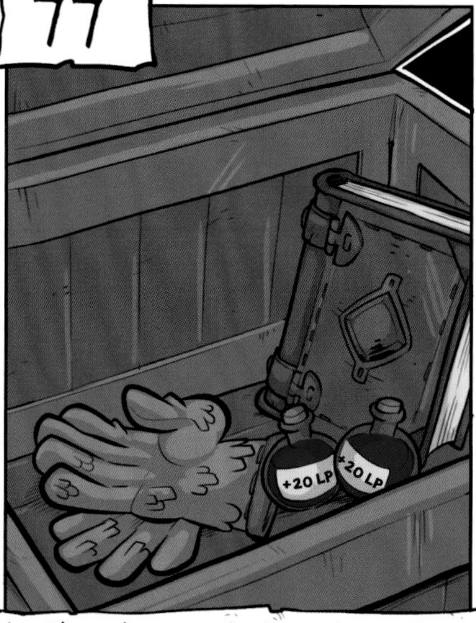
+20 LP
+20 LP

These dragonscale gloves give you 2 additional Resistance points. The grimoire spell book strengthens a mage's Fire spell. Its magic has the power to add 2 Attack points. Now go back to 26.

78

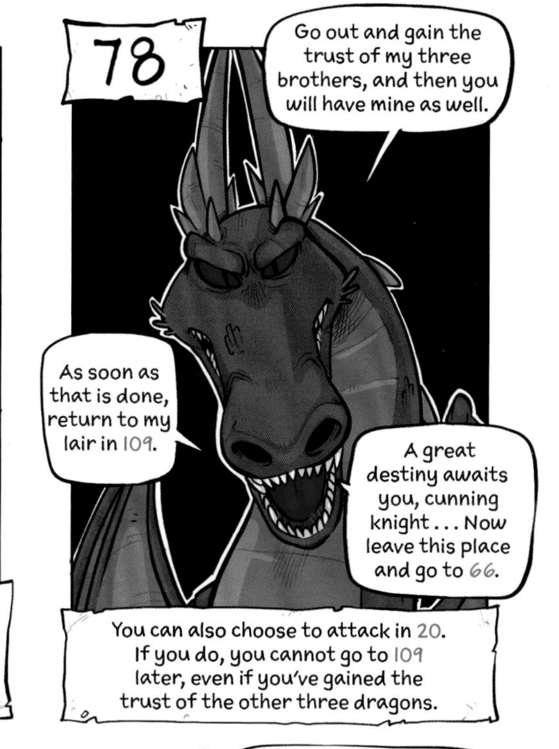
Go out and gain the trust of my three brothers, and then you will have mine as well.
As soon as that is done, return to my lair in 109.
A great destiny awaits you, cunning knight . . . Now leave this place and go to 66.

You can also choose to attack in 20. If you do, you cannot go to 109 later, even if you've gained the trust of the other three dragons.

79

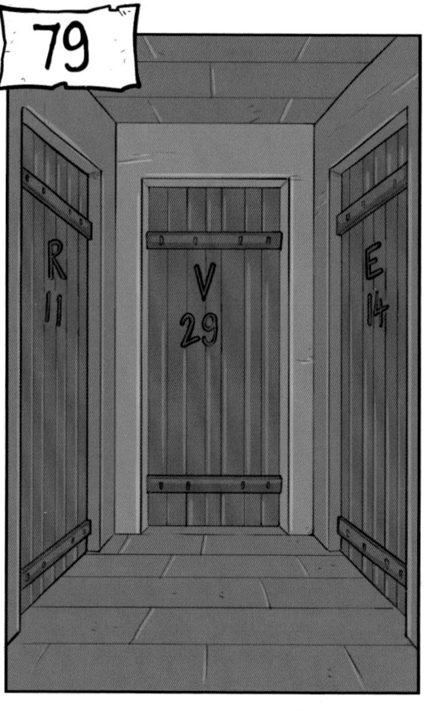
R
11
V
29
E
14

80

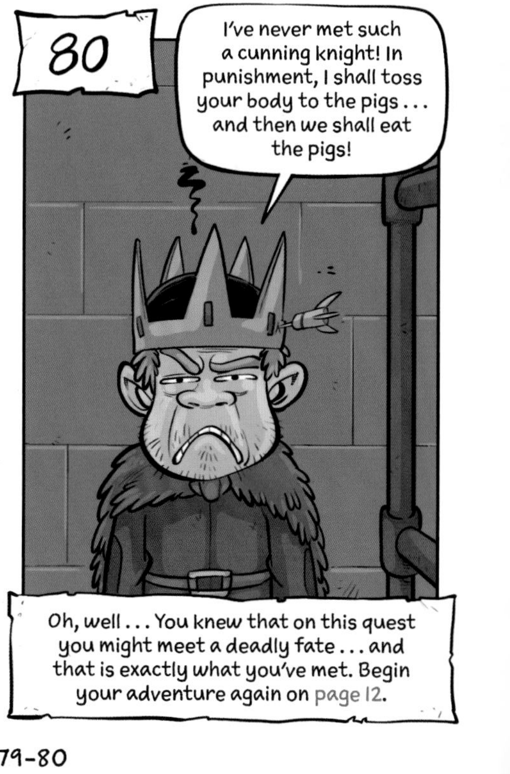
I've never met such a cunning knight! In punishment, I shall toss your body to the pigs . . . and then we shall eat the pigs!

Oh, well . . . You knew that on this quest you might meet a deadly fate . . . and that is exactly what you've met. Begin your adventure again on page 12.

81

MULT	3		
SP	7	SQ	2
ATT	4		
RES	0		
SR	0		
XP	5		
LOOT	0		

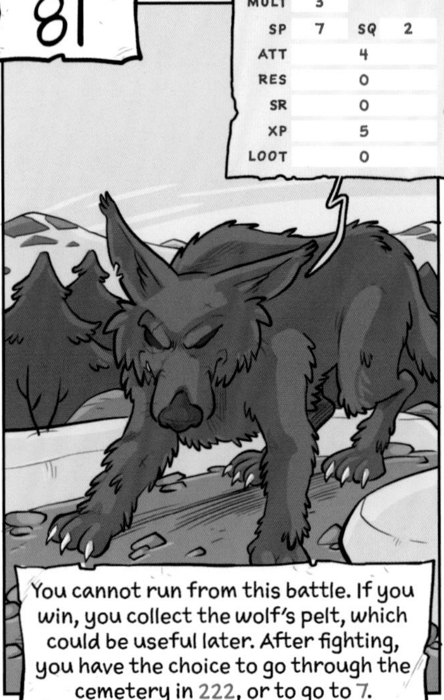
You cannot run from this battle. If you win, you collect the wolf's pelt, which could be useful later. After fighting, you have the choice to go through the cemetery in 222, or to go to 7.

82

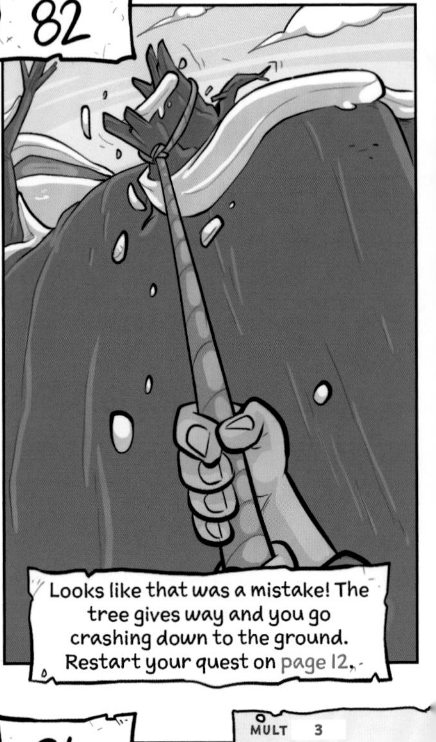
Looks like that was a mistake! The tree gives way and you go crashing down to the ground. Restart your quest on page 12.

83

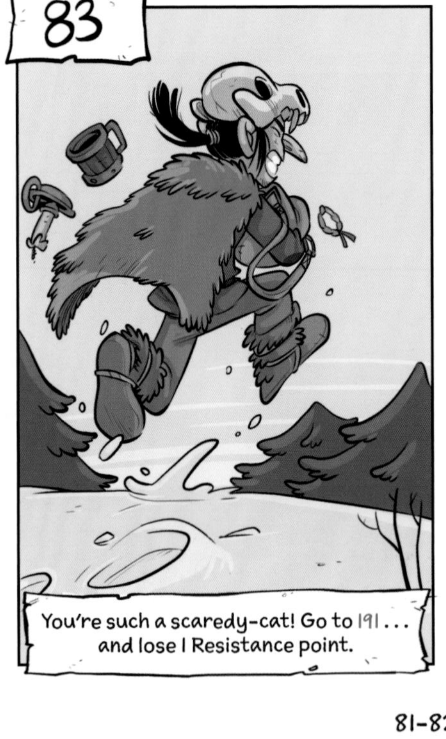
You're such a scaredy-cat! Go to 191 . . . and lose 1 Resistance point.

84

MULT	3		
SP	10	SQ	2
ATT	6		
RES	2		
SR	0		
XP	15		
LOOT	0		

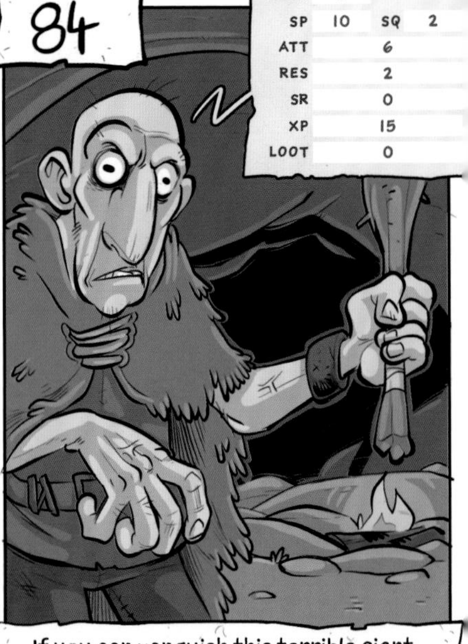
If you can vanquish this terrible giant, you can enter the grotto that he guards in 121. Or take the path at 148.

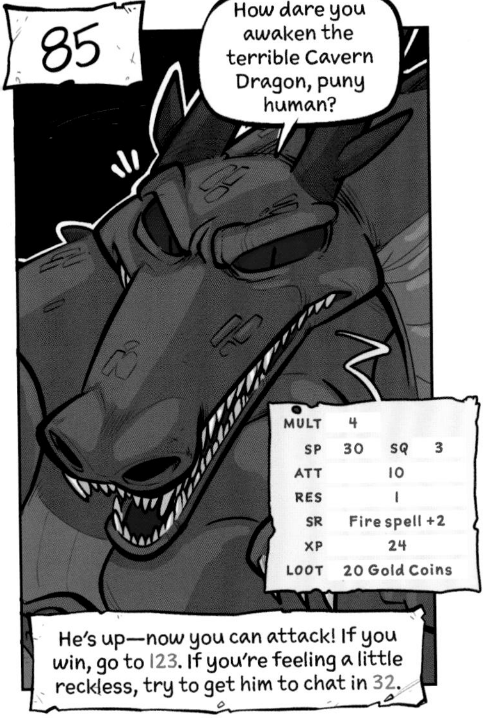
85
How dare you awaken the terrible Cavern Dragon, puny human?
He's up—now you can attack! If you win, go to 123. If you're feeling a little reckless, try to get him to chat in 32.

MULT	4		
SP	30	SQ	3
ATT	10		
RES	1		
SR	Fire spell +2		
XP	24		
LOOT	20 Gold Coins		

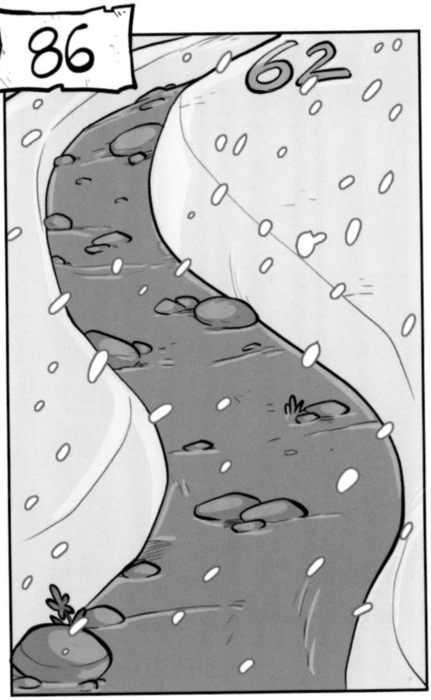
86
62

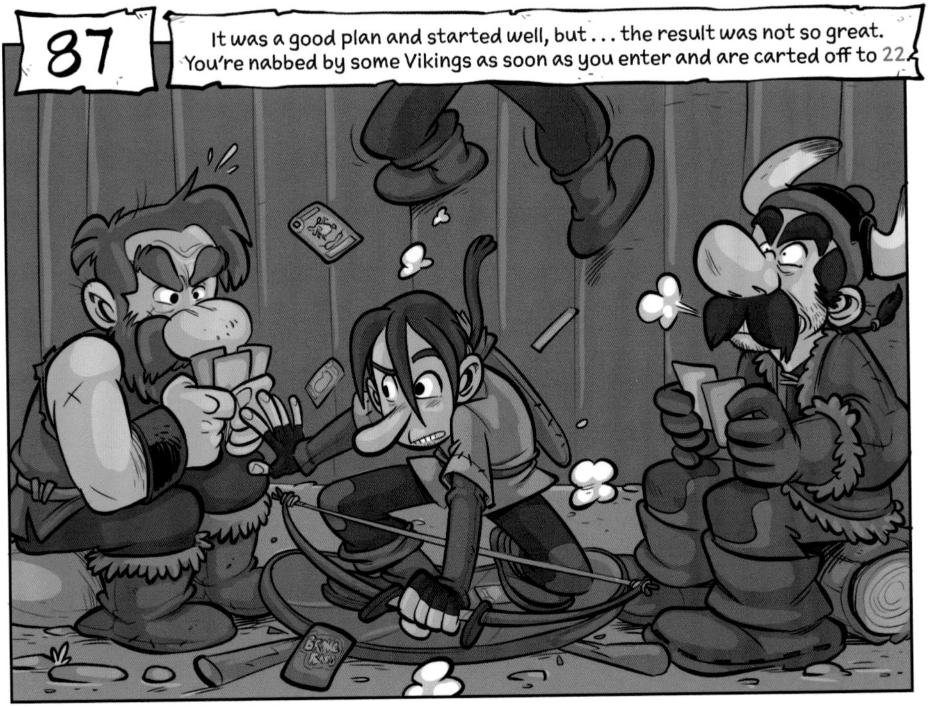
87
It was a good plan and started well, but . . . the result was not so great. You're nabbed by some Vikings as soon as you enter and are carted off to 22.

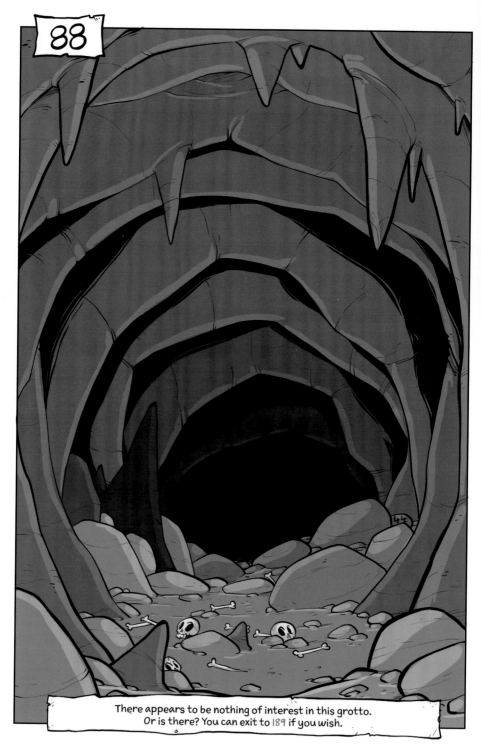

There appears to be nothing of interest in this grotto.
Or is there? You can exit to 189 if you wish.

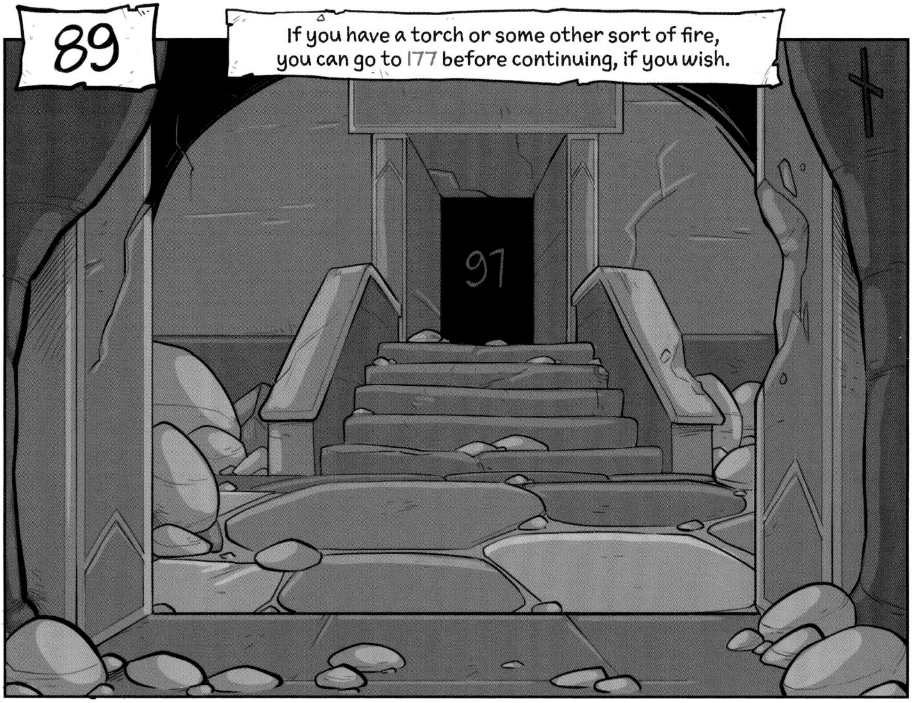
89
If you have a torch or some other sort of fire, you can go to 177 before continuing, if you wish.
97

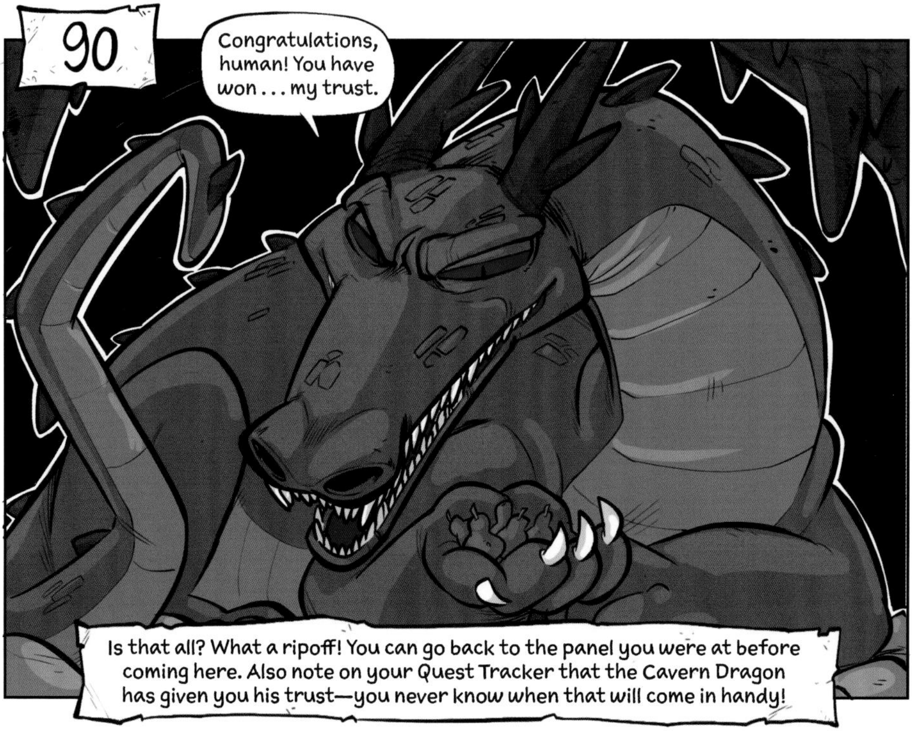
90
Congratulations, human! You have won . . . my trust.
Is that all? What a ripoff! You can go back to the panel you were at before coming here. Also note on your Quest Tracker that the Cavern Dragon has given you his trust—you never know when that will come in handy!

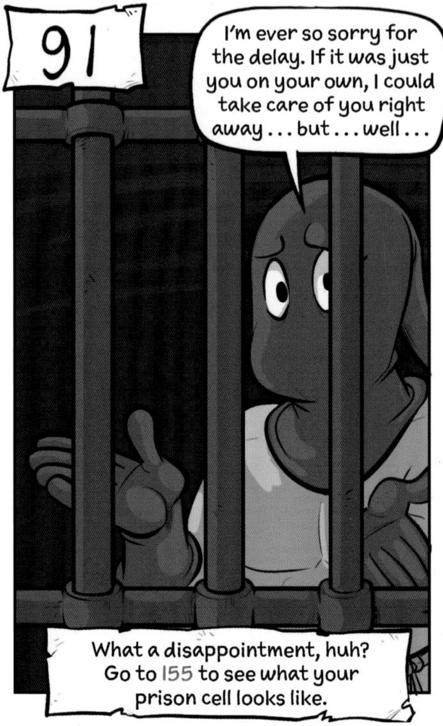
91
I'm ever so sorry for the delay. If it was just you on your own, I could take care of you right away . . . but . . . well . . .
What a disappointment, huh? Go to 155 to see what your prison cell looks like.

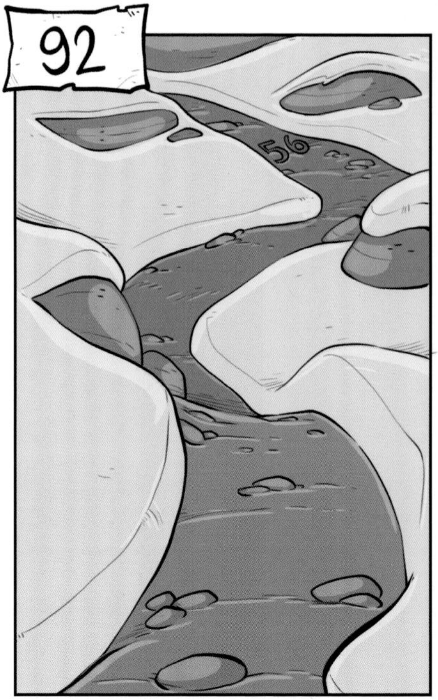
92
56

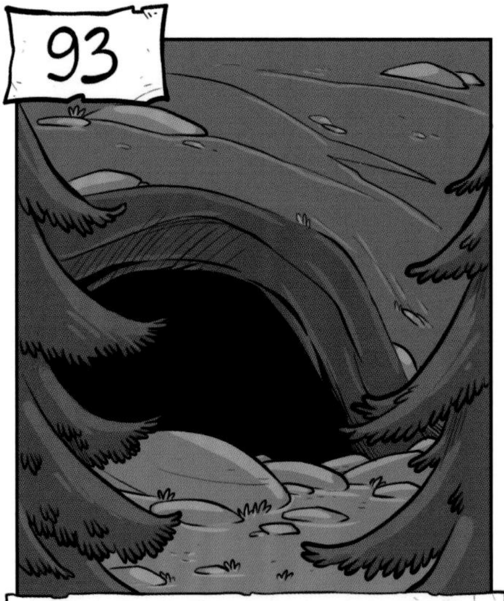
93
If you have a torch, light it and enter the cave in 75. You can also do so if you're a mage because you're skilled in fire. If you want to risk visiting the grotto without light, go to 30. Or you can retrace your steps to 215—why not come back another time, when you're better prepared?

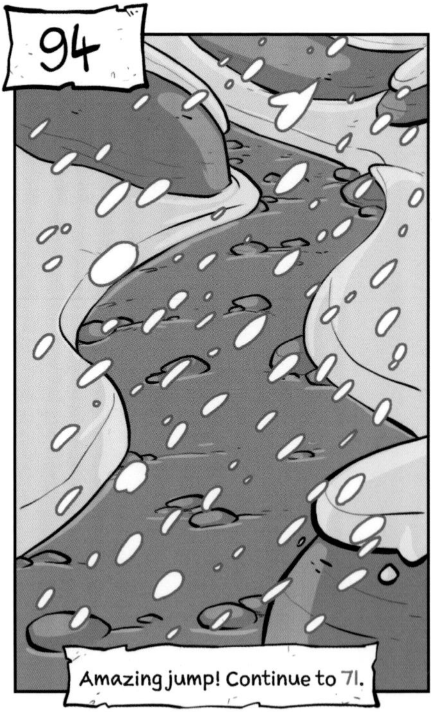
94
Amazing jump! Continue to 71.

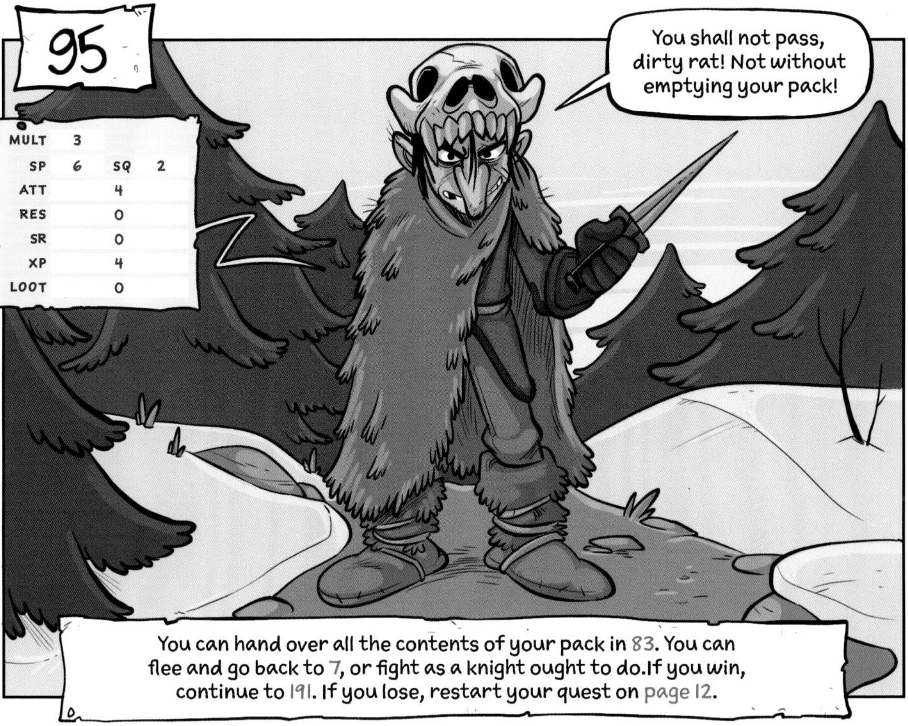
95
You shall not pass, dirty rat! Not without emptying your pack!
You can hand over all the contents of your pack in 83. You can flee and go back to 7, or fight as a knight ought to do.If you win, continue to 191. If you lose, restart your quest on page 12.

MULT	3		
SP	6	SQ	2
ATT		4	
RES		0	
SR		0	
XP		4	
LOOT		0	

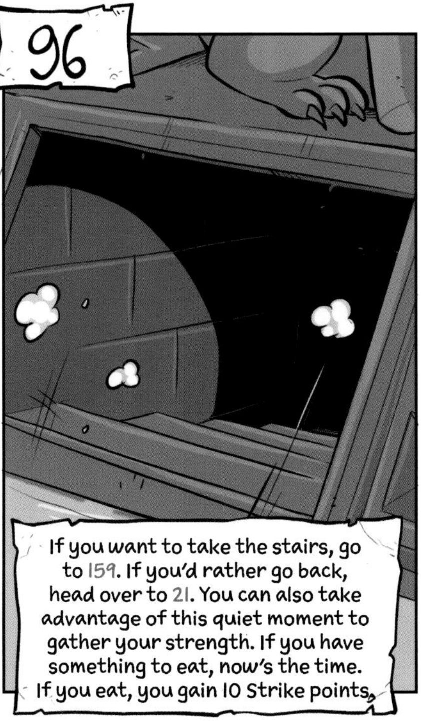
96
If you want to take the stairs, go to 159. If you'd rather go back, head over to 21. You can also take advantage of this quiet moment to gather your strength. If you have something to eat, now's the time. If you eat, you gain 10 Strike points.

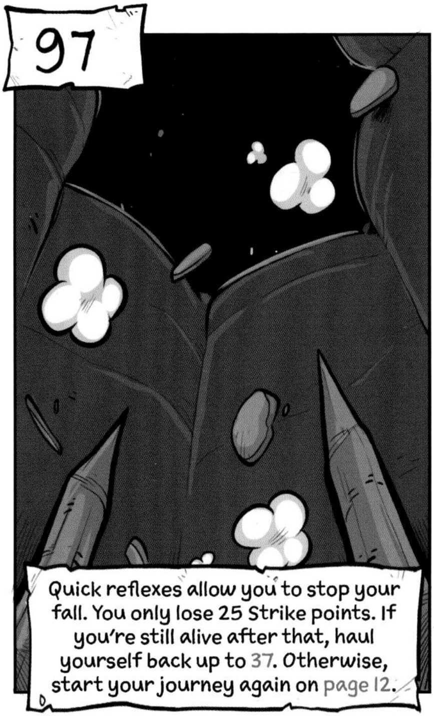
97
Quick reflexes allow you to stop your fall. You only lose 25 Strike points. If you're still alive after that, haul yourself back up to 37. Otherwise, start your journey again on page 12.

Hugin and Munin, my most faithful friends, have reported that the humans have entrusted you with a mission of the utmost importance. I shall give you a mission that is just as worthy, if you wish to proceed in peace through the lands of Asgard:

Learn to recognize what surrounds you. Learn to recognize the names of the deities that will keep you alive. Learn Futhark from the runes that you find along your way. And then you will be able to meet me.

_____ : god of thunder. Mjöllnir is his most powerful ally.

_____ : goddess of the seas and oceans. She will fish you out in her nets if you are drowning.

_____ : goddess of healing. She will help you mix the most useful potions for your survival.

_____ : goddess of the night. It is possible that you will never catch sight of her.

_____ : god of justice and strategy. He won the trust of Fenrir through self-sacrifice.

_____ : god of cookery.

_____ : goddess of death. Her visage is bathed in light and covered in darkness.

_____ : god of hunters and winter. If ever anyone did not feed the cold, it is him.

_____ : goddess of long life. Bite into her apple, and you will be granted many years of life.

_____ : this is not a god, but the king of Jötunheim.

Futhark is the alphabet that the people of these lands use to write. It's the only help I can give you. After making sure to write down the number of this parchment so you can return to it and fill in your discoveries, go to 73.

99

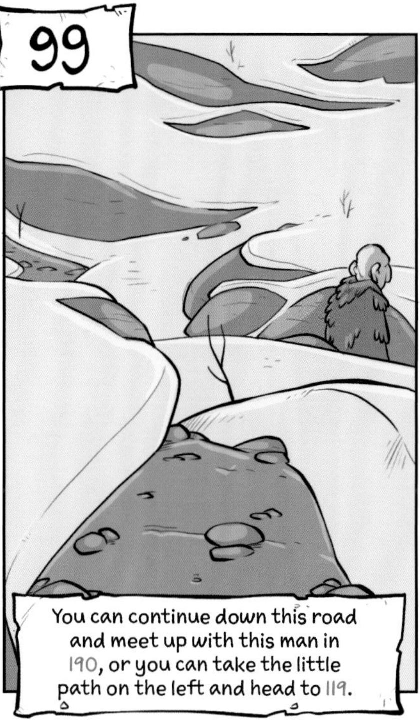
You can continue down this road and meet up with this man in 190, or you can take the little path on the left and head to 119.

100

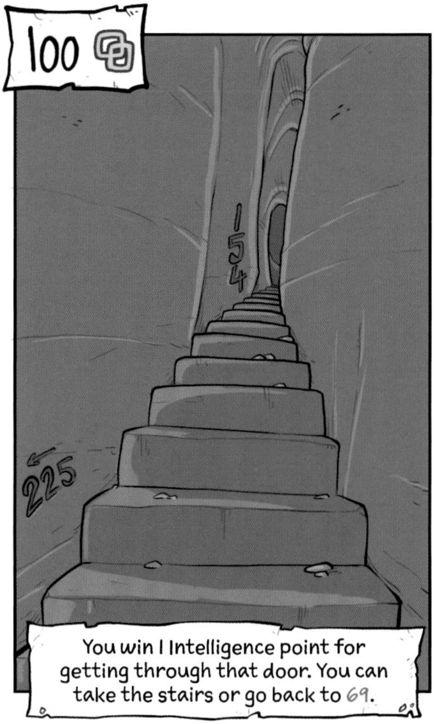
154
225
You win 1 Intelligence point for getting through that door. You can take the stairs or go back to 69.

101

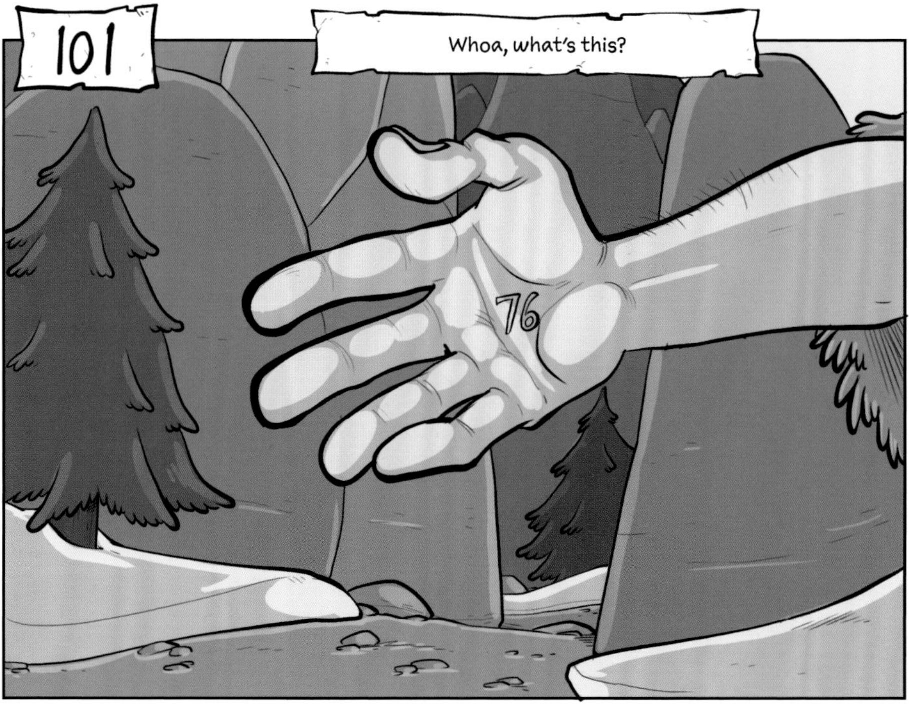
Whoa, what's this?
76

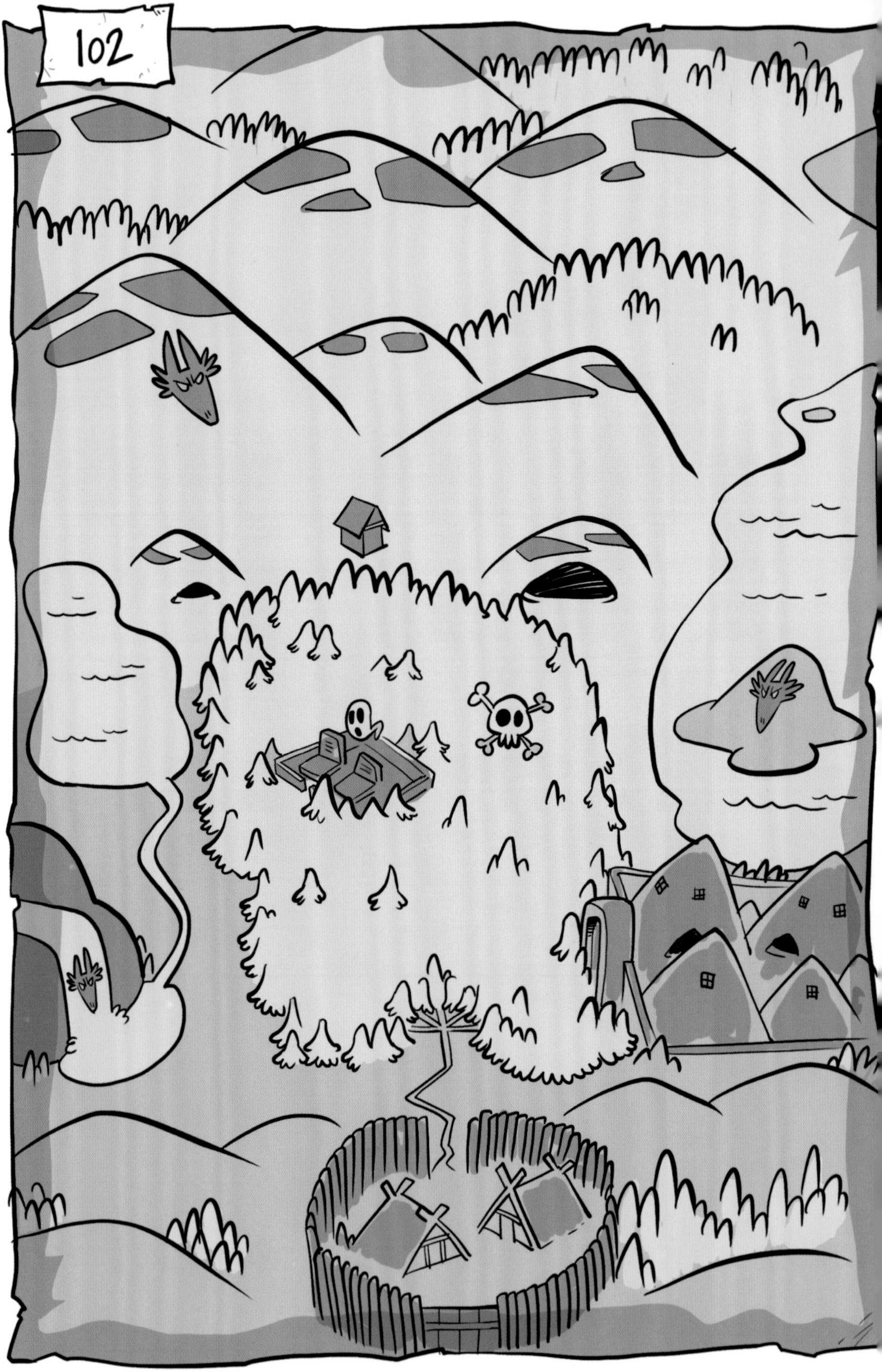
102

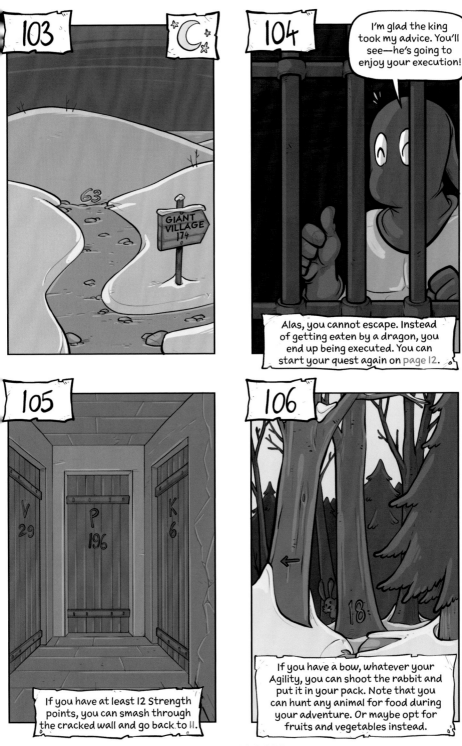

103

63

GIANT
VILLAGE
174

104

I'm glad the king took my advice. You'll see—he's going to enjoy your execution!

Alas, you cannot escape. Instead of getting eaten by a dragon, you end up being executed. You can start your quest again on page 12.

105

V
29

P
196

K
6

If you have at least 12 Strength points, you can smash through the cracked wall and go back to 11.

106

18

If you have a bow, whatever your Agility, you can shoot the rabbit and put it in your pack. Note that you can hunt any animal for food during your adventure. Or maybe opt for fruits and vegetables instead.

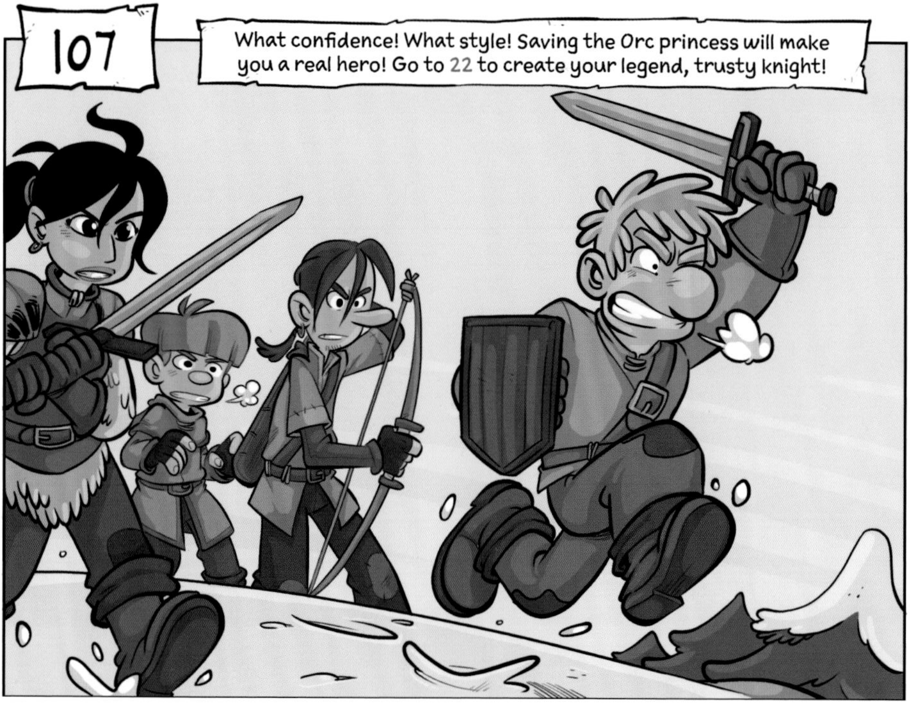
107
What confidence! What style! Saving the Orc princess will make you a real hero! Go to 22 to create your legend, trusty knight!

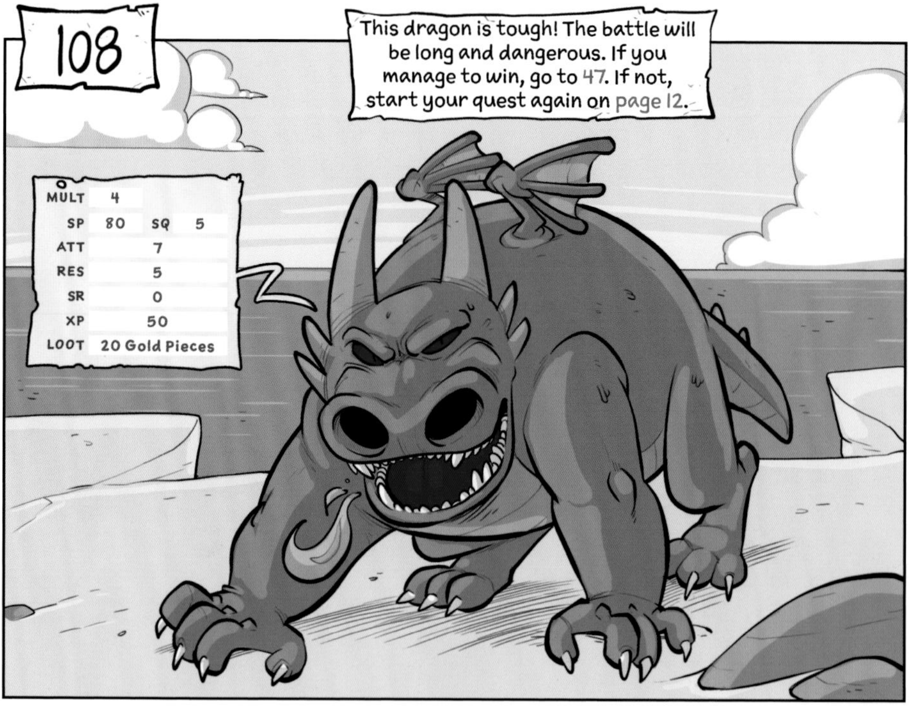
108
This dragon is tough! The battle will be long and dangerous. If you manage to win, go to 47. If not, start your quest again on page 12.
MULT 4
SP 80 SQ 5
ATT 7
RES 5
SR 0
XP 50
LOOT 20 Gold Pieces

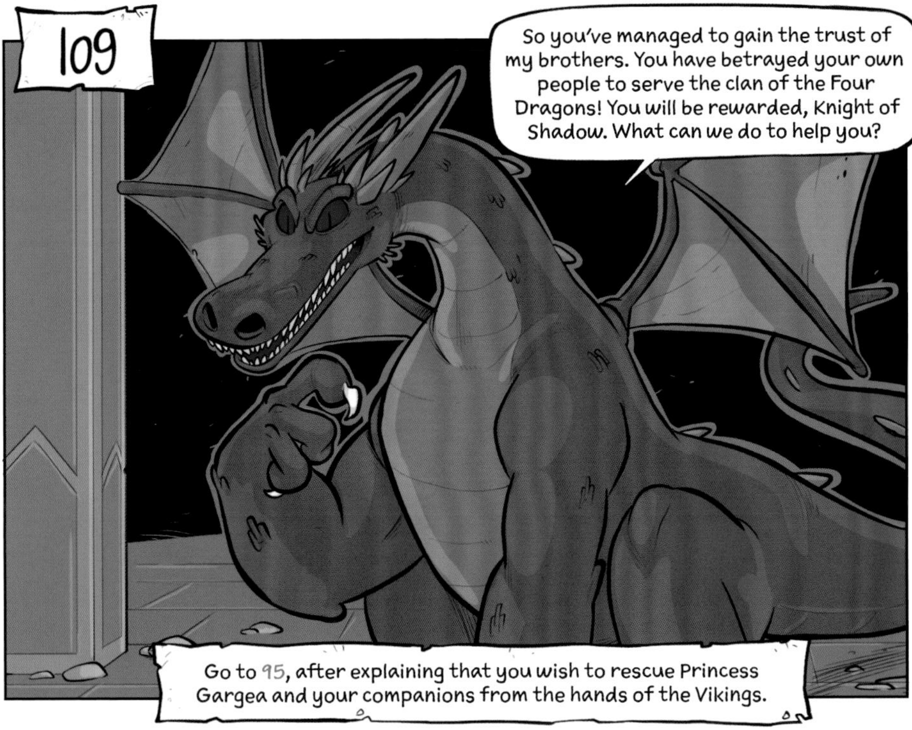
109
So you've managed to gain the trust of my brothers. You have betrayed your own people to serve the clan of the Four Dragons! You will be rewarded, Knight of Shadow. What can we do to help you?
Go to 95, after explaining that you wish to rescue Princess Gargea and your companions from the hands of the Vikings.

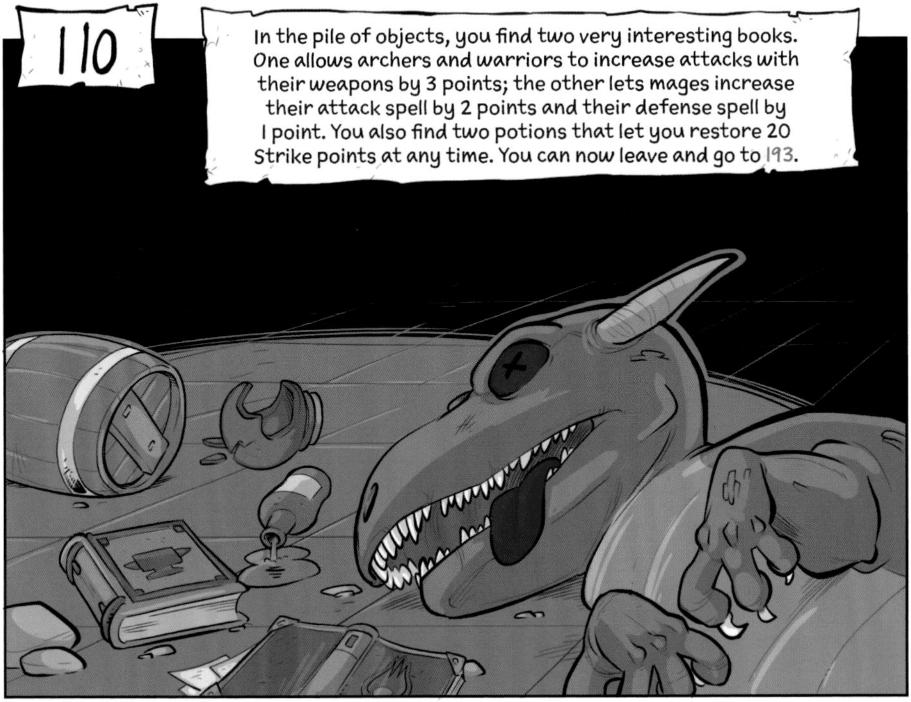
110
In the pile of objects, you find two very interesting books. One allows archers and warriors to increase attacks with their weapons by 3 points; the other lets mages increase their attack spell by 2 points and their defense spell by 1 point. You also find two potions that let you restore 20 Strike points at any time. You can now leave and go to 193.

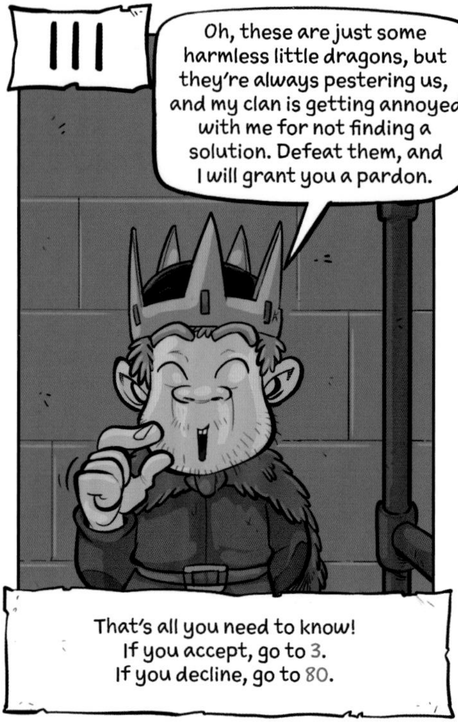
111
Oh, these are just some harmless little dragons, but they're always pestering us, and my clan is getting annoyed with me for not finding a solution. Defeat them, and I will grant you a pardon.
That's all you need to know!
If you accept, go to 3.
If you decline, go to 80.

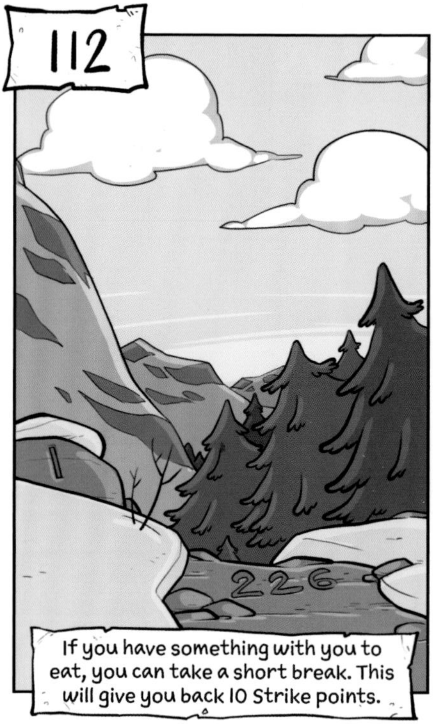
112
226
If you have something with you to eat, you can take a short break. This will give you back 10 Strike points.

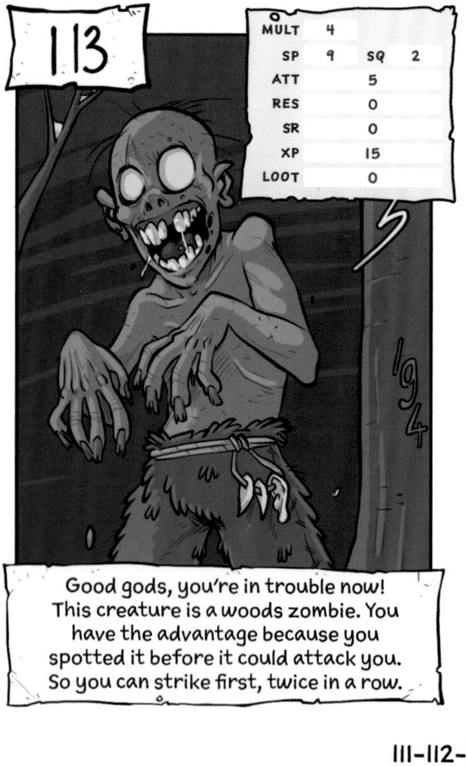
113
194
Good gods, you're in trouble now! This creature is a woods zombie. You have the advantage because you spotted it before it could attack you. So you can strike first, twice in a row.

MULT	4		
SP	9	SQ	2
ATT		5	
RES		0	
SR		0	
XP		15	
LOOT		0	

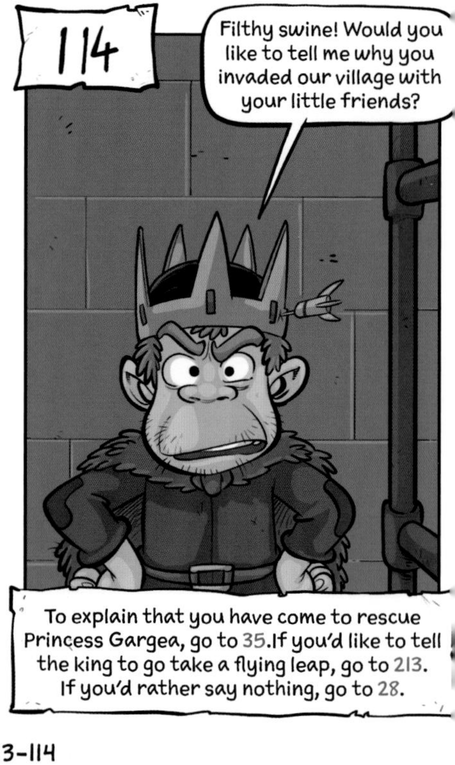
114
Filthy swine! Would you like to tell me why you invaded our village with your little friends?
To explain that you have come to rescue Princess Gargea, go to 35.If you'd like to tell the king to go take a flying leap, go to 213. If you'd rather say nothing, go to 28.

115

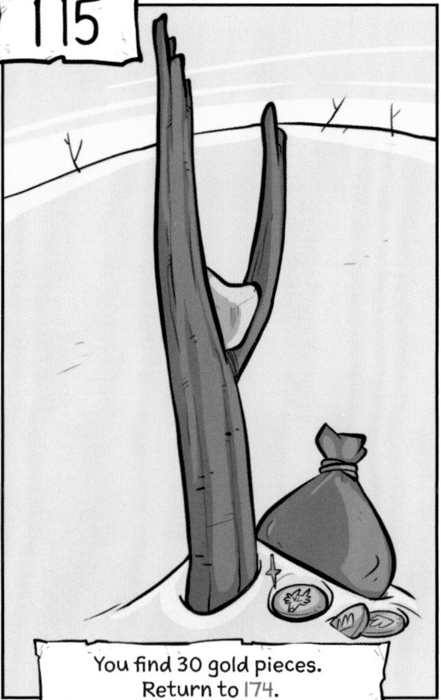

You find 30 gold pieces.
Return to 174.

116

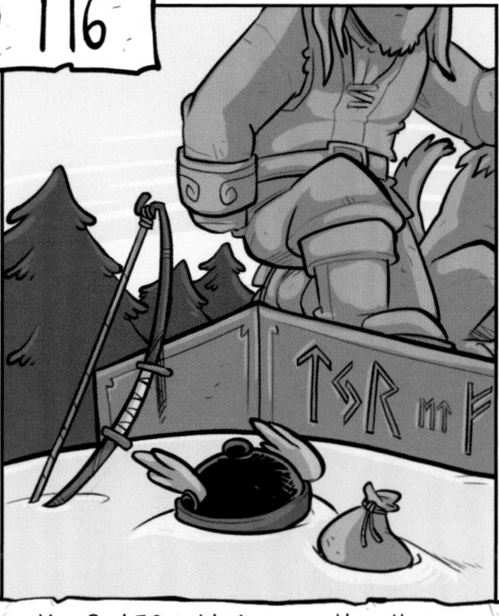

You find 50 gold pieces on the altar, a winged helmet that gives you 2 Resistance points and 1 Agility point while you're wearing it, and a bow that gives 10 Attack points. But take note! To use this bow, you must have a minimum of 15 Agility points. When your pockets are full, go to 199.

117

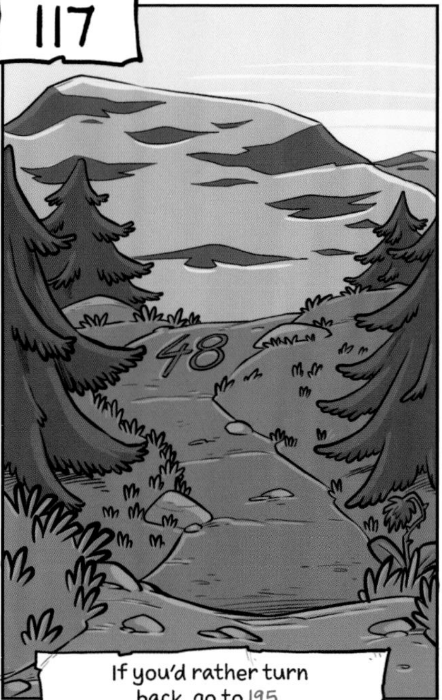
48

If you'd rather turn back, go to 195.

118

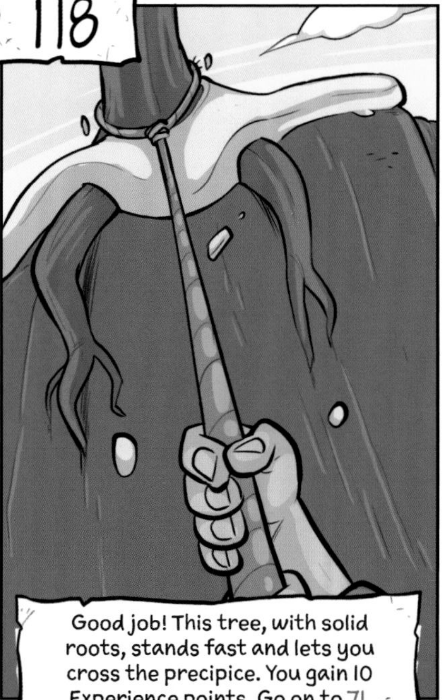

Good job! This tree, with solid roots, stands fast and lets you cross the precipice. You gain 10 Experience points. Go on to 71.

119

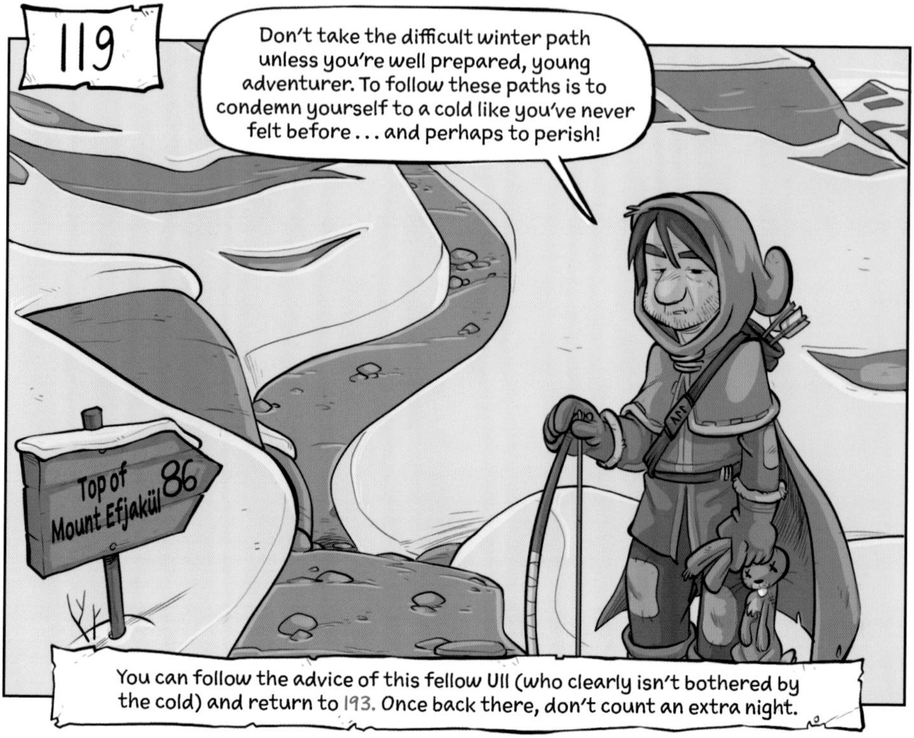
Don't take the difficult winter path unless you're well prepared, young adventurer. To follow these paths is to condemn yourself to a cold like you've never felt before . . . and perhaps to perish!
Top of Mount Efjaköl 86
You can follow the advice of this fellow Ull (who clearly isn't bothered by the cold) and return to 193. Once back there, don't count an extra night.

120

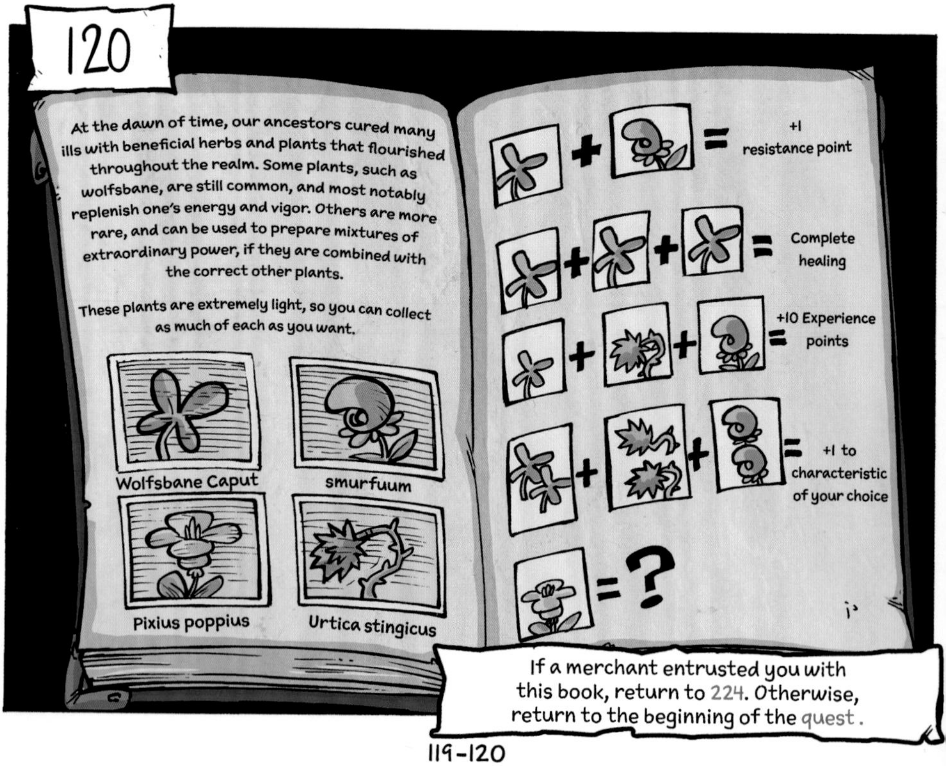
At the dawn of time, our ancestors cured many ills with beneficial herbs and plants that flourished throughout the realm. Some plants, such as wolfsbane, are still common, and most notably replenish one's energy and vigor. Others are more rare, and can be used to prepare mixtures of extraordinary power, if they are combined with the correct other plants.
These plants are extremely light, so you can collect as much of each as you want.
Wolfsbane Caput
smurfuum
Pixius poppius
Urtica stingicus
+1 resistance point
Complete healing
+10 Experience points
+1 to characteristic of your choice
?
If a merchant entrusted you with this book, return to 224. Otherwise, return to the beginning of the quest.

121

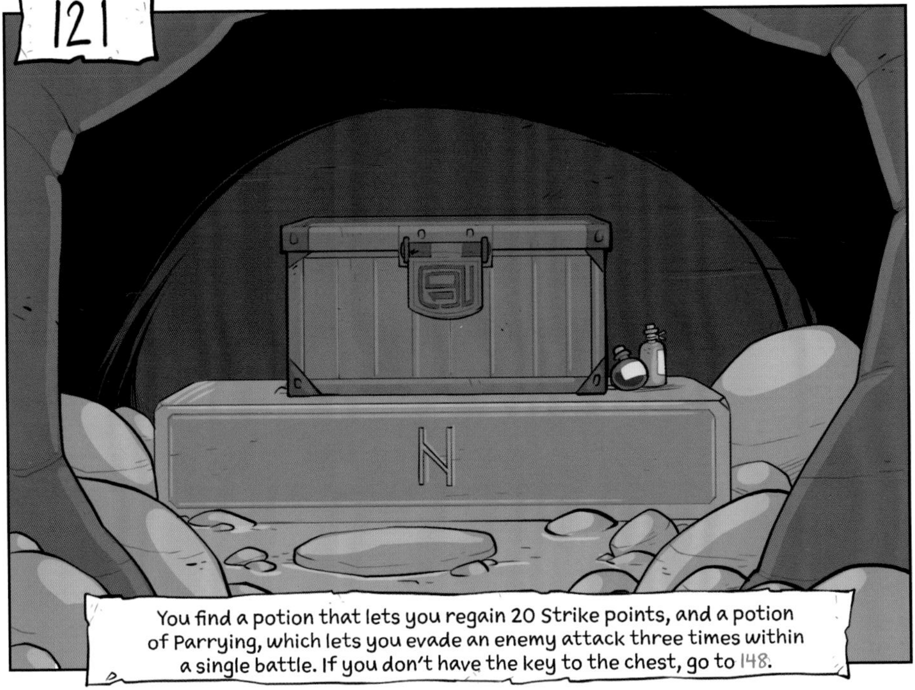
You find a potion that lets you regain 20 Strike points, and a potion of Parrying, which lets you evade an enemy attack three times within a single battle. If you don't have the key to the chest, go to 148.

122

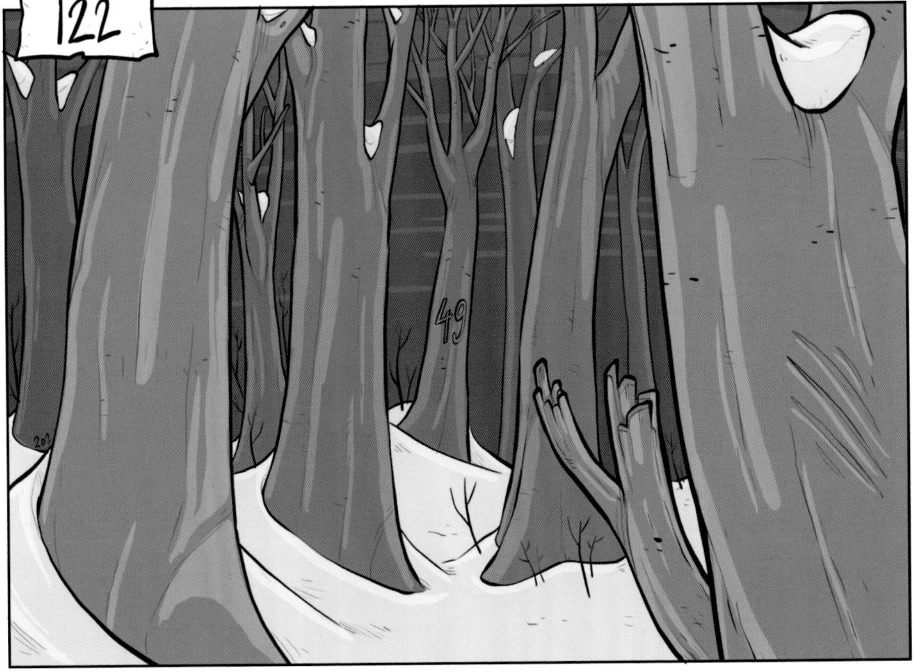
49

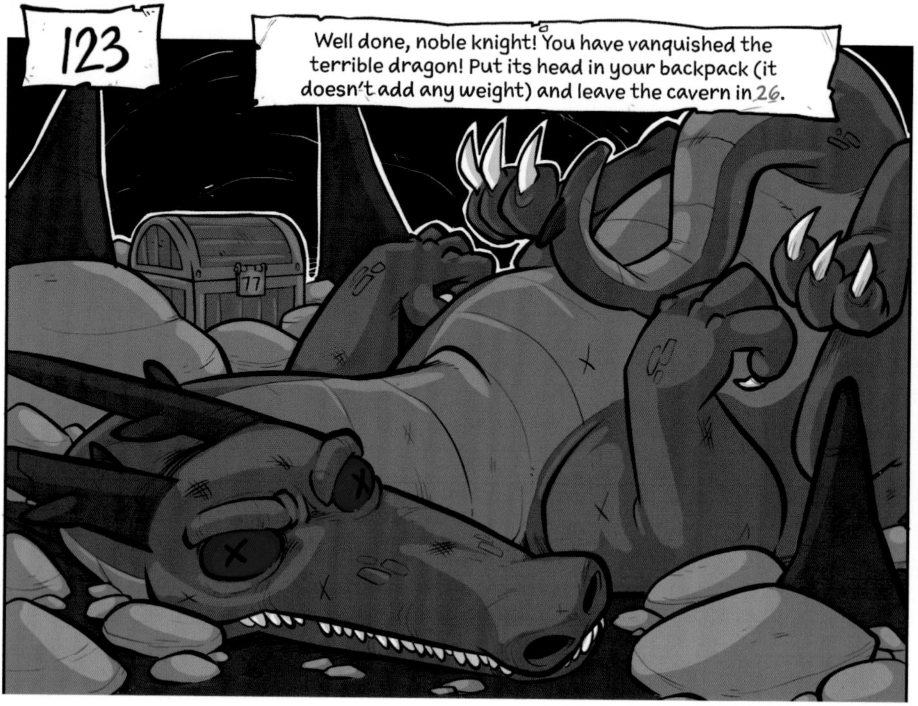
123
Well done, noble knight! You have vanquished the terrible dragon! Put its head in your backpack (it doesn't add any weight) and leave the cavern in 26.
77

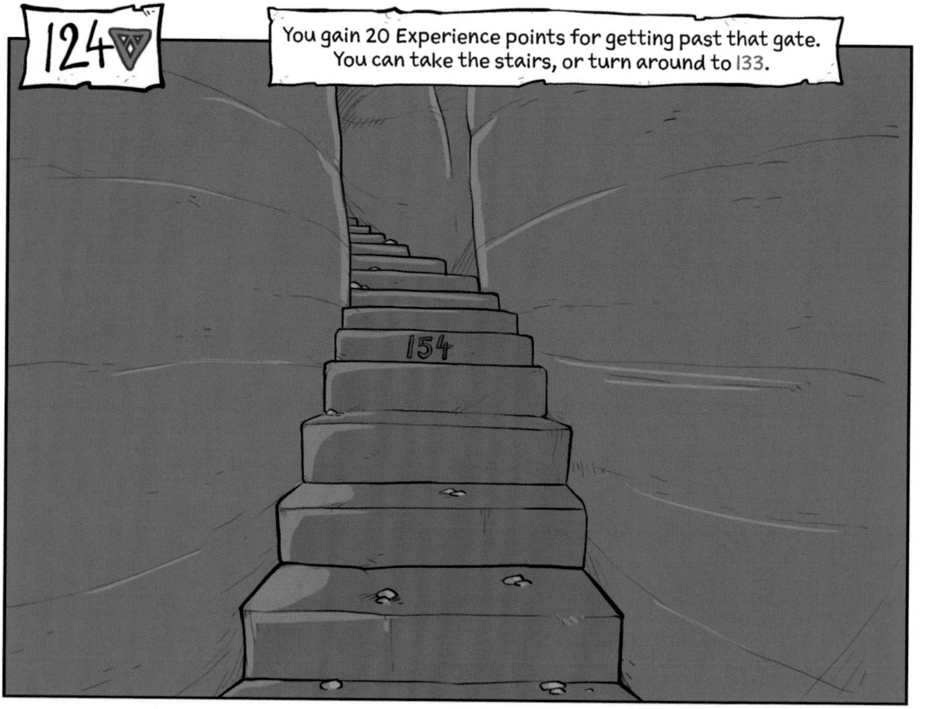
124
You gain 20 Experience points for getting past that gate. You can take the stairs, or turn around to 133.
154

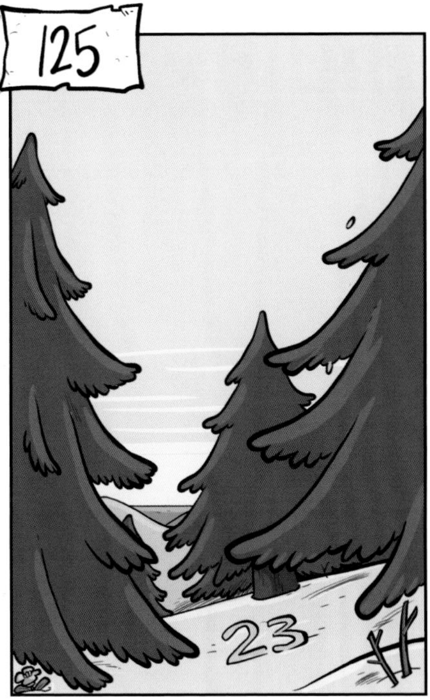
125
23

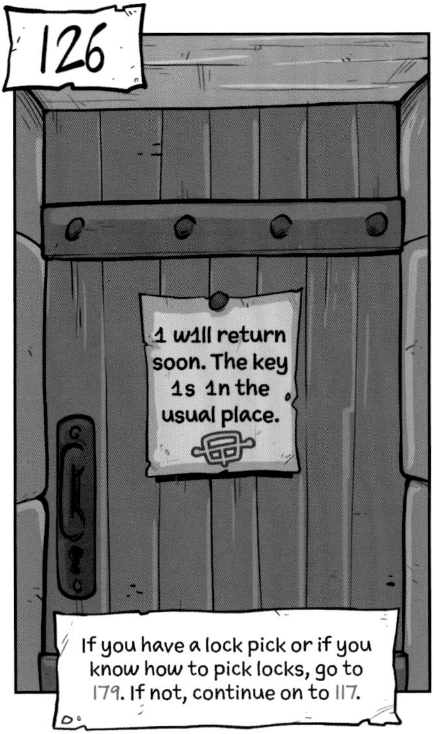
126
1 w1ll return soon. The key 1s 1n the usual place.
If you have a lock pick or if you know how to pick locks, go to 179. If not, continue on to 117.

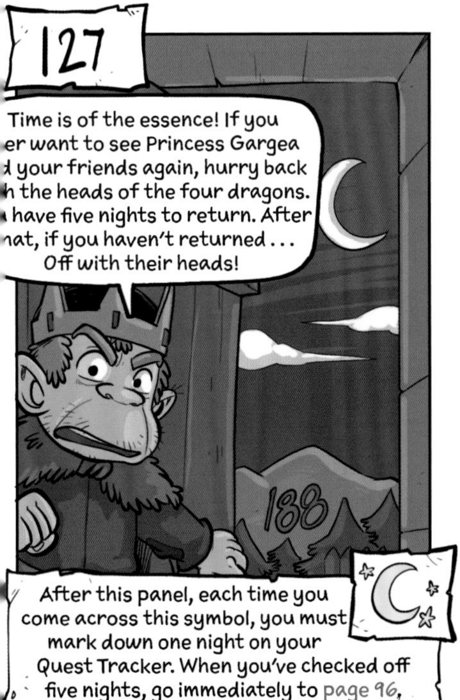
127
Time is of the essence! If you
er want to see Princess Gargea
d your friends again, hurry back
h the heads of the four dragons.
have five nights to return. After
hat, if you haven't returned . . .
Off with their heads!
188
After this panel, each time you come across this symbol, you must mark down one night on your Quest Tracker. When you've checked off five nights, go immediately to page 96.

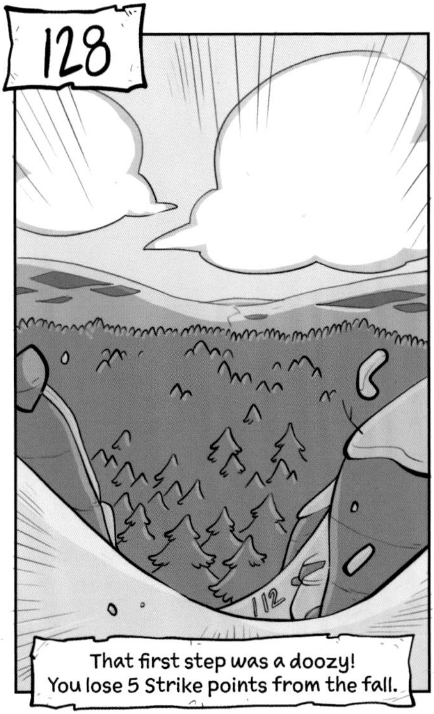
128
112
That first step was a doozy!
You lose 5 Strike points from the fall.

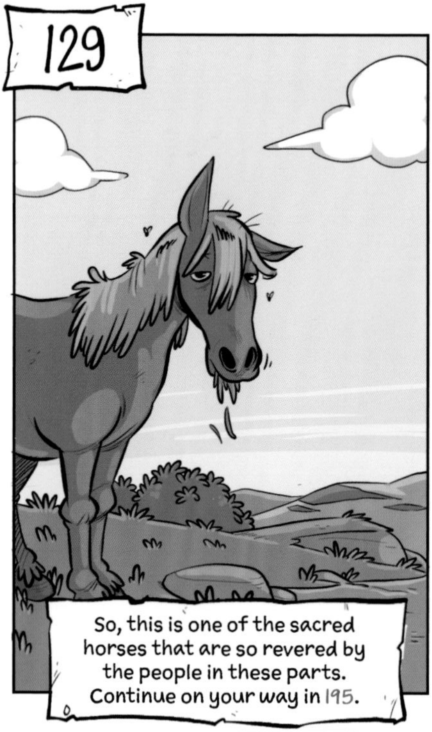
129
So, this is one of the sacred horses that are so revered by the people in these parts. Continue on your way in 195.

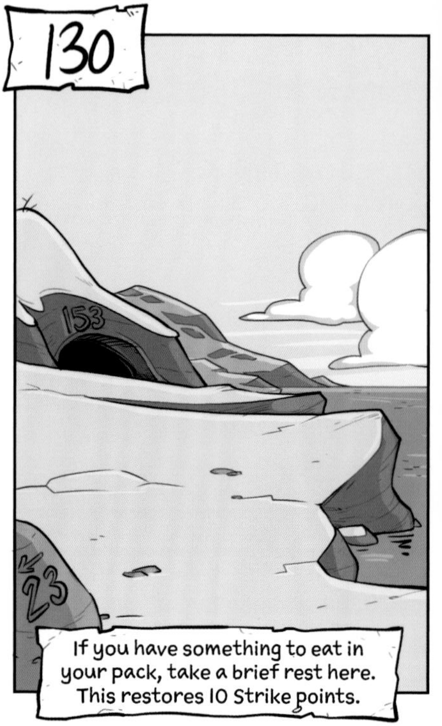
130
153
23
If you have something to eat in your pack, take a brief rest here. This restores 10 Strike points.

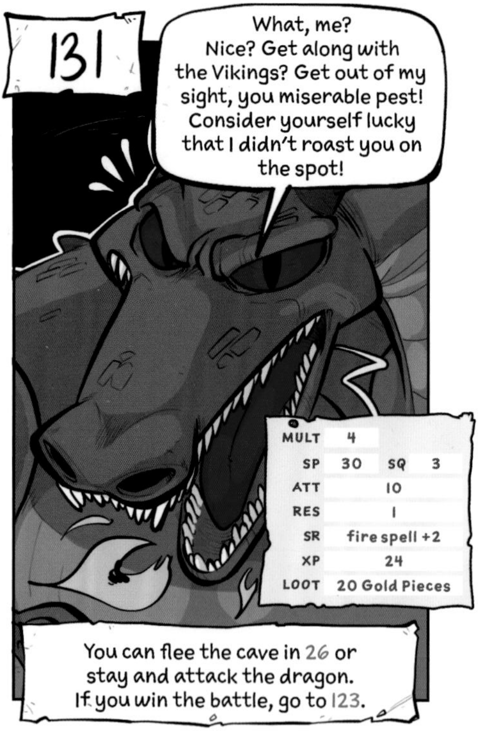
131
What, me? Nice? Get along with the Vikings? Get out of my sight, you miserable pest! Consider yourself lucky that I didn't roast you on the spot!
You can flee the cave in 26 or stay and attack the dragon. If you win the battle, go to 123.

MULT	4		
SP	30	SQ	3
ATT	10		
RES	1		
SR	fire spell +2		
XP	24		
LOOT	20 Gold Pieces		

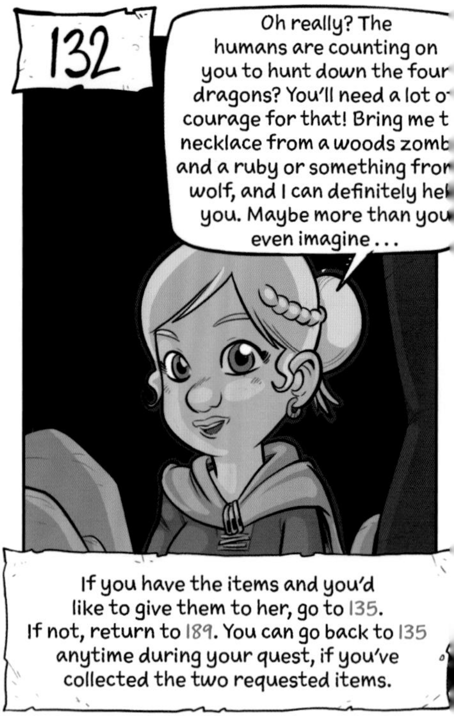
132
Oh really? The humans are counting on you to hunt down the four dragons? You'll need a lot o courage for that! Bring me t necklace from a woods zomb and a ruby or something fror wolf, and I can definitely hel you. Maybe more than you even imagine . . .
If you have the items and you'd like to give them to her, go to 135. If not, return to 189. You can go back to 135 anytime during your quest, if you've collected the two requested items.

133

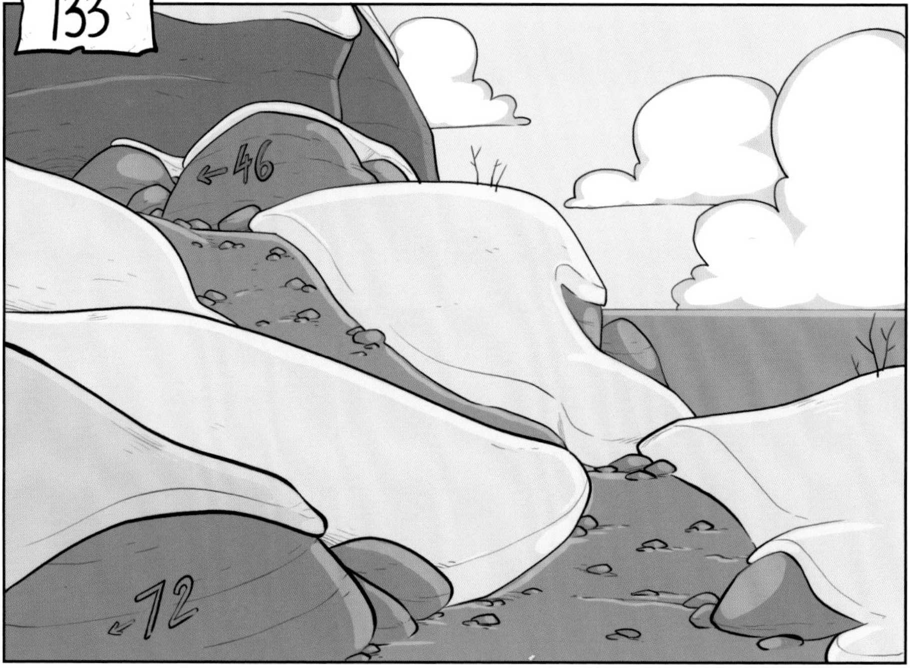

←46
←72

134

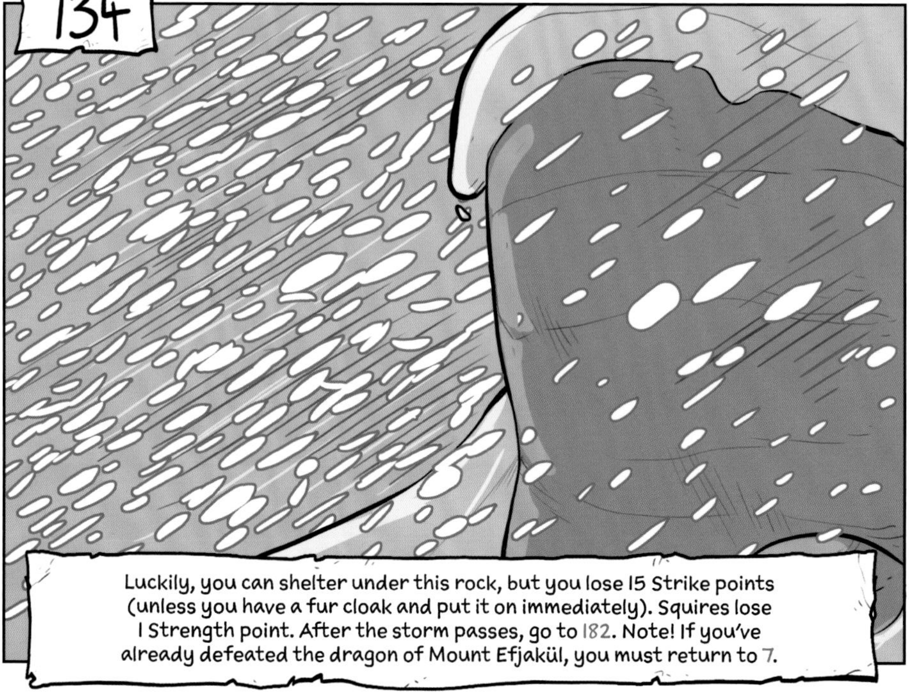

Luckily, you can shelter under this rock, but you lose 15 Strike points (unless you have a fur cloak and put it on immediately). Squires lose 1 Strength point. After the storm passes, go to 182. Note! If you've already defeated the dragon of Mount Efjakül, you must return to 7.

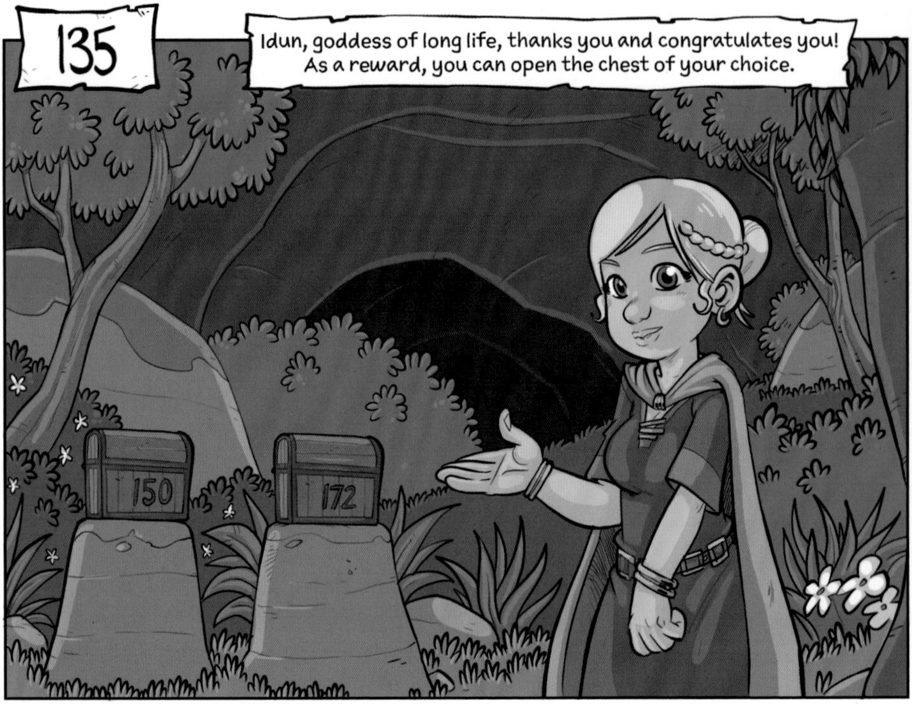
135
Idun, goddess of long life, thanks you and congratulates you! As a reward, you can open the chest of your choice.
150
172

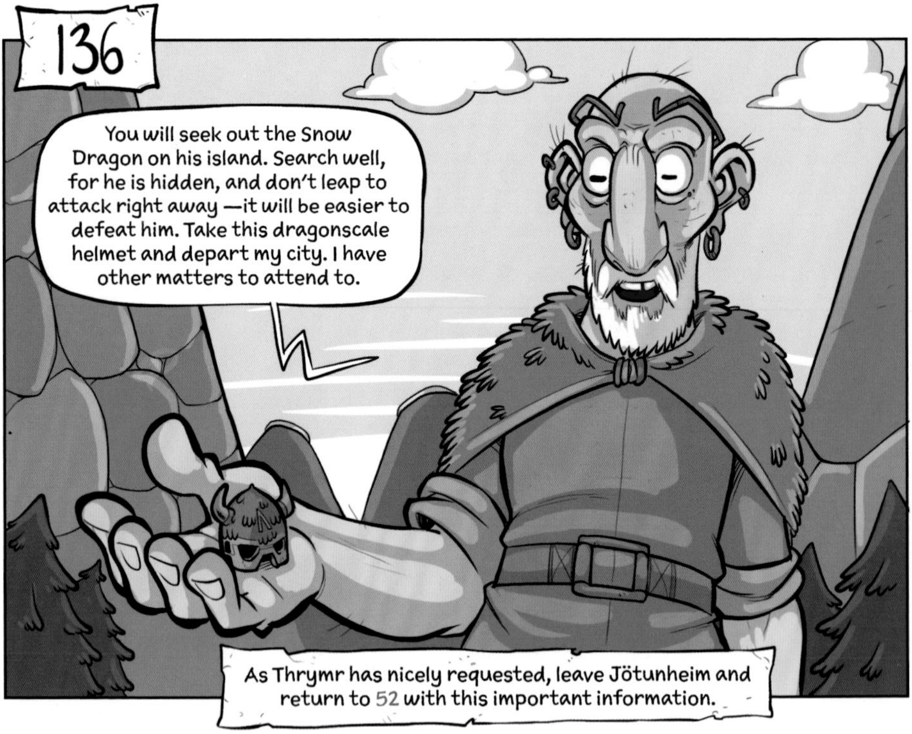
136
You will seek out the Snow Dragon on his island. Search well, for he is hidden, and don't leap to attack right away—it will be easier to defeat him. Take this dragonscale helmet and depart my city. I have other matters to attend to.
As Thrymr has nicely requested, leave Jötunheim and return to 52 with this important information.

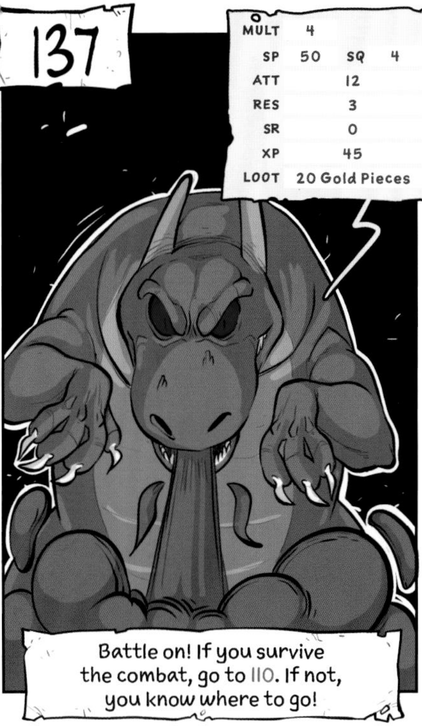
137
MULT 4
SP 50 SQ 4
ATT 12
RES 3
SR 0
XP 45
LOOT 20 Gold Pieces
Battle on! If you survive the combat, go to 110. If not, you know where to go!

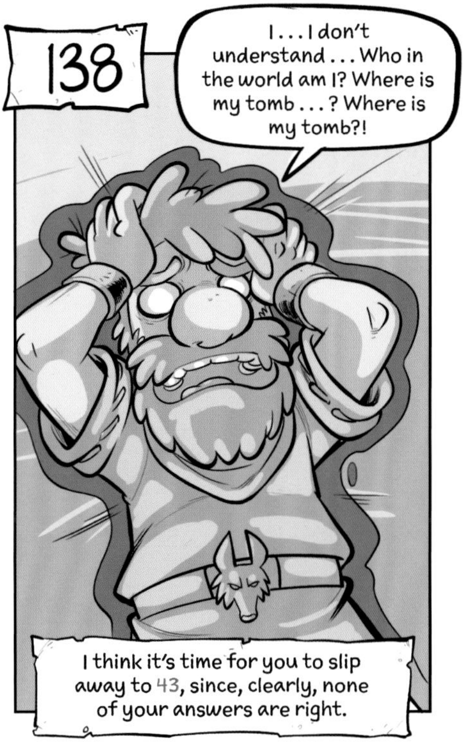
138
I . . . I don't understand . . . Who in the world am I? Where is my tomb . . . ? Where is my tomb?!
I think it's time for you to slip away to 43, since, clearly, none of your answers are right.

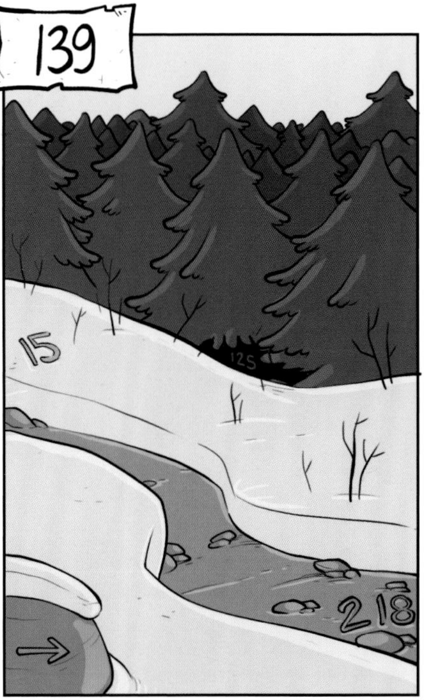
139
15
125
218

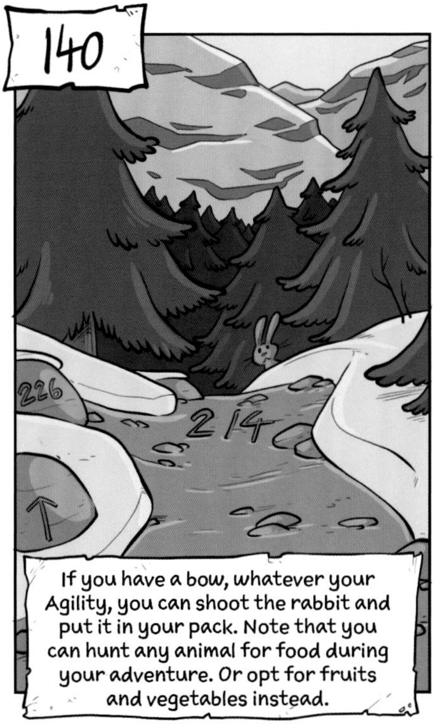
140
226
214
If you have a bow, whatever your Agility, you can shoot the rabbit and put it in your pack. Note that you can hunt any animal for food during your adventure. Or opt for fruits and vegetables instead.

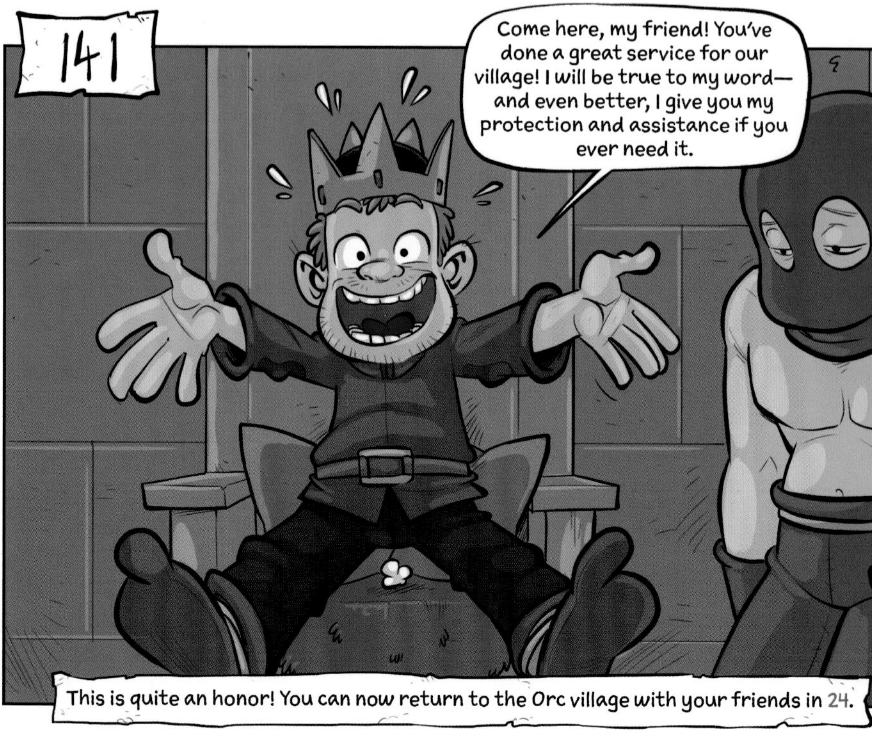
141
Come here, my friend! You've done a great service for our village! I will be true to my word—and even better, I give you my protection and assistance if you ever need it.
This is quite an honor! You can now return to the Orc village with your friends in 24.

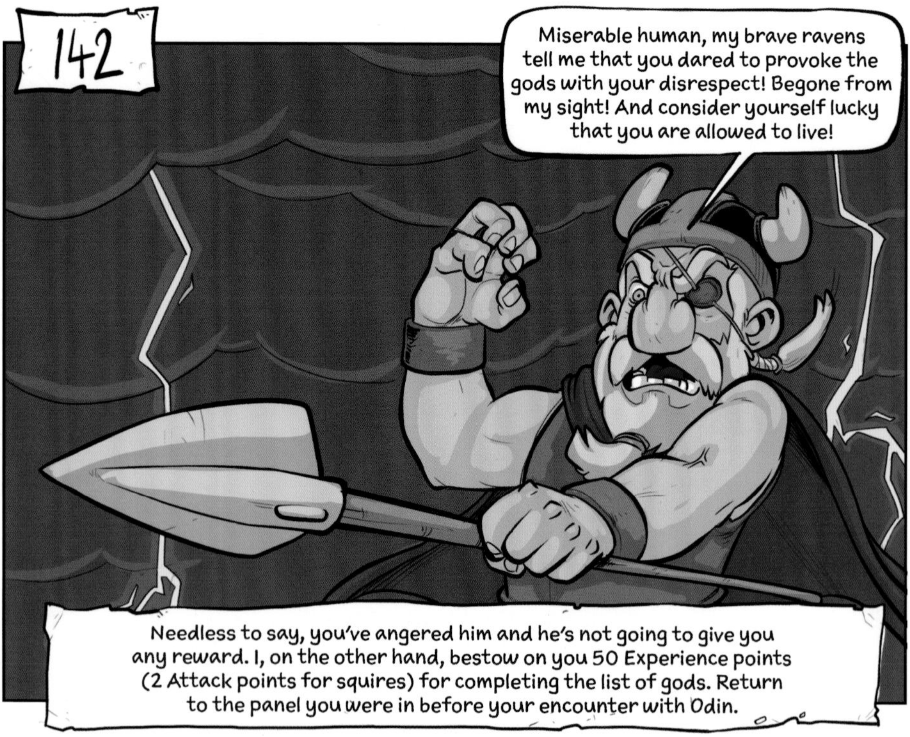
142
Miserable human, my brave ravens tell me that you dared to provoke the gods with your disrespect! Begone from my sight! And consider yourself lucky that you are allowed to live!
Needless to say, you've angered him and he's not going to give you any reward. I, on the other hand, bestow on you 50 Experience points (2 Attack points for squires) for completing the list of gods. Return to the panel you were in before your encounter with Odin.

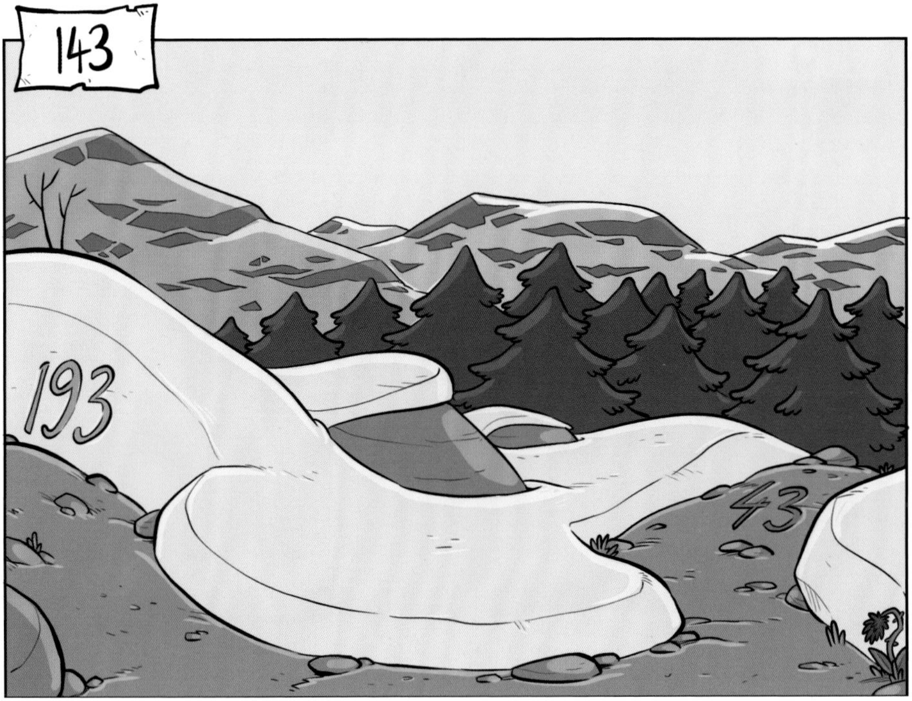
143
193
43

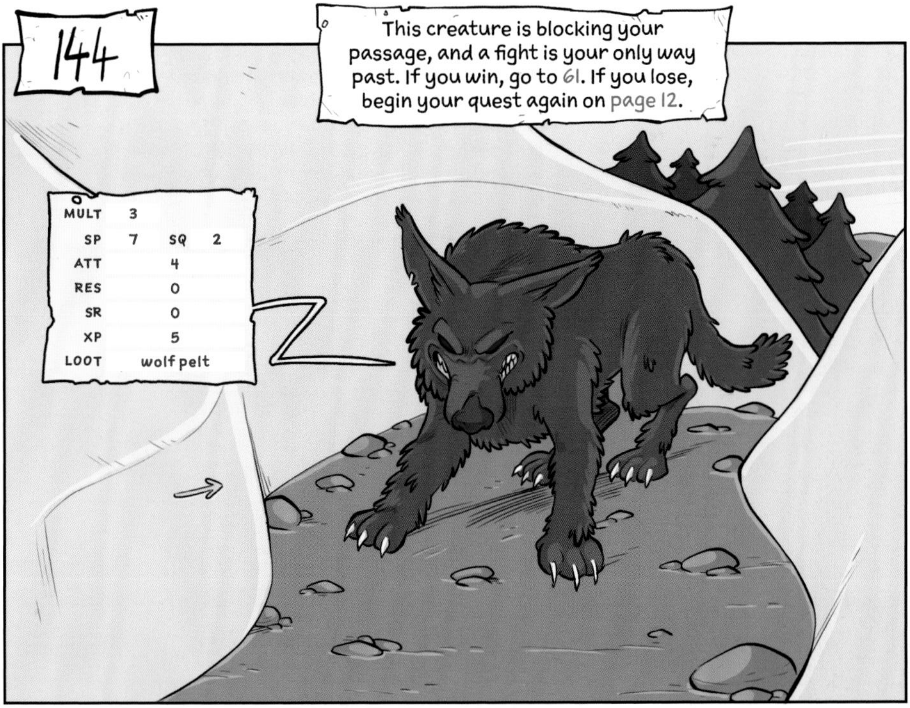
144
This creature is blocking your passage, and a fight is your only way past. If you win, go to 61. If you lose, begin your quest again on page 12.
MULT 3
SP 7 SQ 2
ATT 4
RES 0
SR 0
XP 5
LOOT wolf pelt

145

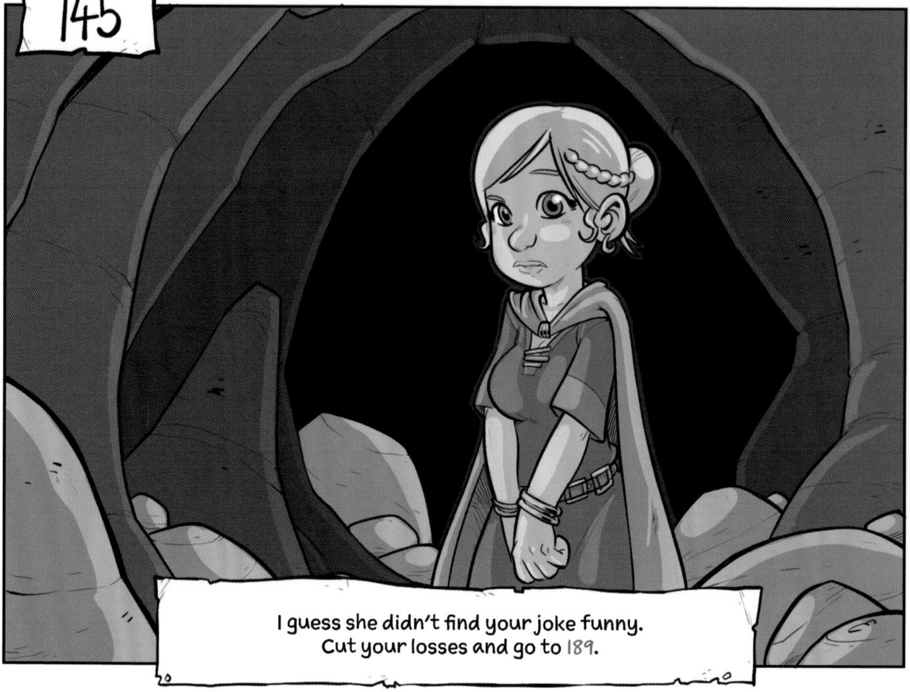
I guess she didn't find your joke funny.
Cut your losses and go to 189.

146

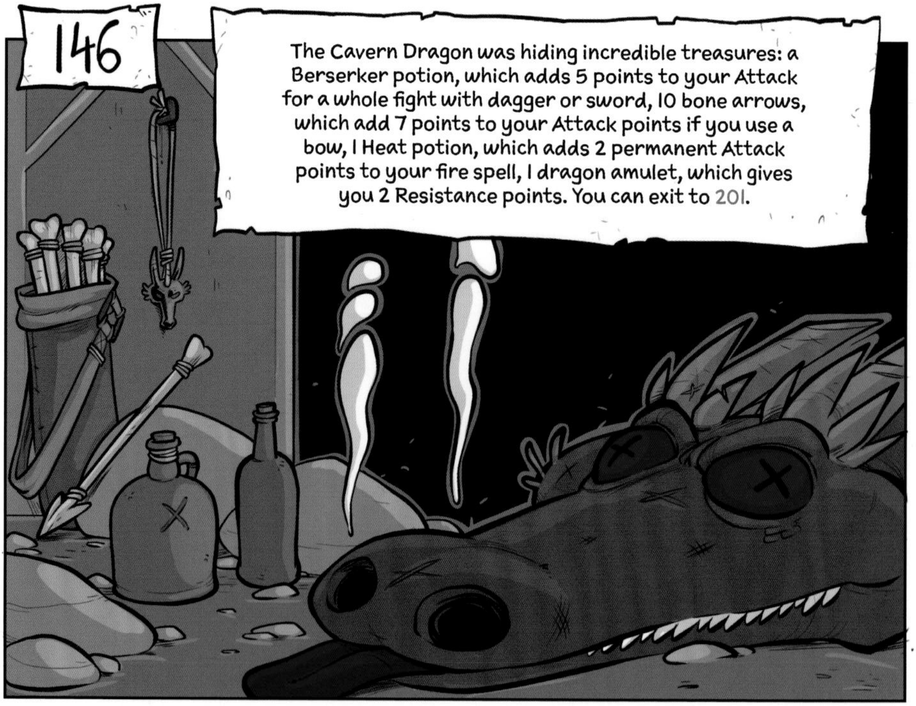
The Cavern Dragon was hiding incredible treasures: a Berserker potion, which adds 5 points to your Attack for a whole fight with dagger or sword, 10 bone arrows, which add 7 points to your Attack points if you use a bow, 1 Heat potion, which adds 2 permanent Attack points to your fire spell, 1 dragon amulet, which gives you 2 Resistance points. You can exit to 201.

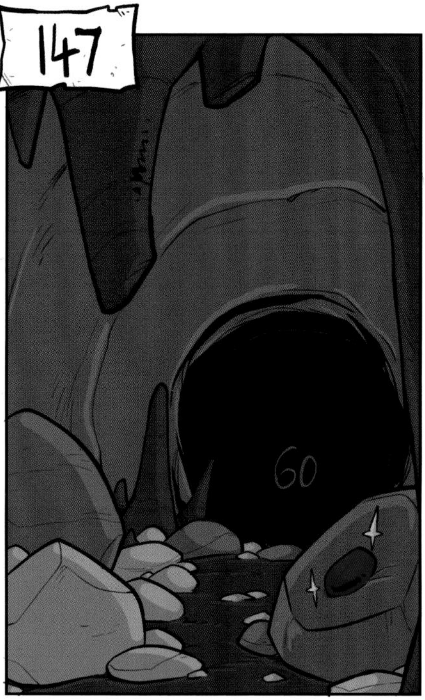
147
60

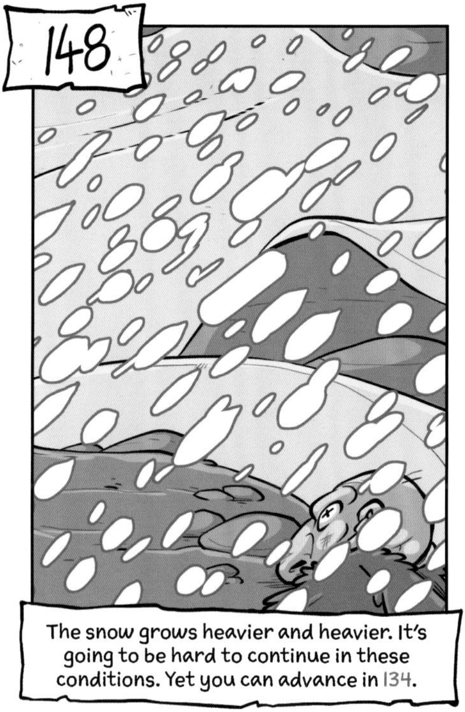
148
The snow grows heavier and heavier. It's going to be hard to continue in these conditions. Yet you can advance in 134.

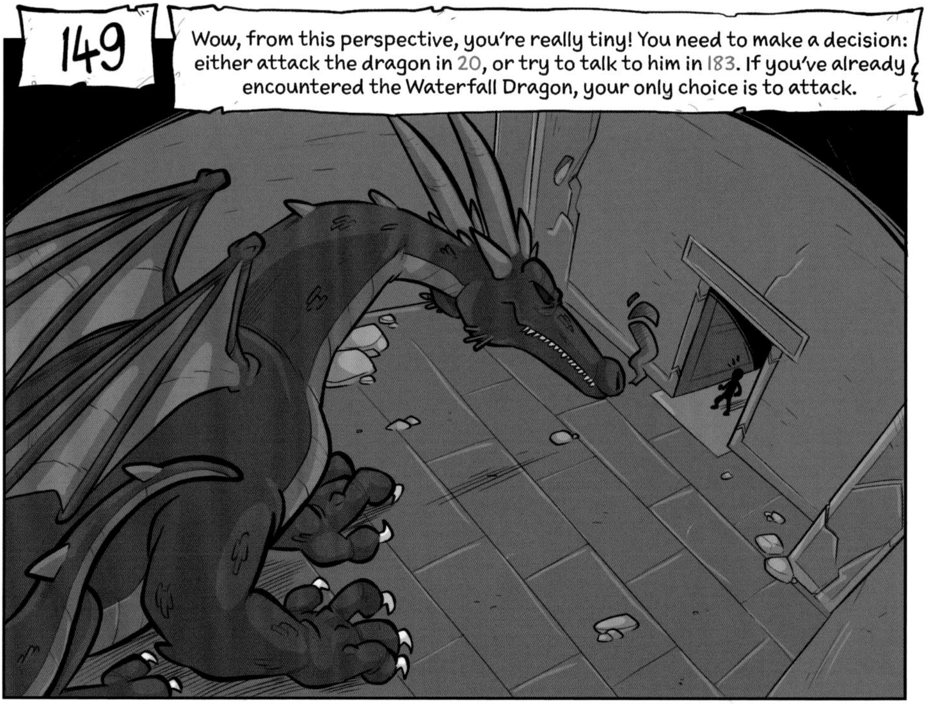
149
Wow, from this perspective, you're really tiny! You need to make a decision: either attack the dragon in 20, or try to talk to him in 183. If you've already encountered the Waterfall Dragon, your only choice is to attack.

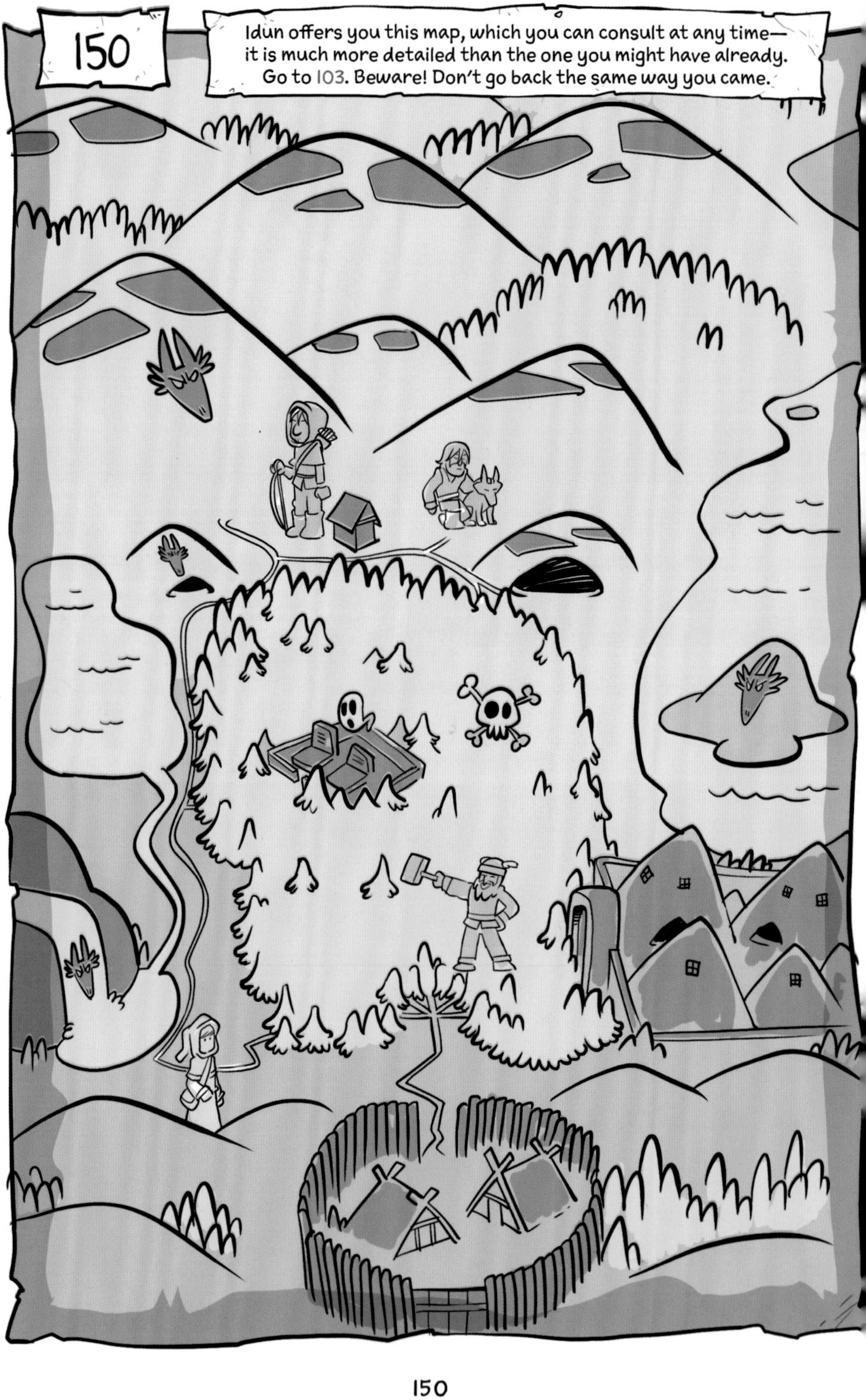
150
Idun offers you this map, which you can consult at any time—
it is much more detailed than the one you might have already.
Go to 103. Beware! Don't go back the same way you came.

151

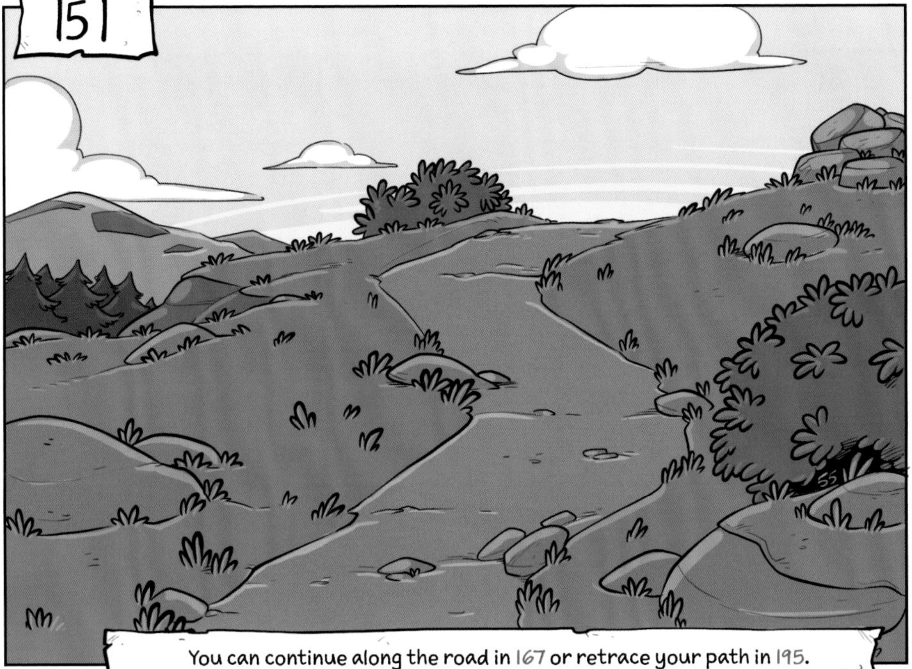
You can continue along the road in 167 or retrace your path in 195.

152

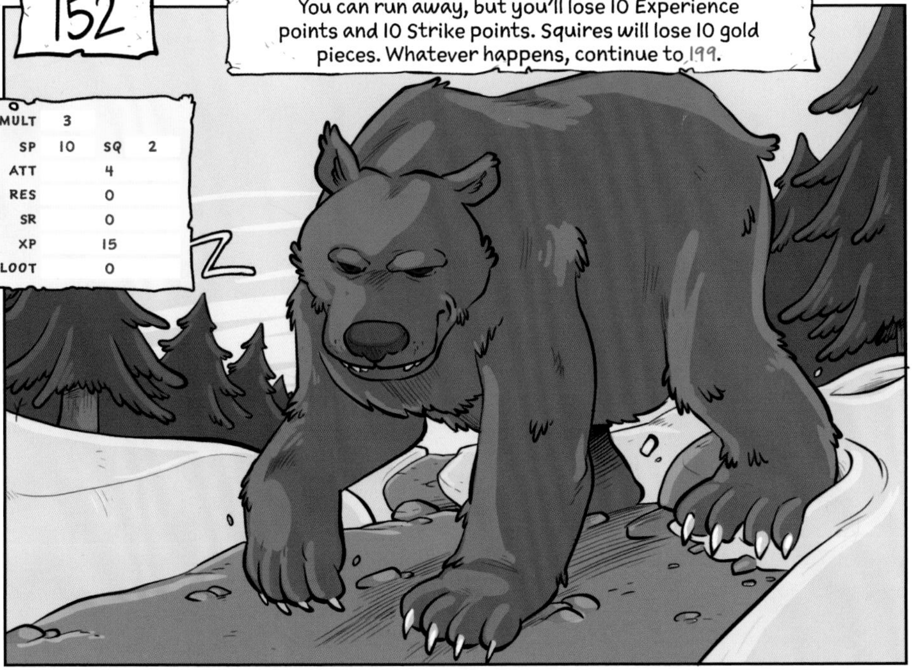
You can run away, but you'll lose 10 Experience points and 10 Strike points. Squires will lose 10 gold pieces. Whatever happens, continue to 199.

MULT	3		
SP	10	SQ	2
ATT		4	
RES		0	
SR		0	
XP		15	
LOOT		0	

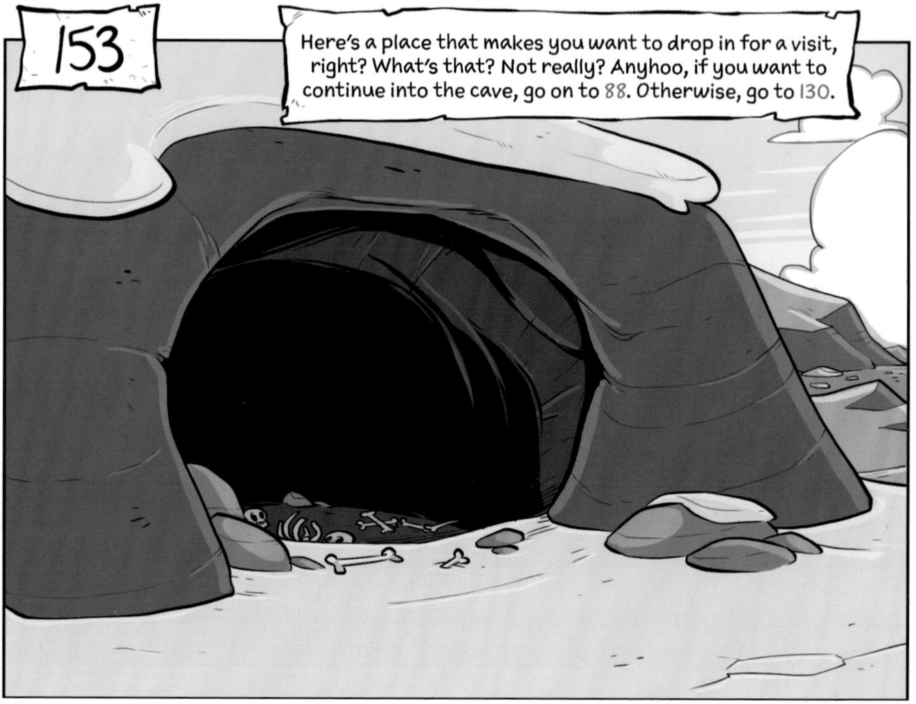
153
Here's a place that makes you want to drop in for a visit, right? What's that? Not really? Anyhoo, if you want to continue into the cave, go on to 88. Otherwise, go to 130.

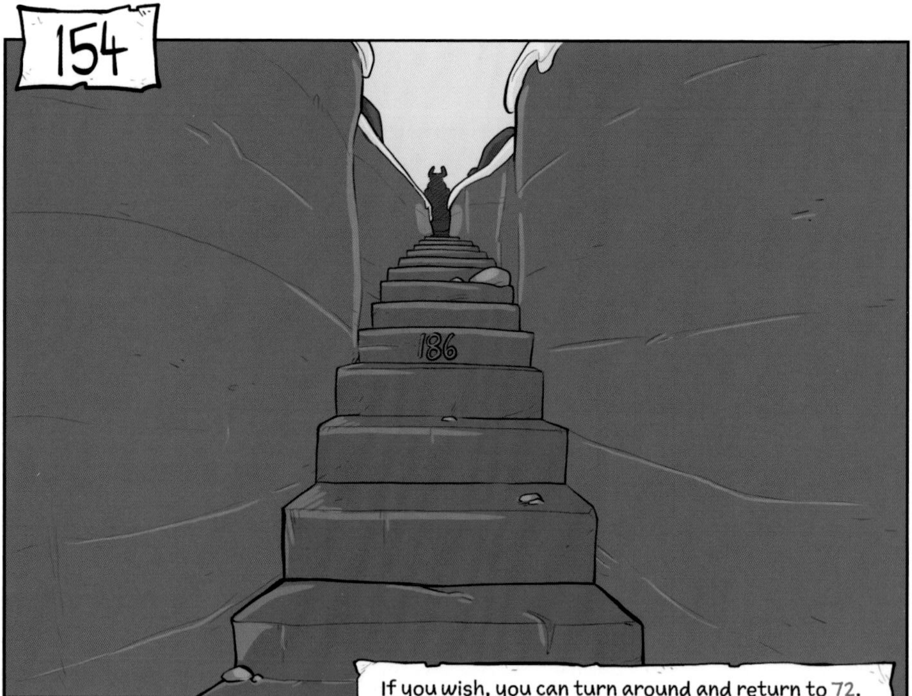
154
186
If you wish, you can turn around and return to 72.

155

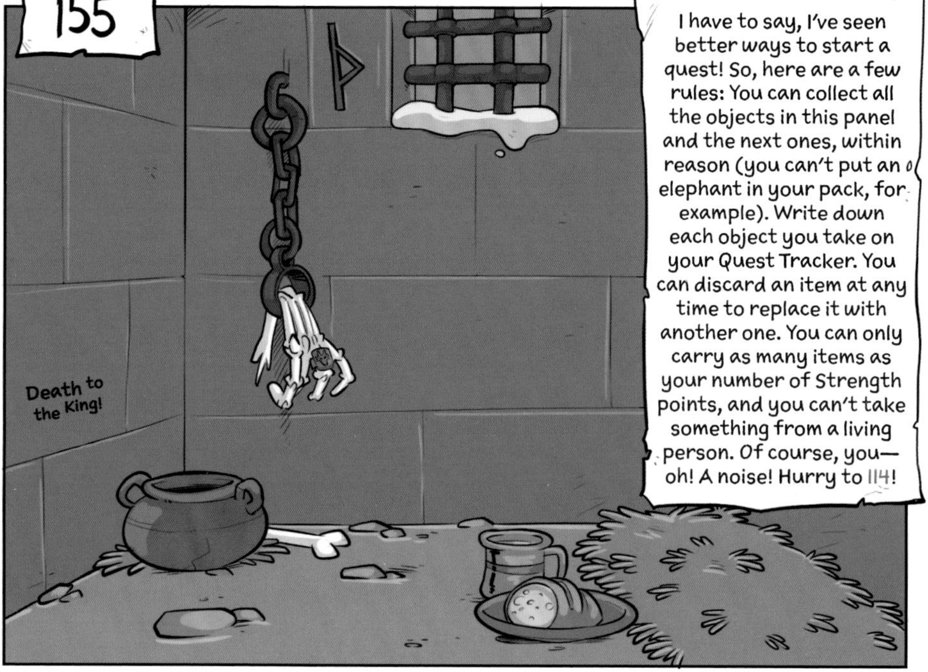

Death to the King!
I have to say, I've seen better ways to start a quest! So, here are a few rules: You can collect all the objects in this panel and the next ones, within reason (you can't put an elephant in your pack, for example). Write down each object you take on your Quest Tracker. You can discard an item at any time to replace it with another one. You can only carry as many items as your number of Strength points, and you can't take something from a living person. Of course, you—oh! A noise! Hurry to 114!

156

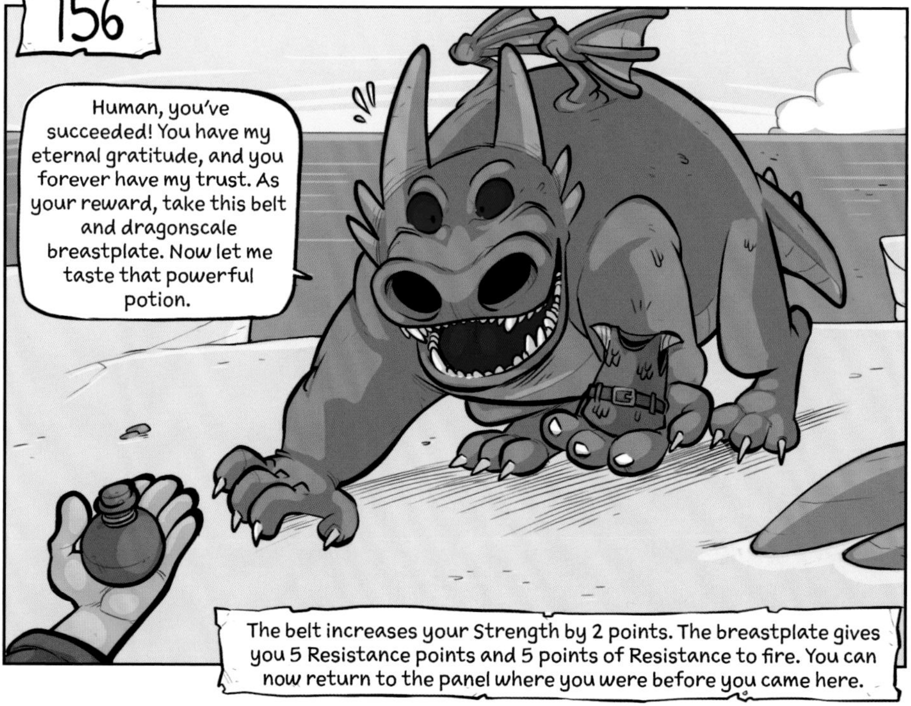

Human, you've succeeded! You have my eternal gratitude, and you forever have my trust. As your reward, take this belt and dragonscale breastplate. Now let me taste that powerful potion.
The belt increases your Strength by 2 points. The breastplate gives you 5 Resistance points and 5 points of Resistance to fire. You can now return to the panel where you were before you came here.

157

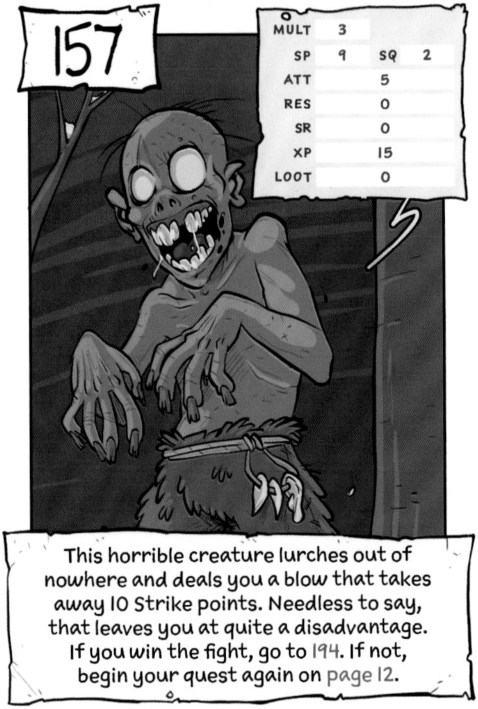

MULT	3		
SP	9	SQ	2
ATT	5		
RES	0		
SR	0		
XP	15		
LOOT	0		

This horrible creature lurches out of nowhere and deals you a blow that takes away 10 Strike points. Needless to say, that leaves you at quite a disadvantage. If you win the fight, go to 194. If not, begin your quest again on page 12.

158

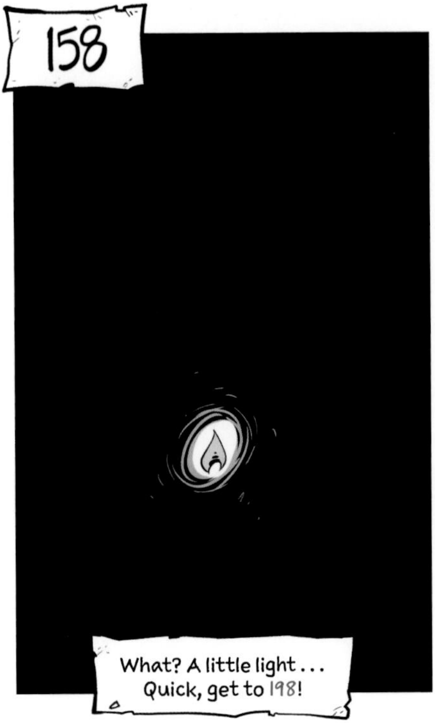
What? A little light . . . Quick, get to 198!

159

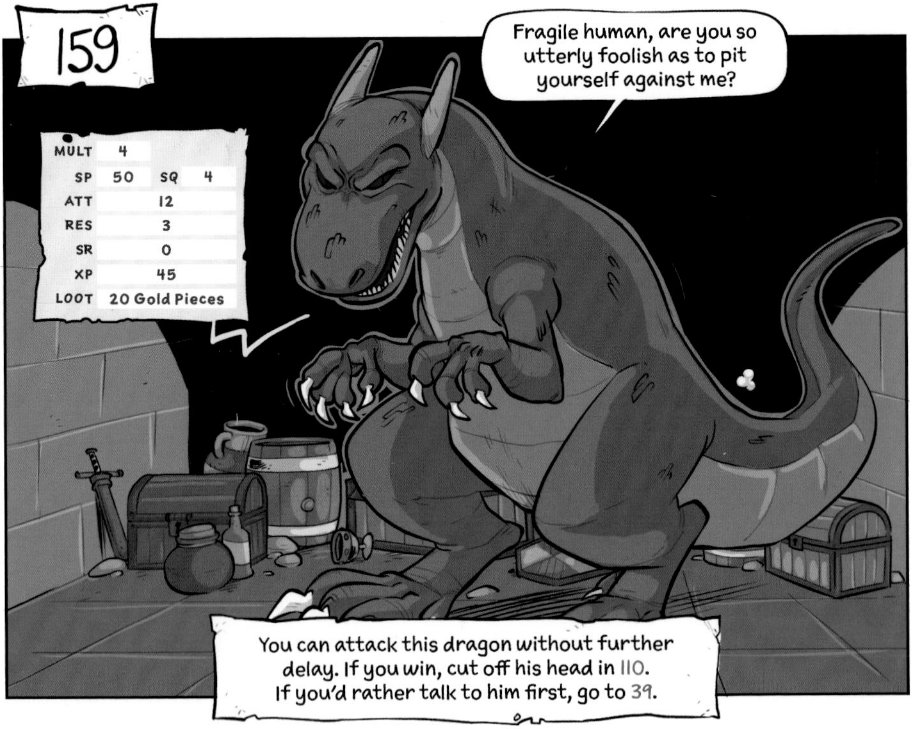
Fragile human, are you so utterly foolish as to pit yourself against me?

MULT	4		
SP	50	SQ	4
ATT	12		
RES	3		
SR	0		
XP	45		
LOOT	20 Gold Pieces		

You can attack this dragon without further delay. If you win, cut off his head in 110. If you'd rather talk to him first, go to 39.

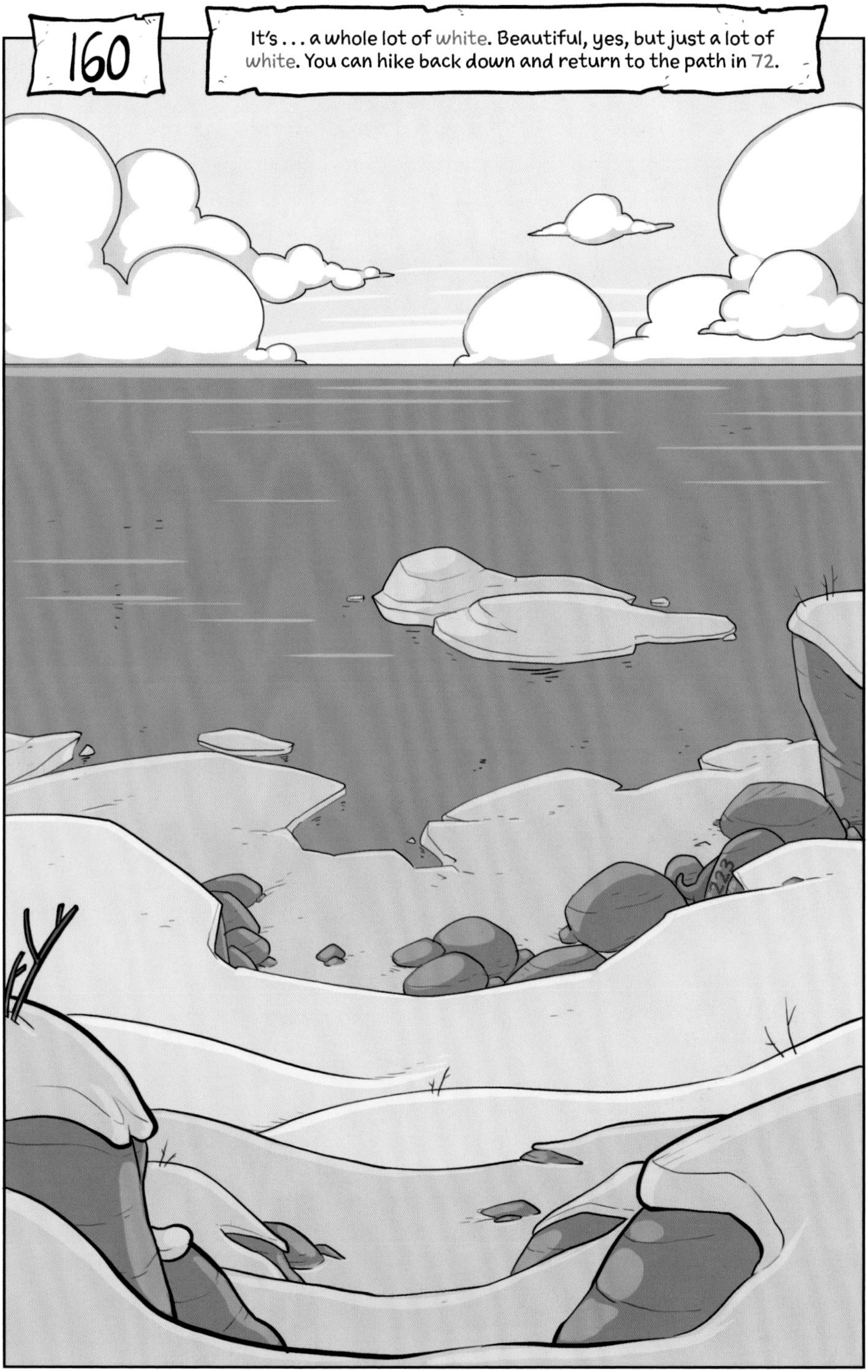
160
It's . . . a whole lot of white. Beautiful, yes, but just a lot of white. You can hike back down and return to the path in 72.
223

161

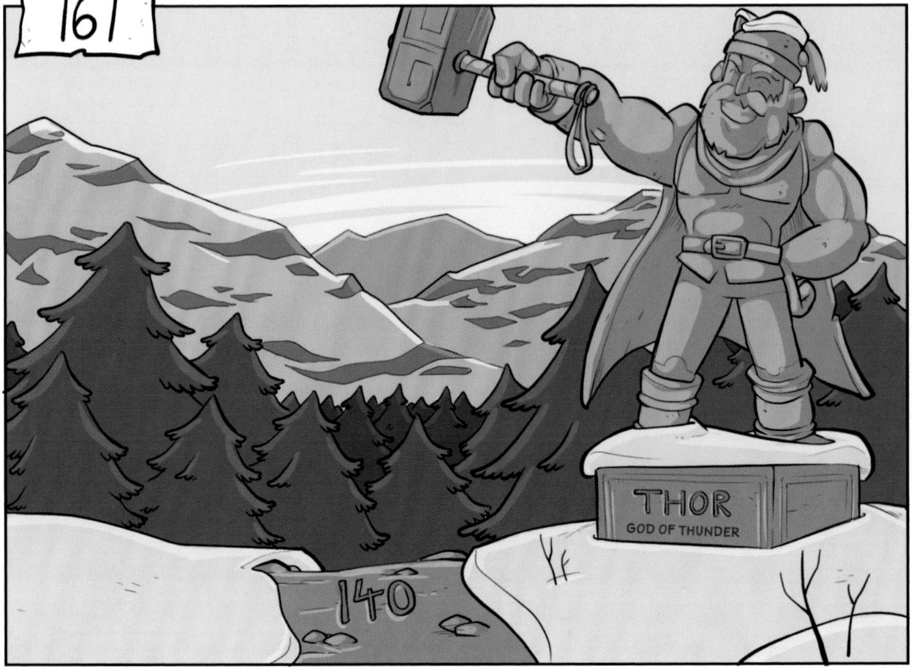
THOR
GOD OF THUNDER
140

162

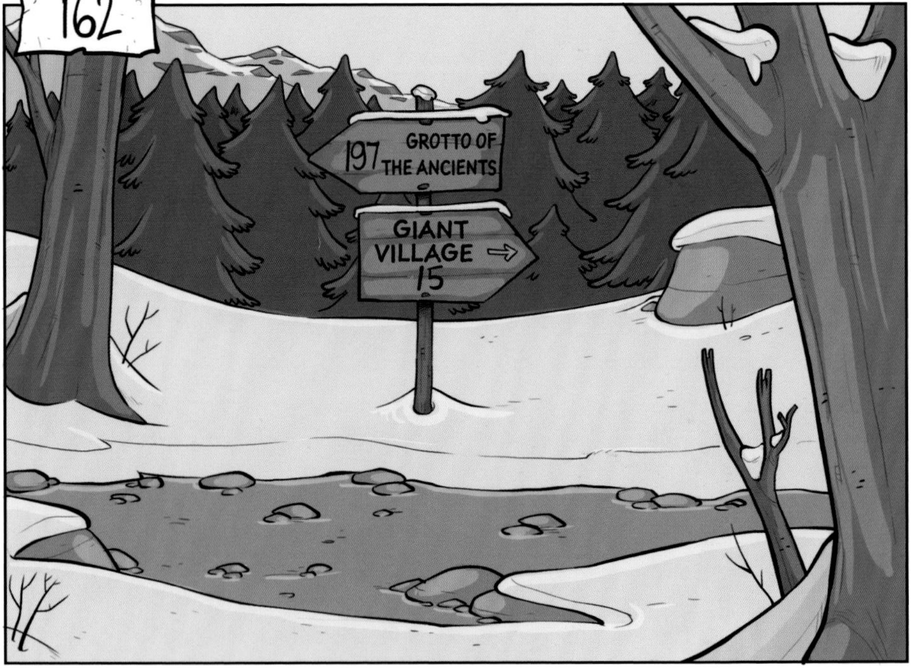
197 GROTTO OF THE ANCIENTS
GIANT VILLAGE 15

163

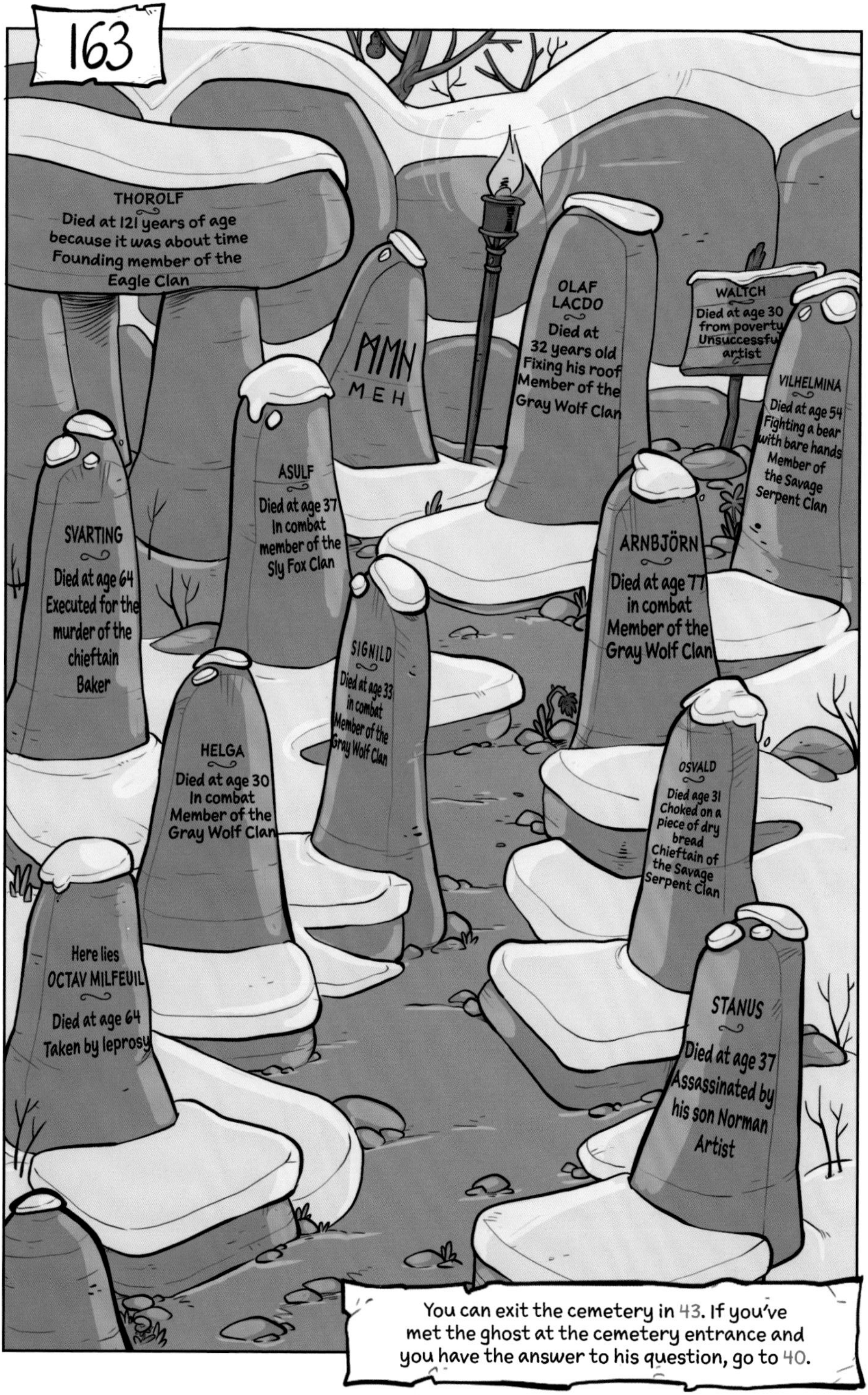

THOROLF
Died at 121 years of age because it was about time Founding member of the Eagle Clan
MMN
MEH
OLAF LACDO
Died at 32 years old Fixing his roof Member of the Gray Wolf Clan
WALTCH
Died at age 30 from poverty Unsuccessful artist
VILHELMINA
Died at age 54 Fighting a bear with bare hands Member of the Savage Serpent Clan
ASULF
Died at age 37 In combat member of the Sly Fox Clan
SVARTING
Died at age 64 Executed for the murder of the chieftain Baker
ARNBJÖRN
Died at age 77 in combat Member of the Gray Wolf Clan
SIGNILD
Died at age 33 in combat Member of the Gray Wolf Clan
HELGA
Died at age 30 In combat Member of the Gray Wolf Clan
OSVALD
Died age 31 Choked on a piece of dry bread Chieftain of the Savage Serpent Clan
Here lies OCTAV MILFEUIL
Died at age 64 Taken by leprosy
STANUS
Died at age 37 Assassinated by his son Norman Artist

You can exit the cemetery in 43. If you've met the ghost at the cemetery entrance and you have the answer to his question, go to 40.

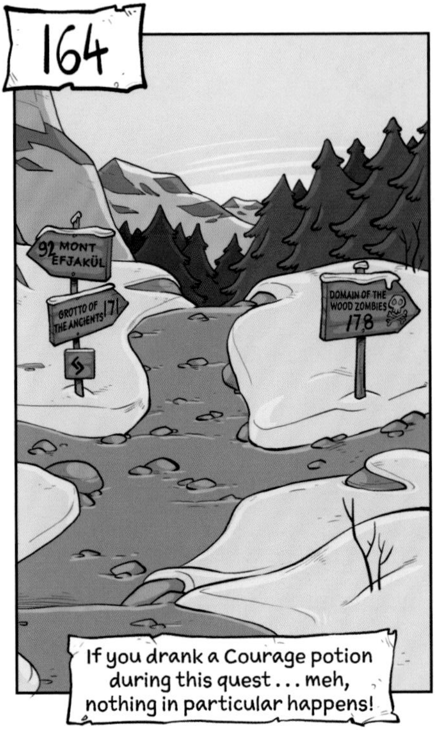
164
92 MONT EFJAKÜL
GROTTO OF THE ANCIENTS 171
DOMAIN OF THE WOOD ZOMBIES 178
If you drank a Courage potion during this quest . . . meh, nothing in particular happens!

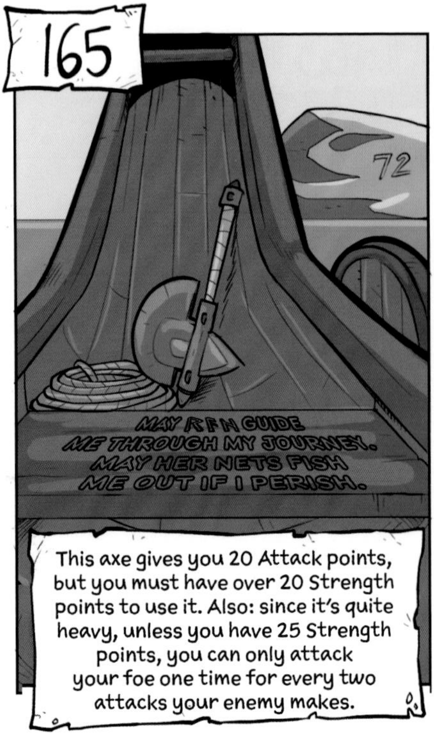
165
72
ME THROUGH MY JOURNEY.
MAY HER NETS FISH
ME OUT IF I PERISH.
This axe gives you 20 Attack points, but you must have over 20 Strength points to use it. Also: since it's quite heavy, unless you have 25 Strength points, you can only attack your foe one time for every two attacks your enemy makes.

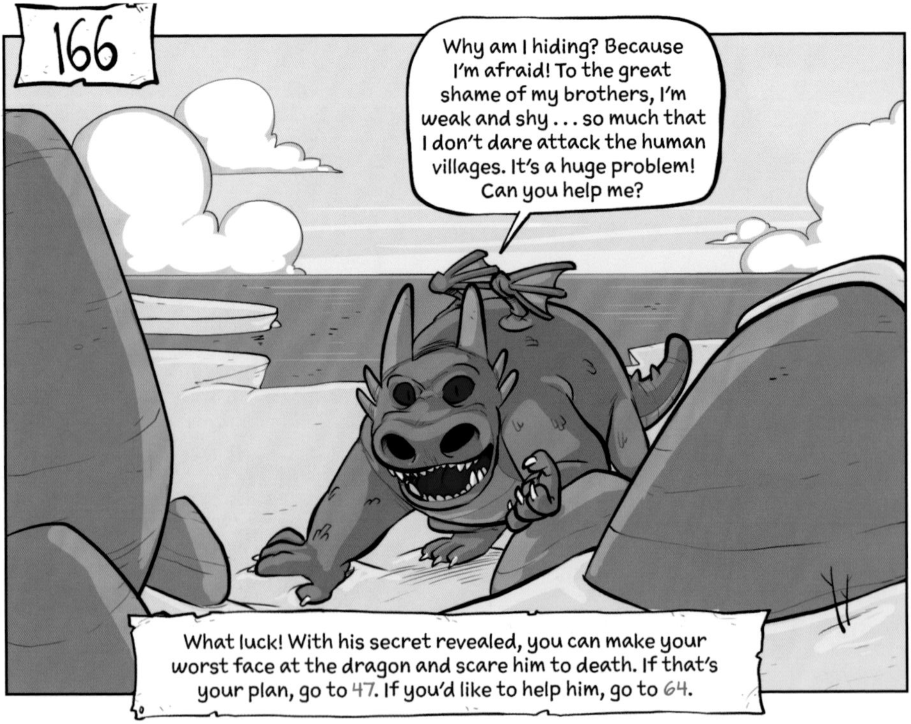
166
Why am I hiding? Because I'm afraid! To the great shame of my brothers, I'm weak and shy . . . so much that I don't dare attack the human villages. It's a huge problem! Can you help me?
What luck! With his secret revealed, you can make your worst face at the dragon and scare him to death. If that's your plan, go to 47. If you'd like to help him, go to 64.

167

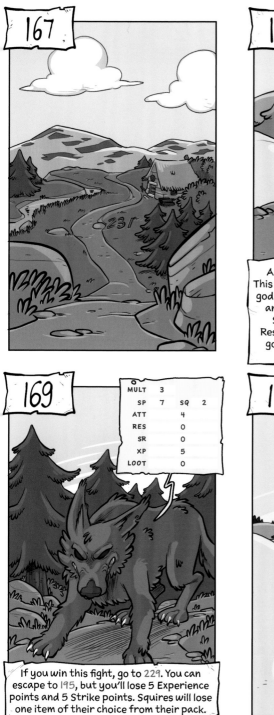

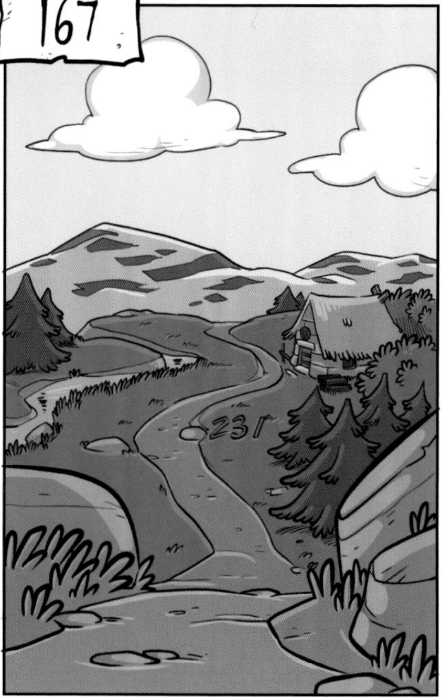
231

168

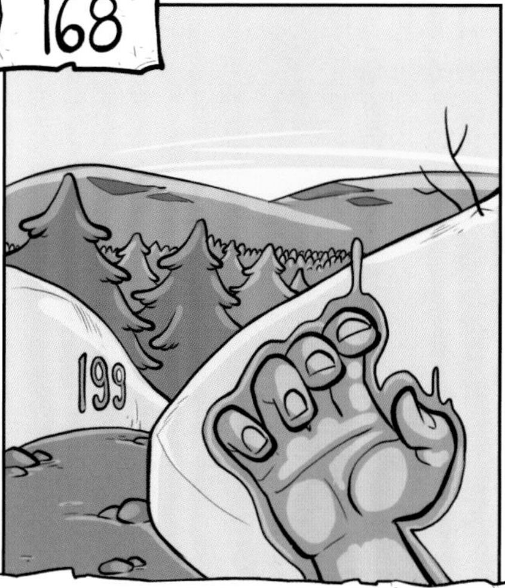
199

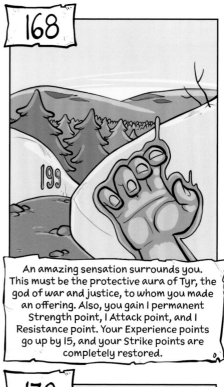

An amazing sensation surrounds you. This must be the protective aura of Tyr, the god of war and justice, to whom you made an offering. Also, you gain 1 permanent Strength point, 1 Attack point, and 1 Resistance point. Your Experience points go up by 15, and your Strike points are completely restored.

169

MULT	3		
SP	7	SQ	2
ATT		4	
RES		0	
SR		0	
XP		5	
LOOT		0	

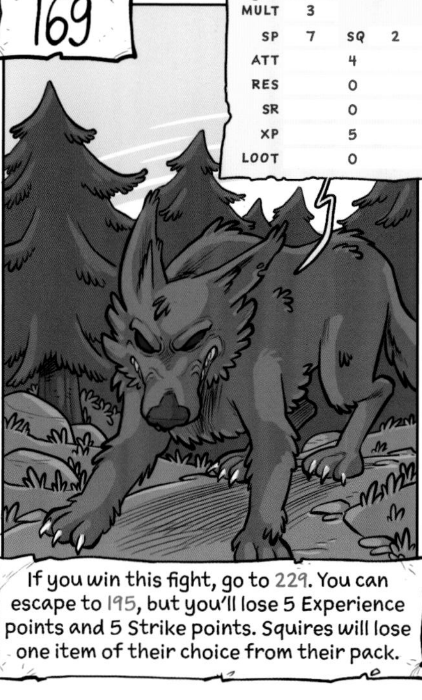

If you win this fight, go to 229. You can escape to 195, but you'll lose 5 Experience points and 5 Strike points. Squires will lose one item of their choice from their pack.

170

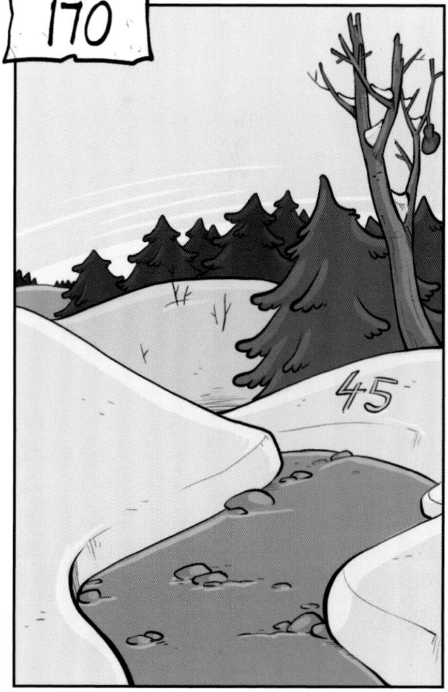
45

171

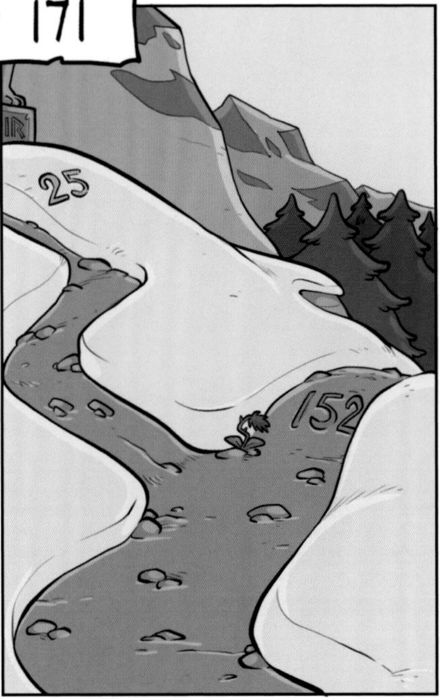
25
152

172

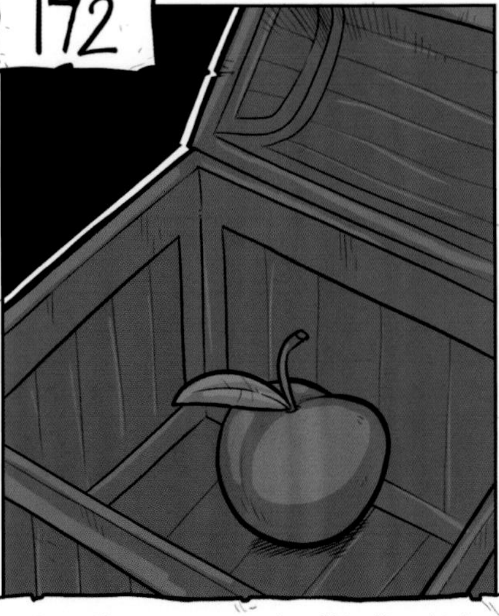

Idun offers you an Apple of Youth, which has the ability to rejuvenate whoever eats it. Even the gods like tasty things! This fruit adds 2 points to the ability of your choice, and 1 point each to two others. Go to 103—and take care not to follow the same path again.

173

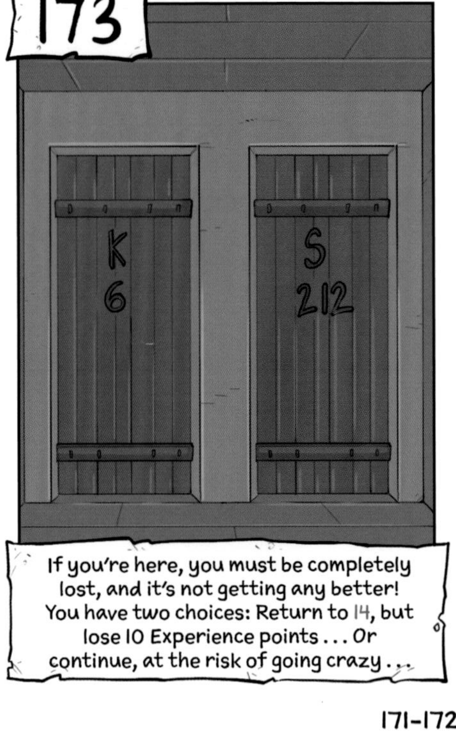
K
6
S
212

If you're here, you must be completely lost, and it's not getting any better! You have two choices: Return to 14, but lose 10 Experience points . . . Or continue, at the risk of going crazy . . .

174

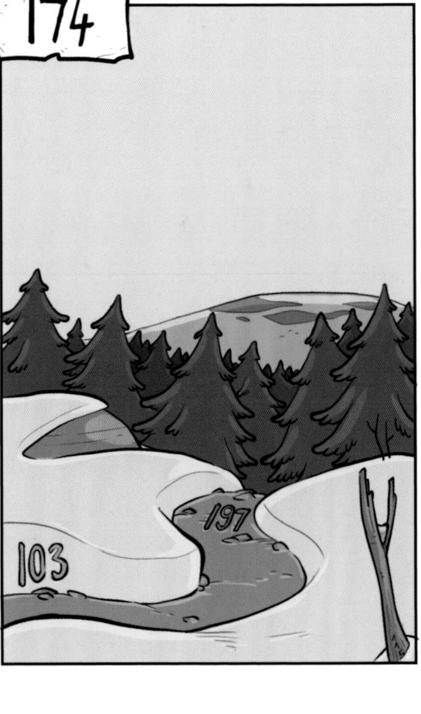
197
103

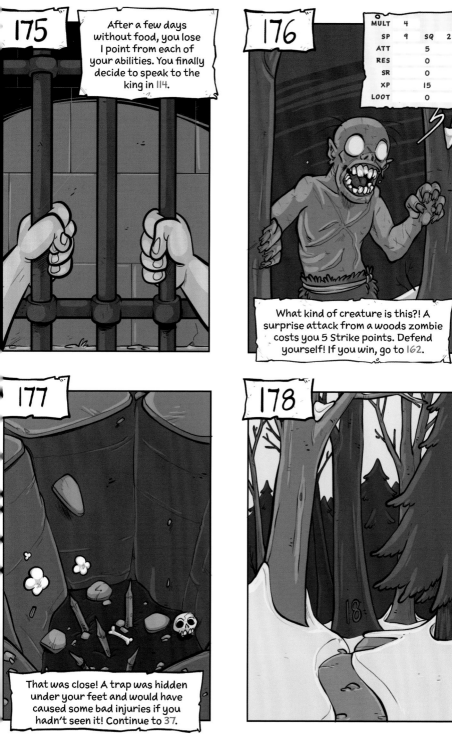

175

After a few days without food, you lose 1 point from each of your abilities. You finally decide to speak to the king in 114.

176

MULT	4		
SP	9	SQ	2
ATT	5		
RES	0		
SR	0		
XP	15		
LOOT	0		

What kind of creature is this?! A surprise attack from a woods zombie costs you 5 Strike points. Defend yourself! If you win, go to 162.

177

That was close! A trap was hidden under your feet and would have caused some bad injuries if you hadn't seen it! Continue to 37.

178

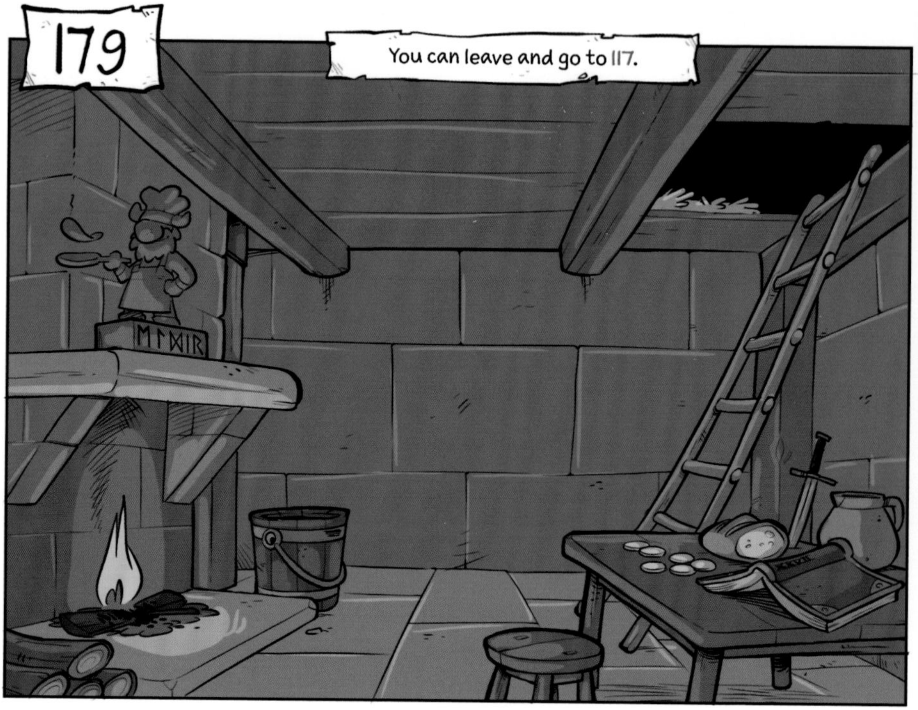
179
You can leave and go to 117.

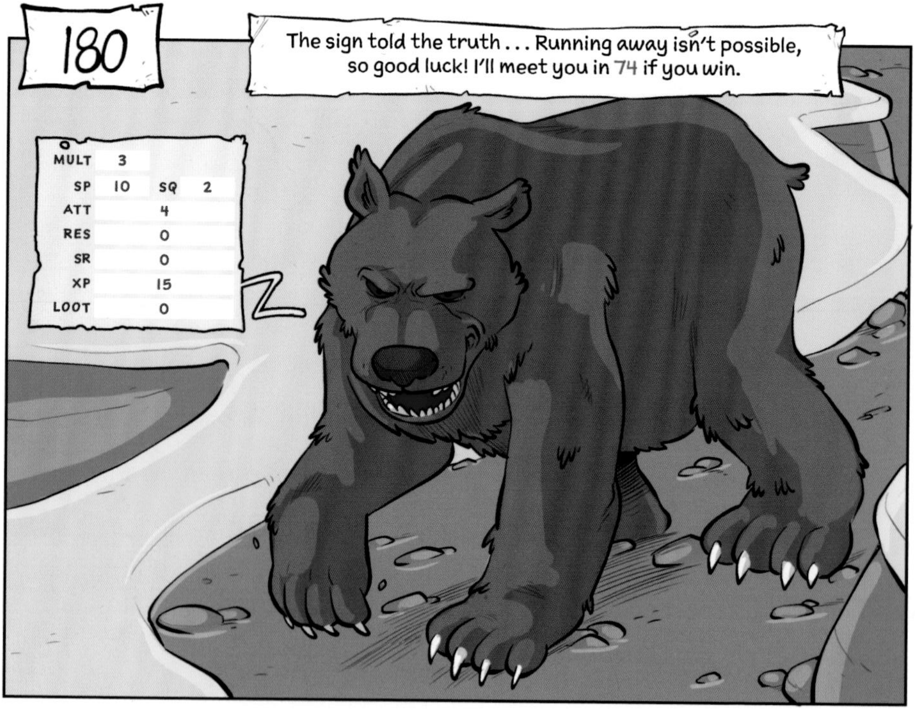
180
The sign told the truth . . . Running away isn't possible,
so good luck! I'll meet you in 74 if you win.

MULT	3		
SP	10	SQ	2
ATT	4		
RES	0		
SR	0		
XP	15		
LOOT	0		

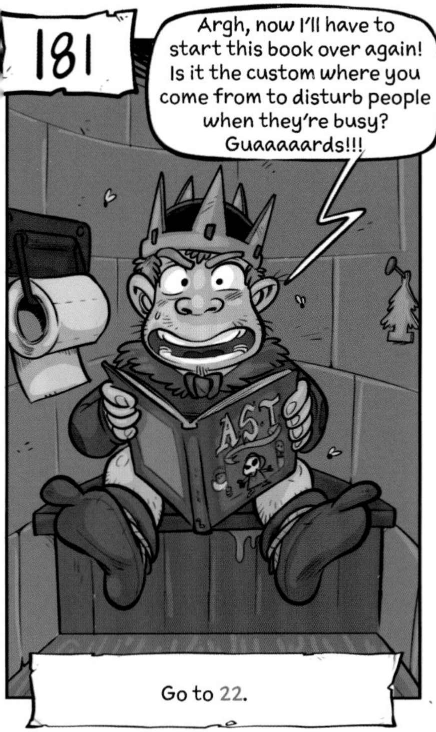
181
Argh, now I'll have to start this book over again! Is it the custom where you come from to disturb people when they're busy? Guaaaaards!!!
Go to 22.

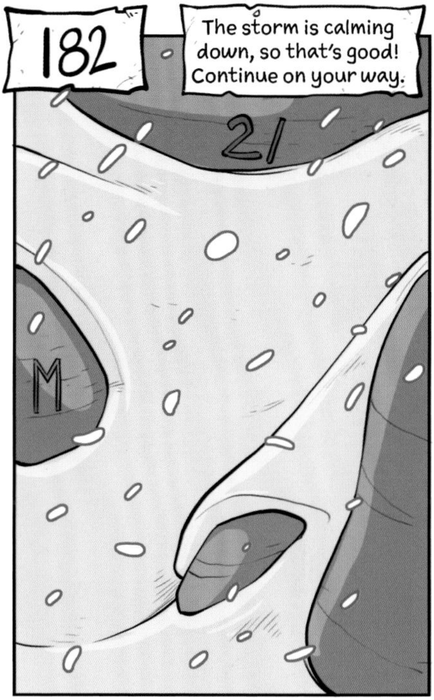
182
The storm is calming down, so that's good! Continue on your way.

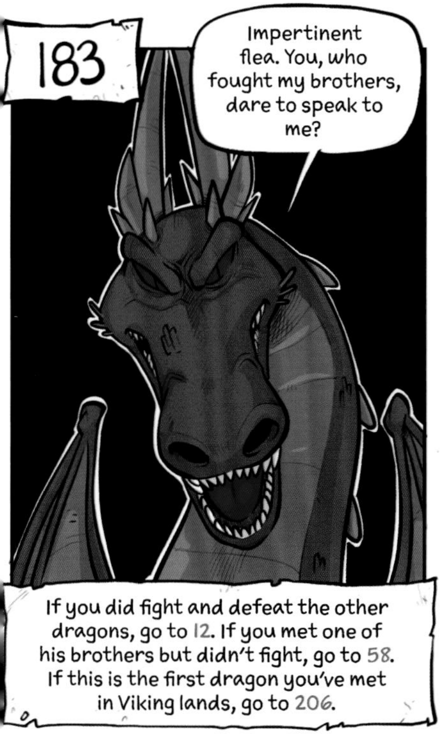
183
Impertinent flea. You, who fought my brothers, dare to speak to me?
If you did fight and defeat the other dragons, go to 12. If you met one of his brothers but didn't fight, go to 58. If this is the first dragon you've met in Viking lands, go to 206.

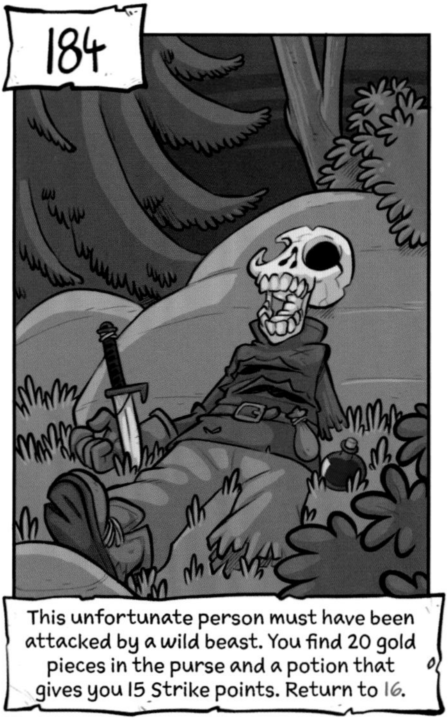
184
This unfortunate person must have been attacked by a wild beast. You find 20 gold pieces in the purse and a potion that gives you 15 Strike points. Return to 16.

185

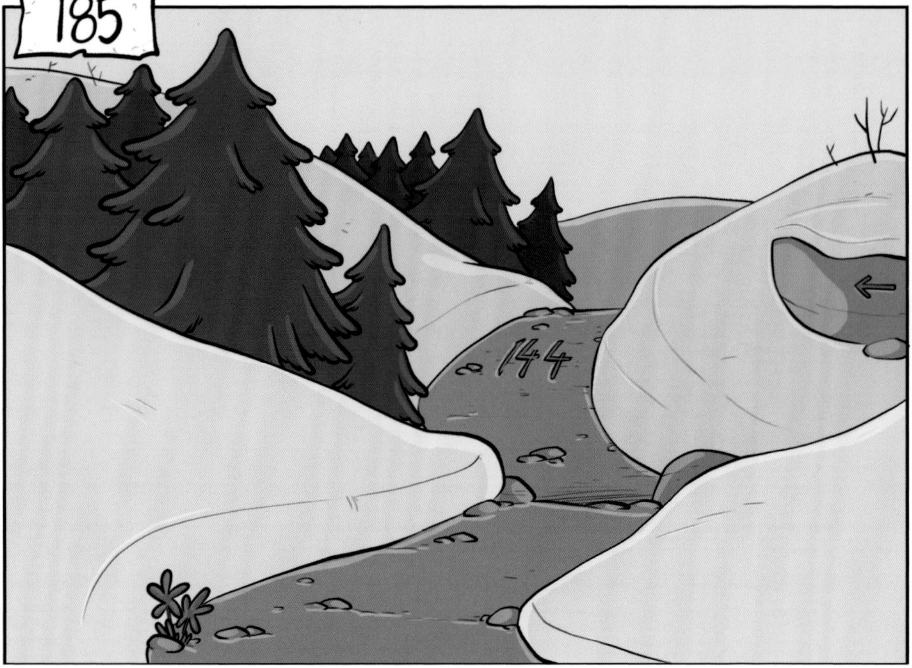

144
←

186

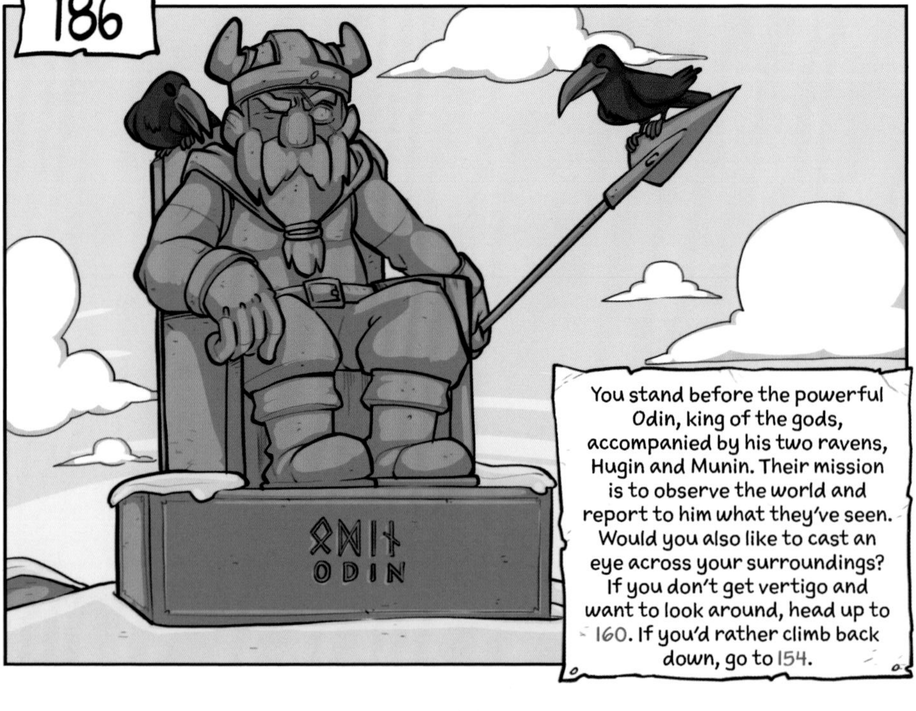

ODIN
You stand before the powerful Odin, king of the gods, accompanied by his two ravens, Hugin and Munin. Their mission is to observe the world and report to him what they've seen. Would you also like to cast an eye across your surroundings? If you don't get vertigo and want to look around, head up to 160. If you'd rather climb back down, go to 154.

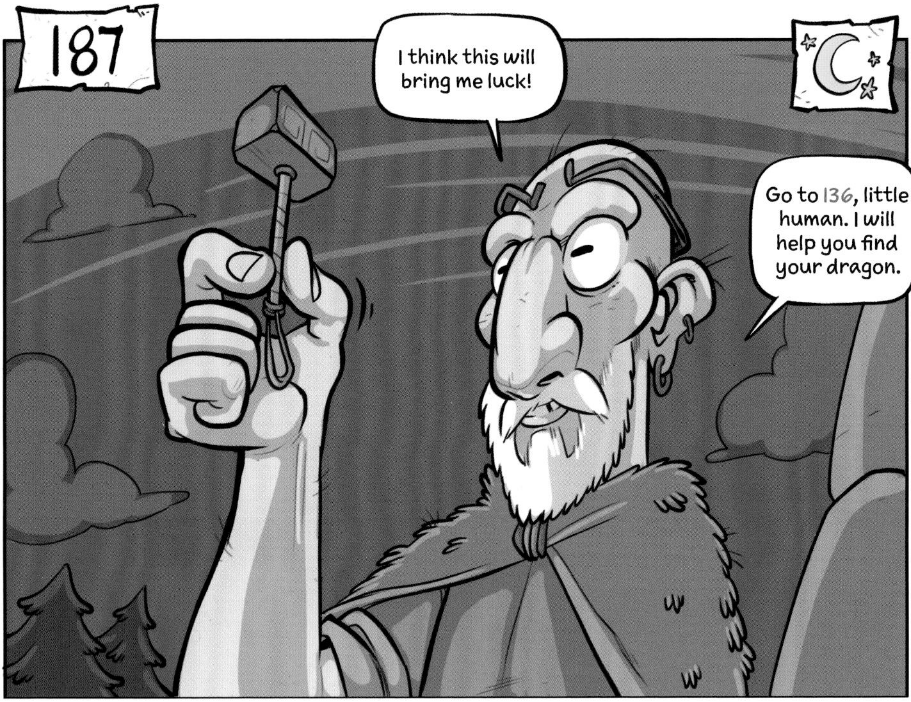
187
I think this will bring me luck!
Go to 136, little human. I will help you find your dragon.

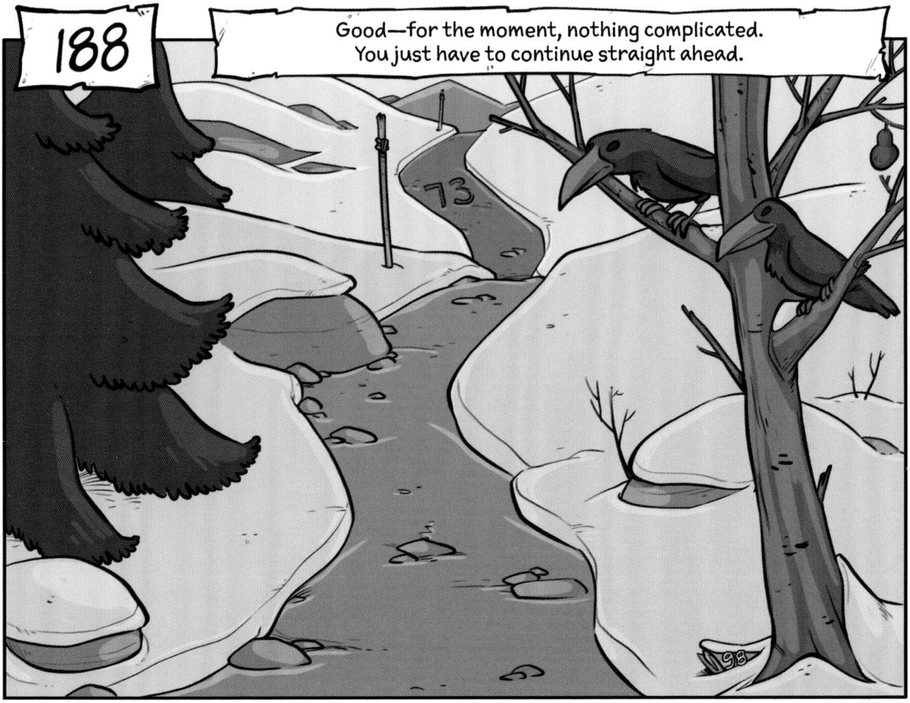
188
Good—for the moment, nothing complicated. You just have to continue straight ahead.
73
98

189

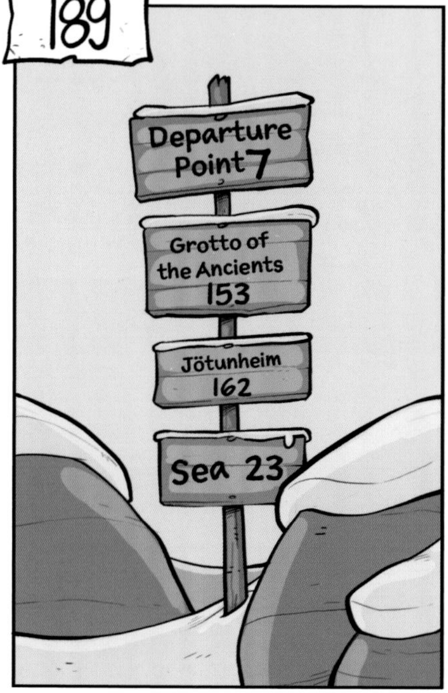
Departure Point 7
Grotto of the Ancients 153
Jötunheim 162
Sea 23

190

MULT	3		
SP	10	SQ	2
ATT	4		
RES	0		
SR	0		
XP	15		
LOOT	0		

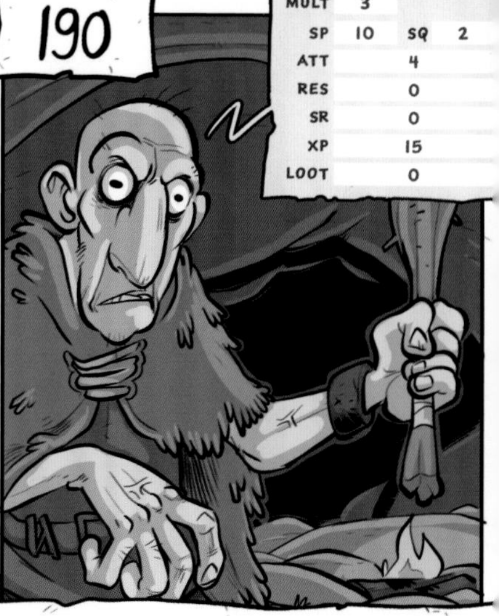

The giant doesn't give you time to raise your weapon before he strikes, but you can still parry if you have 10 Strength points. If not, you lose 10 Strike points. You can now continue the battle and go to 121 if you win, or you can flee down the mountain in 128.

191

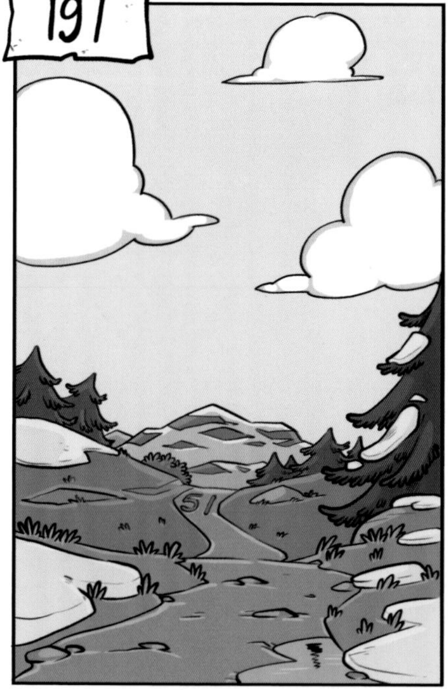
51

192

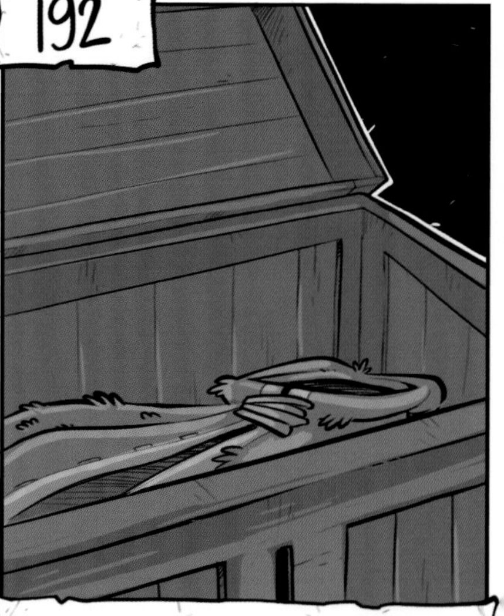

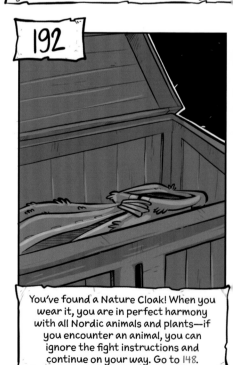

You've found a Nature Cloak! When you wear it, you are in perfect harmony with all Nordic animals and plants—if you encounter an animal, you can ignore the fight instructions and continue on your way. Go to 148.

193

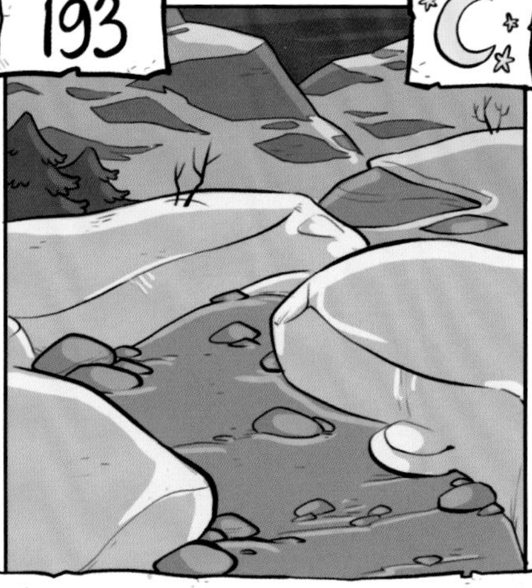

The goddess Nott compels you to stop, enveloping you in her dark arms. If you hunted along the way, eating a bit now restores all your Strike points and gives you 5 Experience points. After a brief sleep, you can start again toward Mount Efjakül in 34 (unless you've already visited it) or toward the cemetery in 143.

194

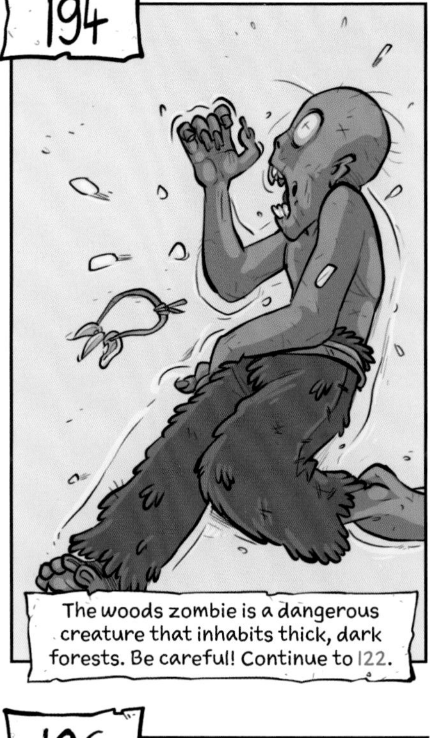

The woods zombie is a dangerous creature that inhabits thick, dark forests. Be careful! Continue to 122.

195

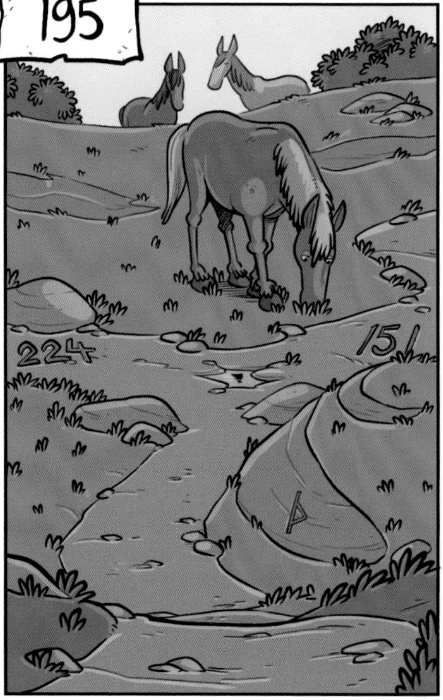
224
151

196

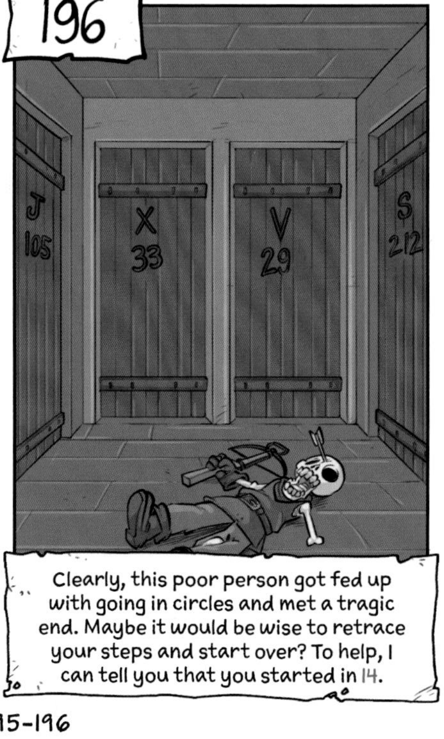
J
105
X
33
V
29
S
212

Clearly, this poor person got fed up with going in circles and met a tragic end. Maybe it would be wise to retrace your steps and start over? To help, I can tell you that you started in 14.

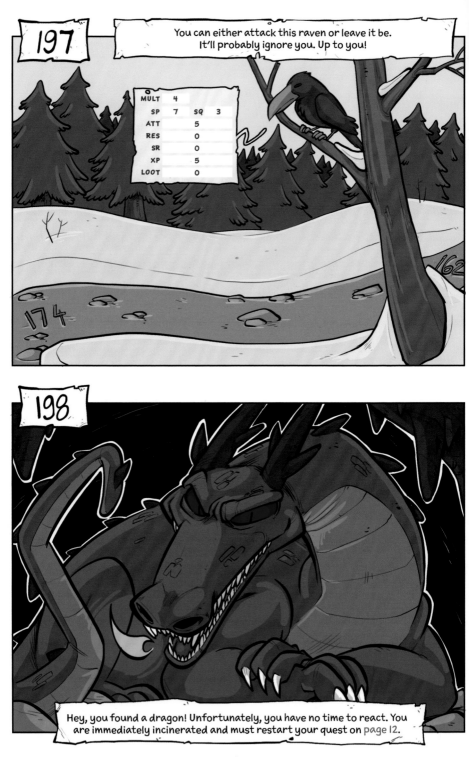

197

You can either attack this raven or leave it be. It'll probably ignore you. Up to you!

MULT	4		
SP	7	SQ	3
ATT	5		
RES	0		
SR	0		
XP	5		
LOOT	0		

198

Hey, you found a dragon! Unfortunately, you have no time to react. You are immediately incinerated and must restart your quest on page 12.

199

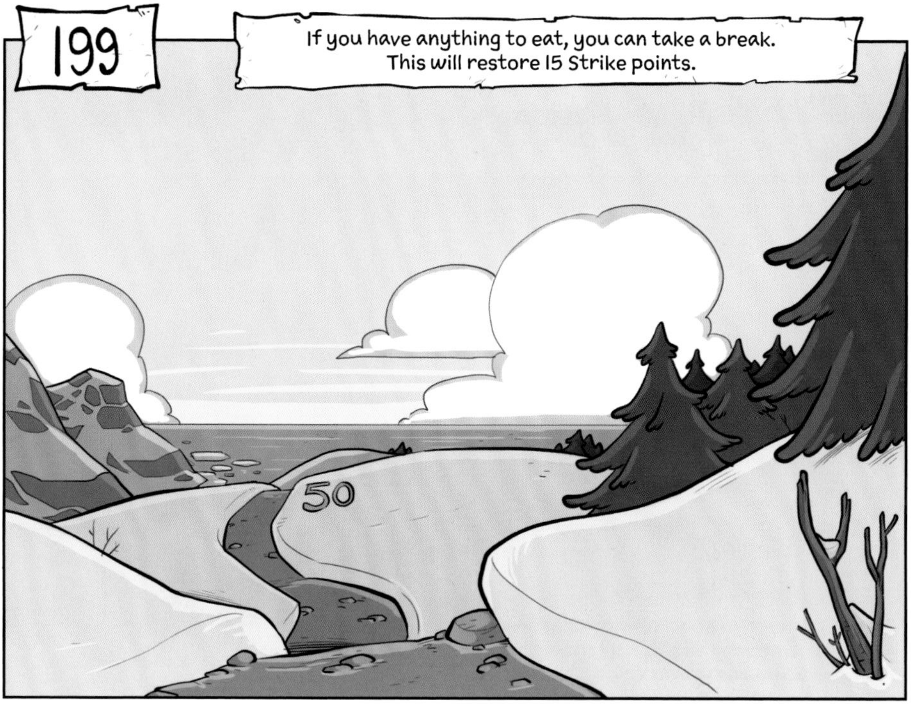
If you have anything to eat, you can take a break. This will restore 15 Strike points.
50

200

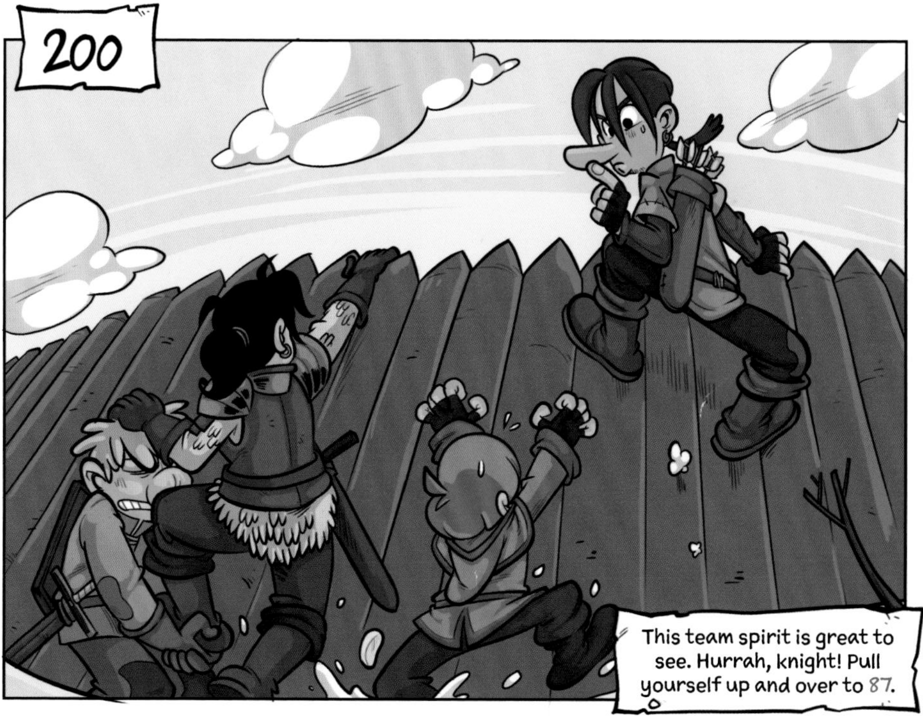
This team spirit is great to see. Hurrah, knight! Pull yourself up and over to 87.

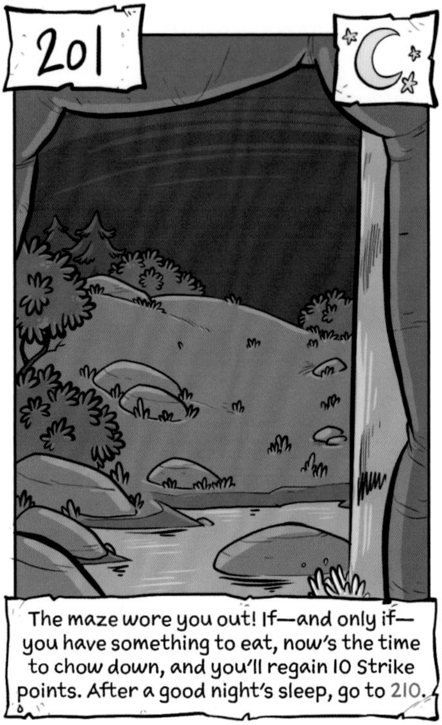
201
The maze wore you out! If—and only if—you have something to eat, now's the time to chow down, and you'll regain 10 Strike points. After a good night's sleep, go to 210.

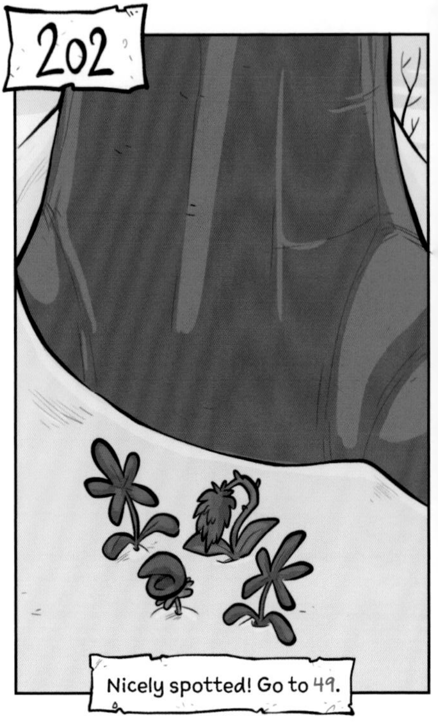
202
Nicely spotted! Go to 49.

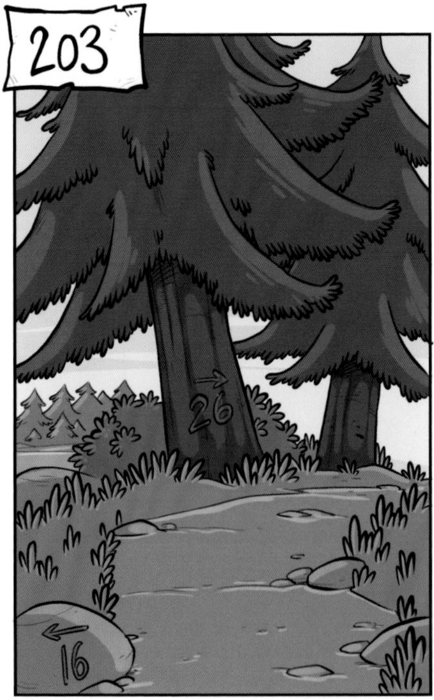
203
26
16

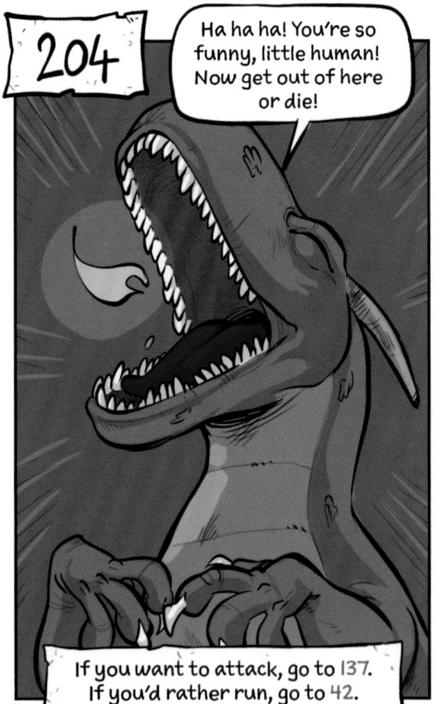
204
Ha ha ha! You're so funny, little human! Now get out of here or die!
If you want to attack, go to 137.
If you'd rather run, go to 42.

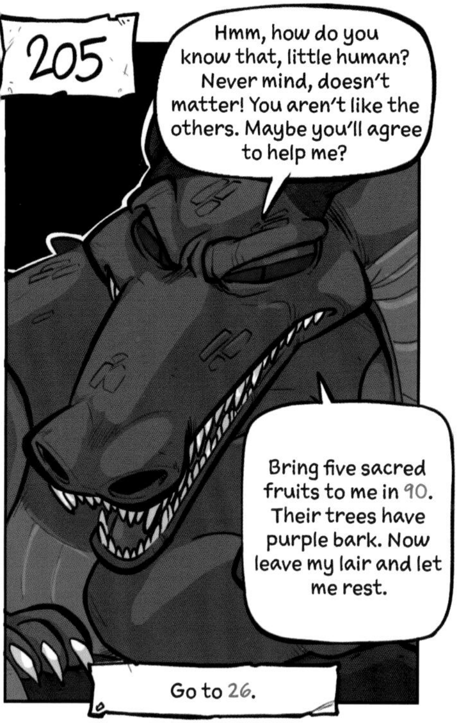
205
Hmm, how do you know that, little human? Never mind, doesn't matter! You aren't like the others. Maybe you'll agree to help me?
Bring five sacred fruits to me in 90. Their trees have purple bark. Now leave my lair and let me rest.
Go to 26.

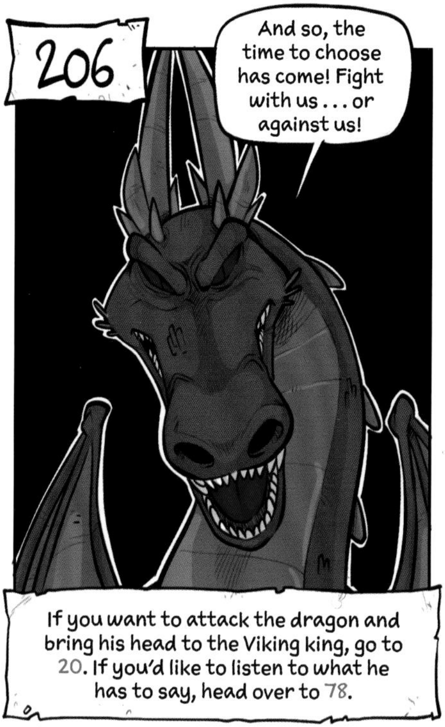
206
And so, the time to choose has come! Fight with us . . . or against us!
If you want to attack the dragon and bring his head to the Viking king, go to 20. If you'd like to listen to what he has to say, head over to 78.

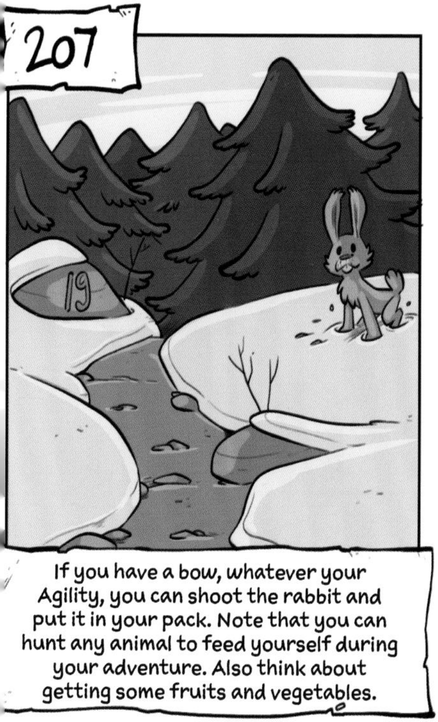
207
19
If you have a bow, whatever your Agility, you can shoot the rabbit and put it in your pack. Note that you can hunt any animal to feed yourself during your adventure. Also think about getting some fruits and vegetables.

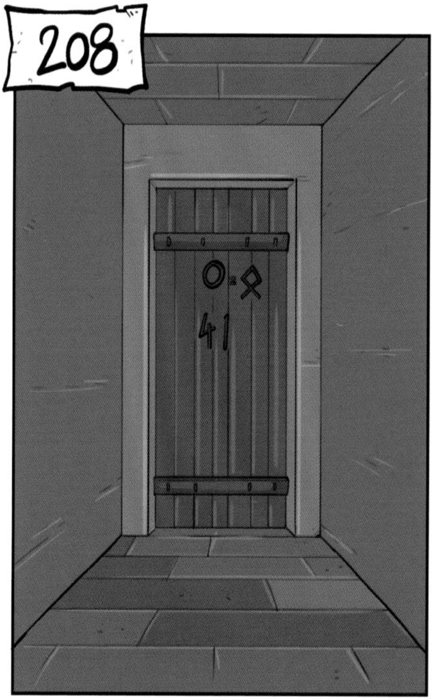
208
41

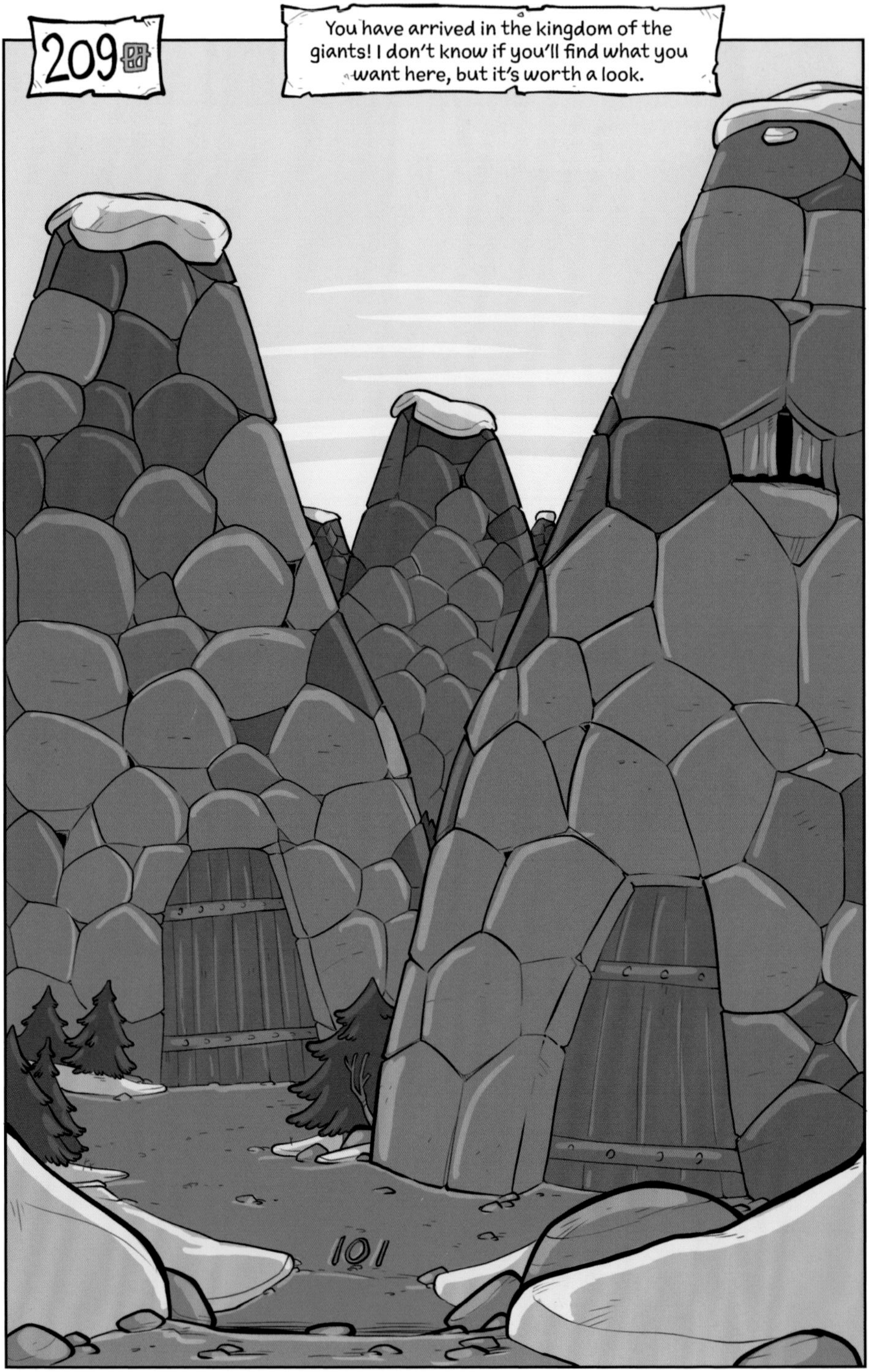
209
You have arrived in the kingdom of the giants! I don't know if you'll find what you want here, but it's worth a look.
101

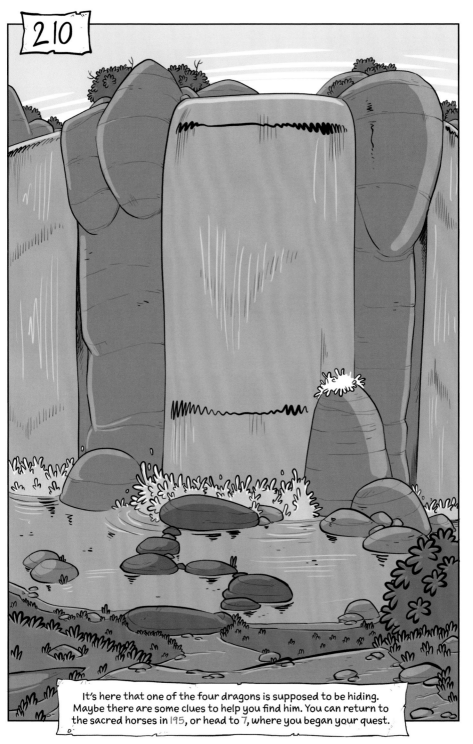

It's here that one of the four dragons is supposed to be hiding. Maybe there are some clues to help you find him. You can return to the sacred horses in 195, or head to 7, where you began your quest.

211

Ah yes, I remember now! Thank you, my friend. To reward you, here is a potion of Courage. I can't drink it. It's no use to me.

You can drink the potion (and perhaps discover some unknown side effects) or you can just put it in your pack. To leave the cemetery, go to 43.

212

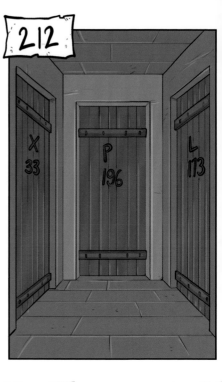

213

A flying leap? What does that mean? Don't get smart with me or I'll cut you in two and then execute you anyway! Last chance for you to have a decent fate: Why are you here?

To say that you came to rescue Princess Gargea, go to 35. To stick out your tongue at the king, go to 80. To stay silent, go to 28.

214

MULT	3		
SP	7	SQ	2
ATT		4	
RES		0	
SR		0	
XP		5	
LOOT		wolf pelt	

Running away is impossible. Fight valiantly, then go to 164, or begin the quest again on page 12 if you're defeated.

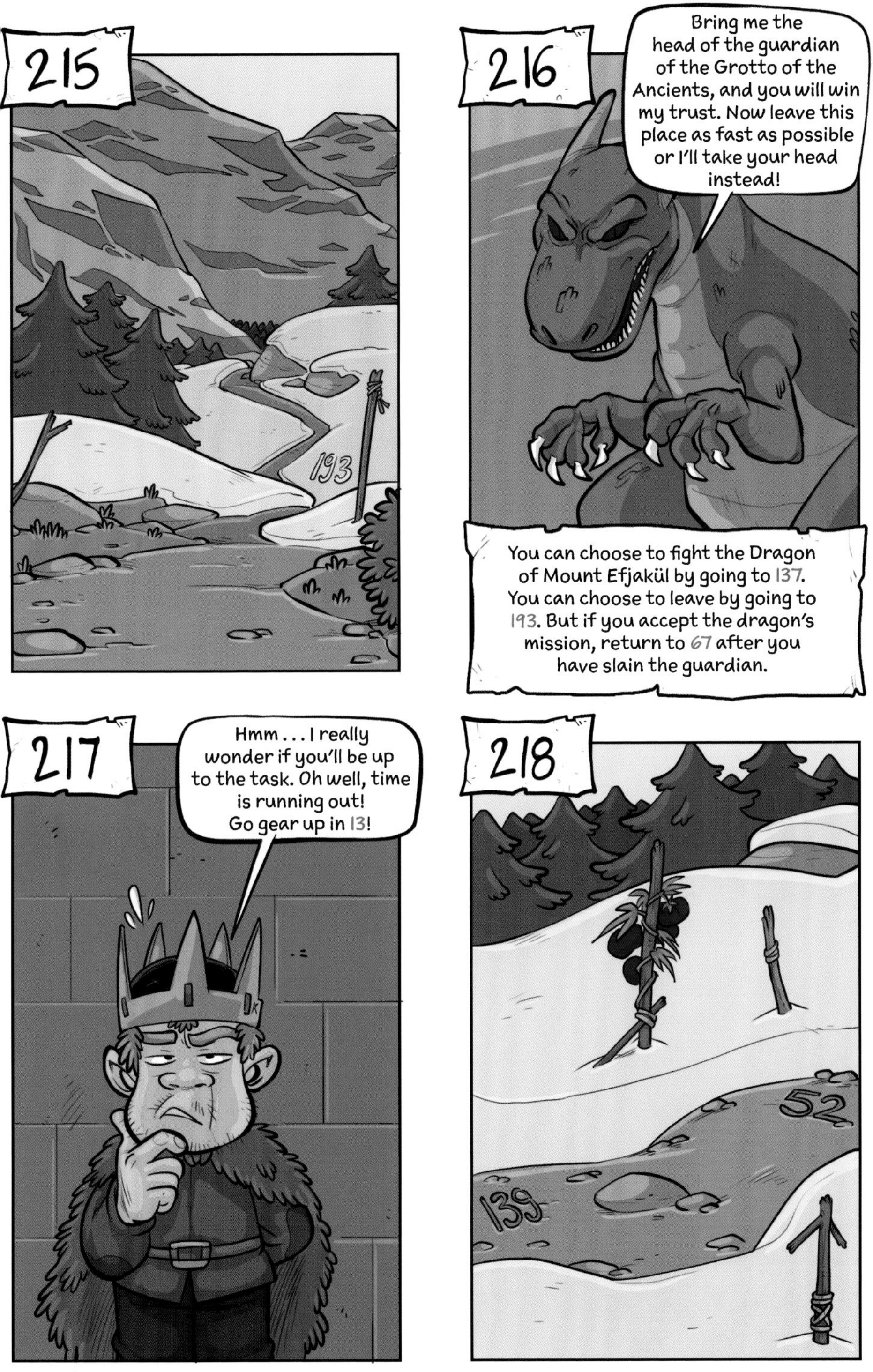
215
193
216
Bring me the head of the guardian of the Grotto of the Ancients, and you will win my trust. Now leave this place as fast as possible or I'll take your head instead!
You can choose to fight the Dragon of Mount Efjakül by going to 137. You can choose to leave by going to 193. But if you accept the dragon's mission, return to 67 after you have slain the guardian.
217
Hmm . . . I really wonder if you'll be up to the task. Oh well, time is running out! Go gear up in 13!
218
52
139

219

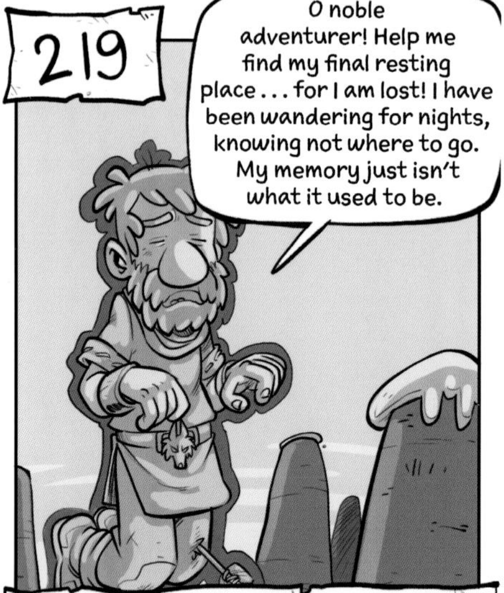
O noble adventurer! Help me find my final resting place . . . for I am lost! I have been wandering for nights, knowing not where to go. My memory just isn't what it used to be.

To help this unfortunate soul, go to 163, then head to 40 when you think you have the answer. If you don't want to help him, but still want to visit the cemetery, go to 163. If you'd like to turn back, go to 43. If you're playing as a squire or have at least 12 Intelligence points, get a clue in 53.

220

MULT	4		
SP	9	SQ	2
ATT	5		
RES	0		
SR	0		
XP	15		
LOOT	0		

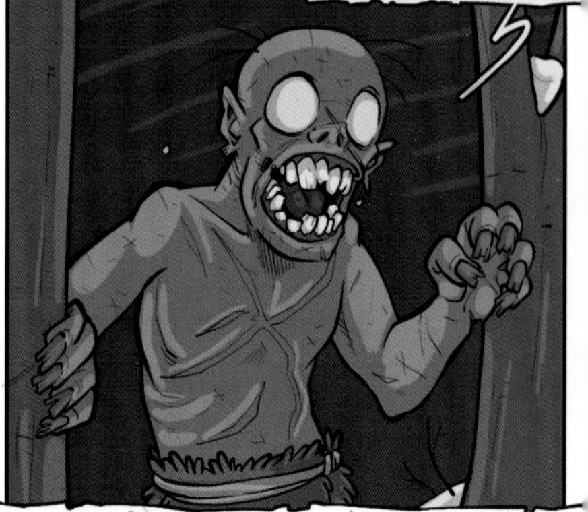

Another woods zombie! You attack first. If your first strike hits, you slice 6 Strike points from him (24 points if you're using a character from a previous adventure). If you win, go to 162.

221

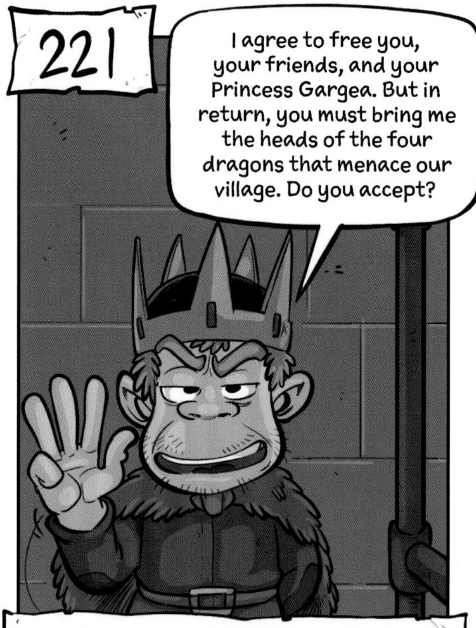
I agree to free you, your friends, and your Princess Gargea. But in return, you must bring me the heads of the four dragons that menace our village. Do you accept?

If you accept the mission without hesitation, go to 3. If you want to know more about the dragons, go to 111. To turn him down, go to 80.

222

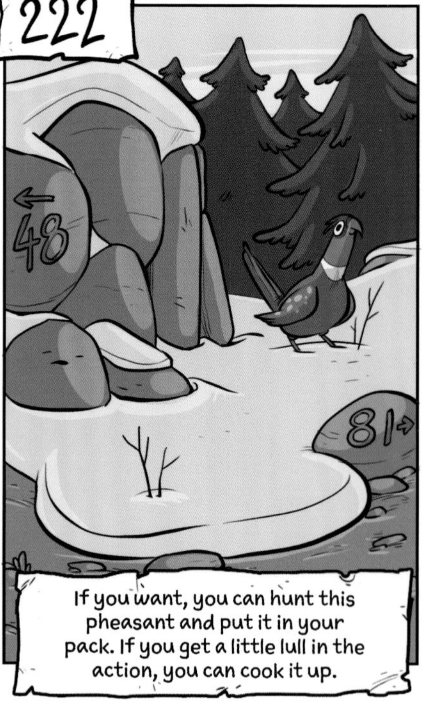
48
81

If you want, you can hunt this pheasant and put it in your pack. If you get a little lull in the action, you can cook it up.

223

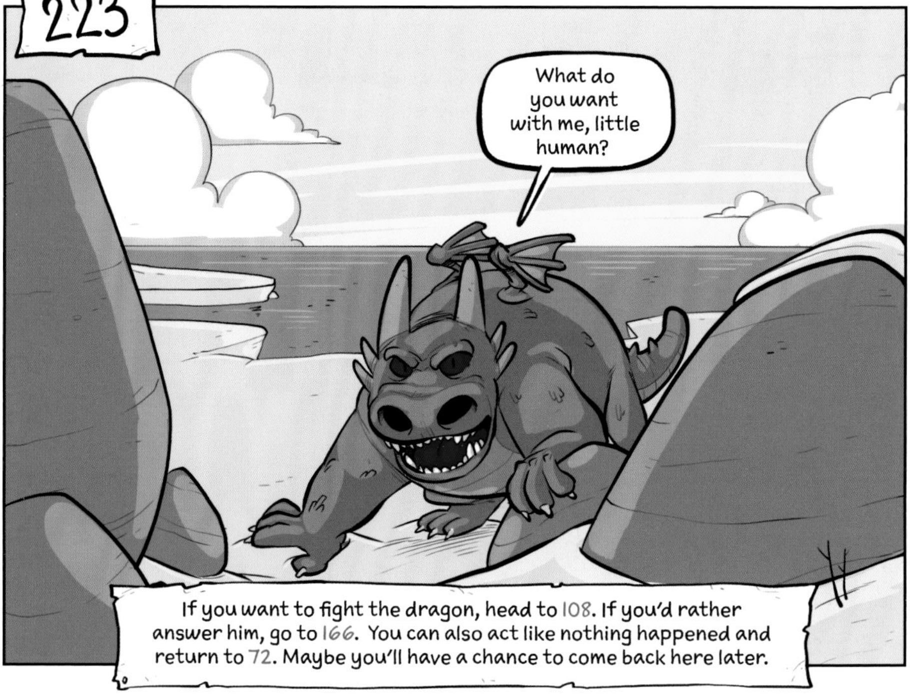
What do you want with me, little human?
If you want to fight the dragon, head to 108. If you'd rather answer him, go to 166. You can also act like nothing happened and return to 72. Maybe you'll have a chance to come back here later.

224

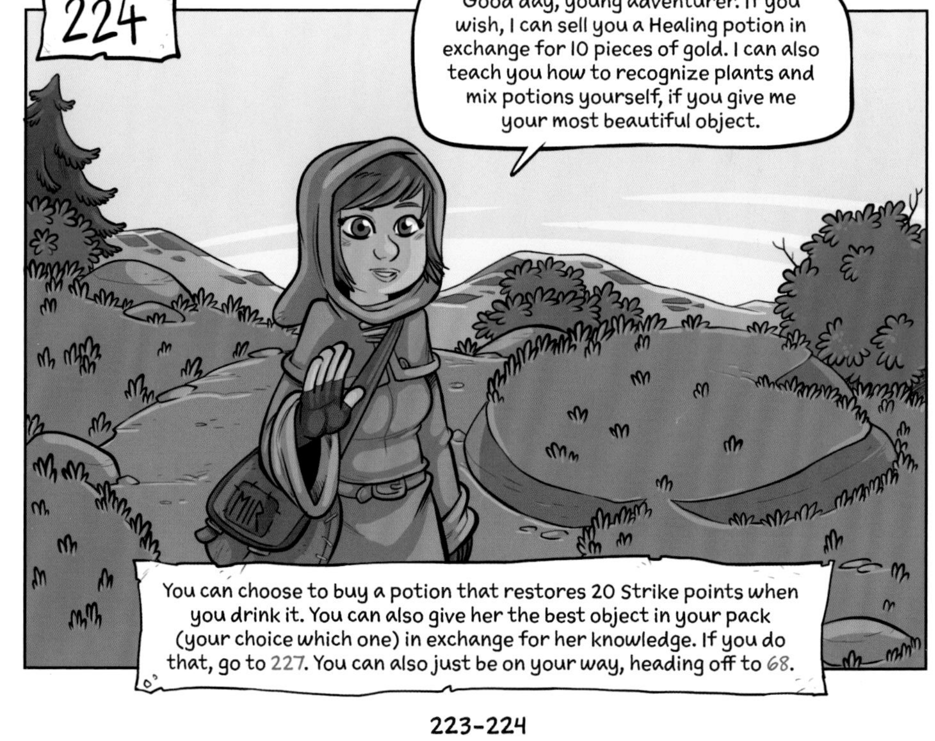
Good day, young adventurer. If you wish, I can sell you a Healing potion in exchange for 10 pieces of gold. I can also teach you how to recognize plants and mix potions yourself, if you give me your most beautiful object.
MIR
You can choose to buy a potion that restores 20 Strike points when you drink it. You can also give her the best object in your pack (your choice which one) in exchange for her knowledge. If you do that, go to 227. You can also just be on your way, heading off to 68.

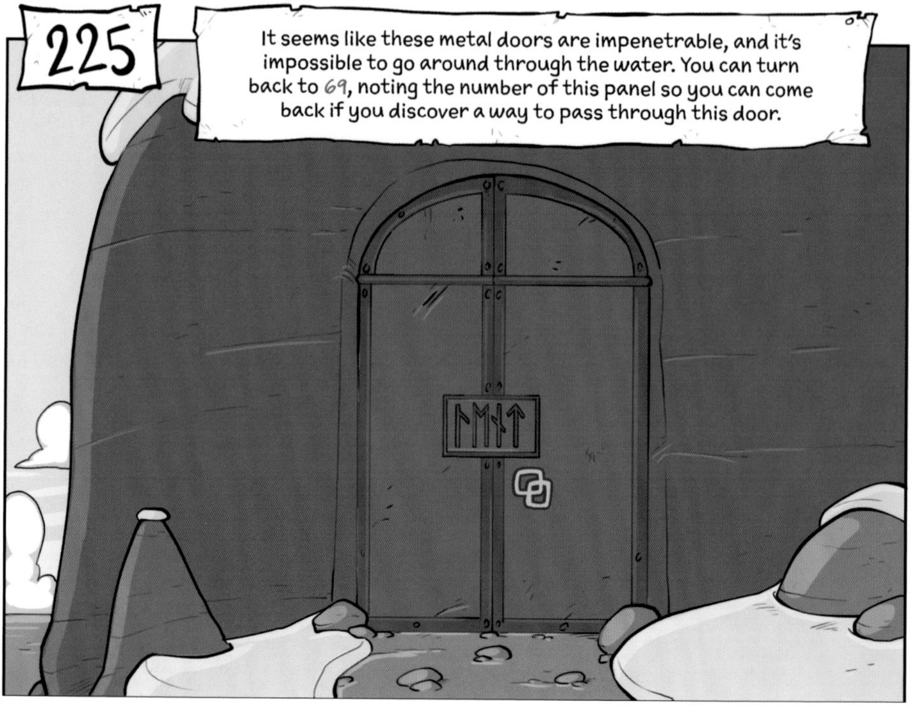
225
It seems like these metal doors are impenetrable, and it's impossible to go around through the water. You can turn back to 69, noting the number of this panel so you can come back if you discover a way to pass through this door.

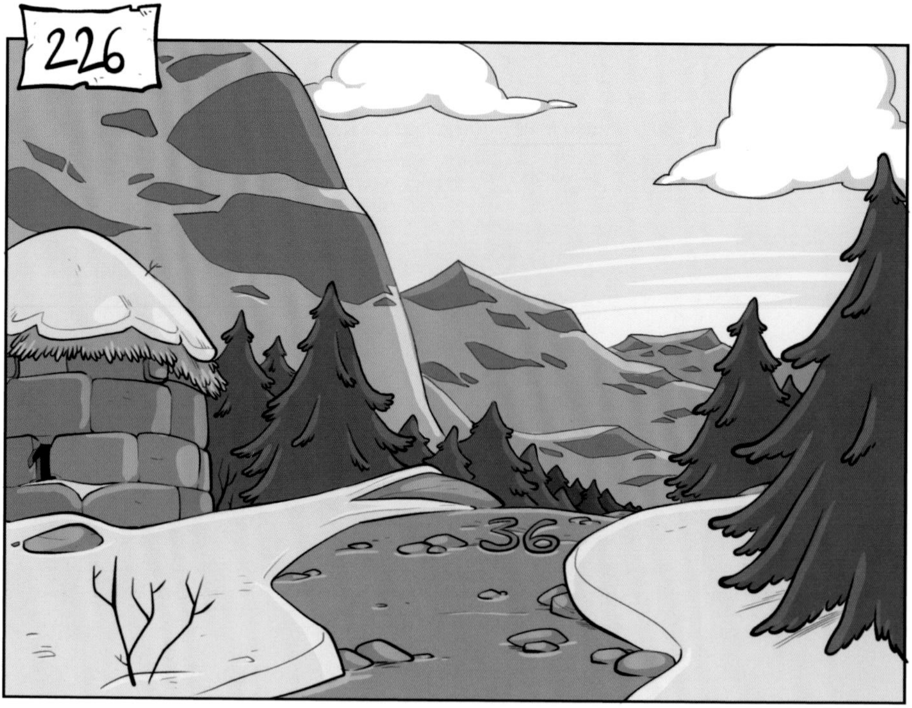
226
36

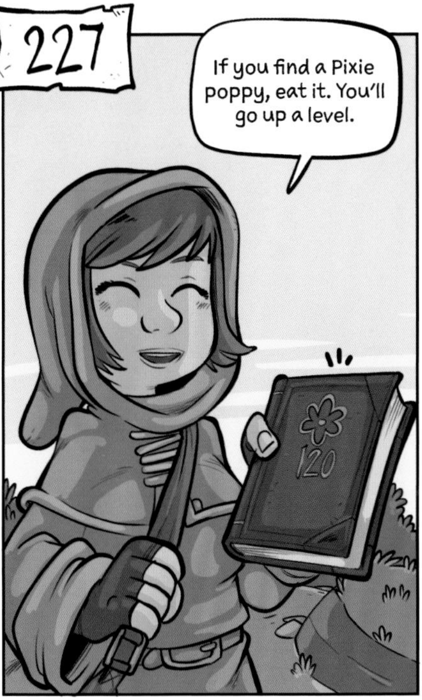
227
If you find a Pixie poppy, eat it. You'll go up a level.
120

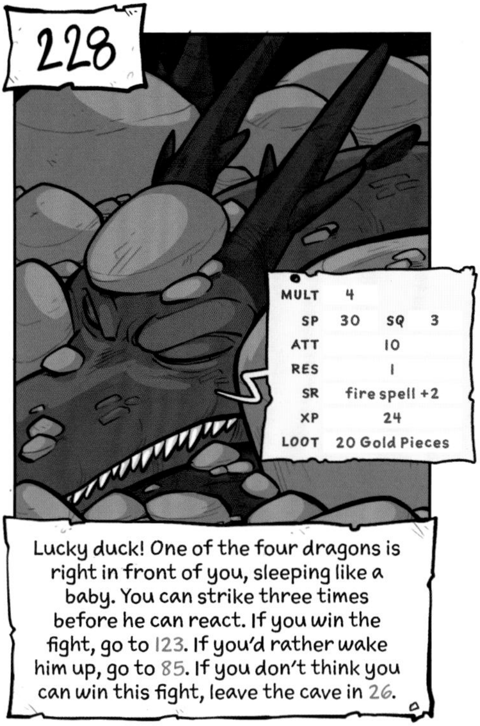
228
MULT 4
SP 30 SQ 3
ATT 10
RES 1
SR fire spell +2
XP 24
LOOT 20 Gold Pieces
Lucky duck! One of the four dragons is right in front of you, sleeping like a baby. You can strike three times before he can react. If you win the fight, go to 123. If you'd rather wake him up, go to 85. If you don't think you can win this fight, leave the cave in 26.

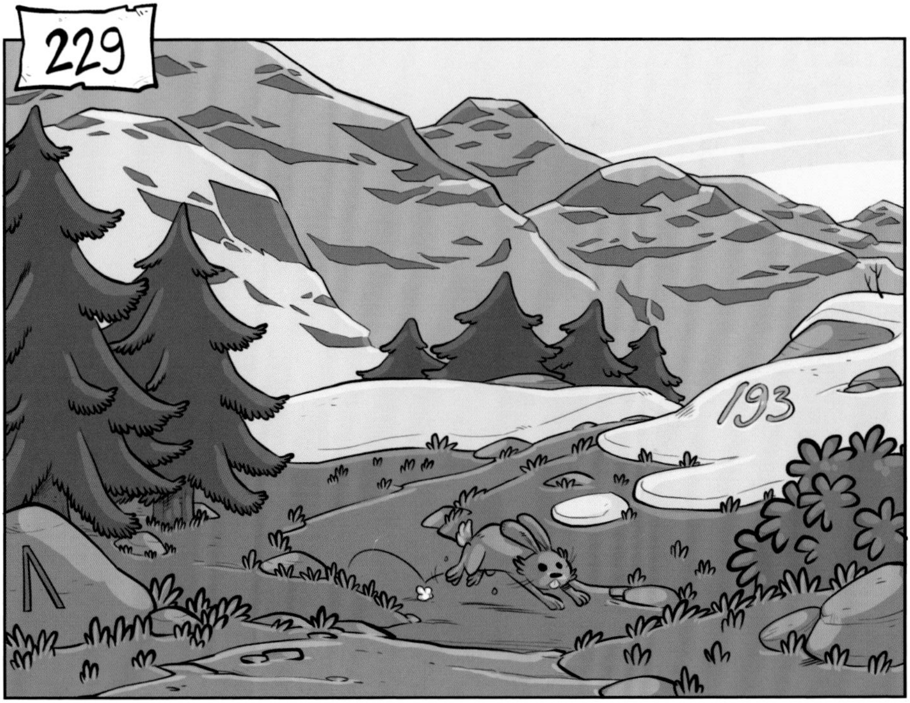
229
193

230

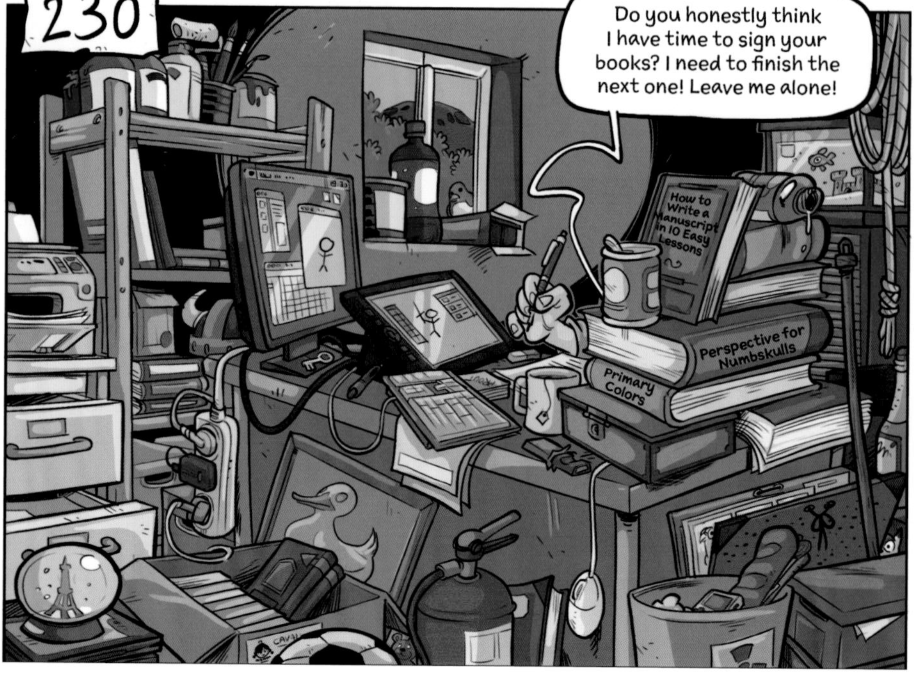
Do you honestly think I have time to sign your books? I need to finish the next one! Leave me alone!
How to Write a Manuscript in 10 Easy Lessons
Perspective for Numbskulls
Primary Colors

231

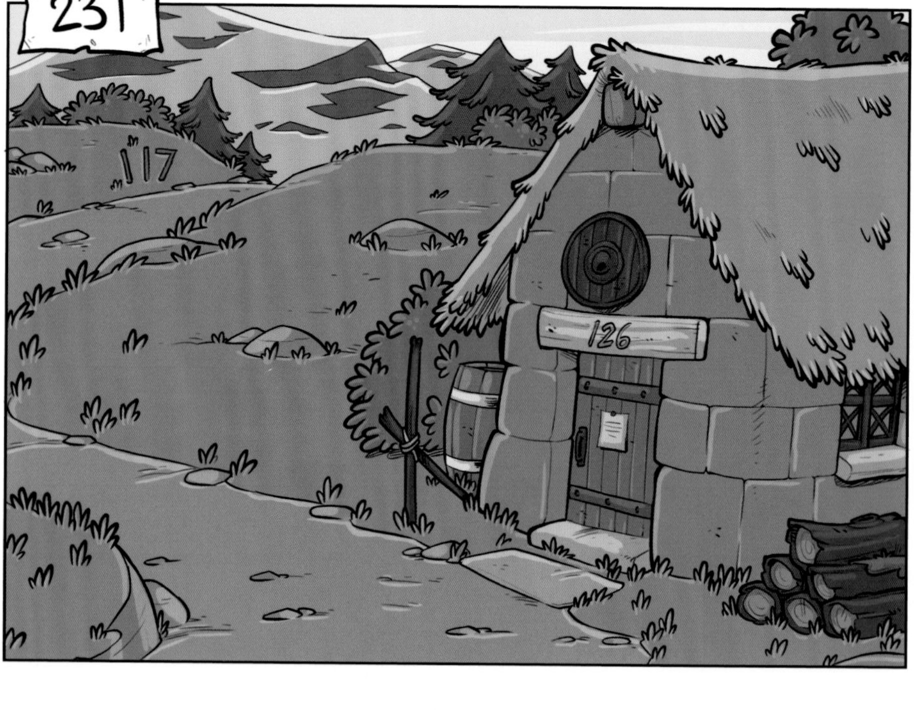
117
126

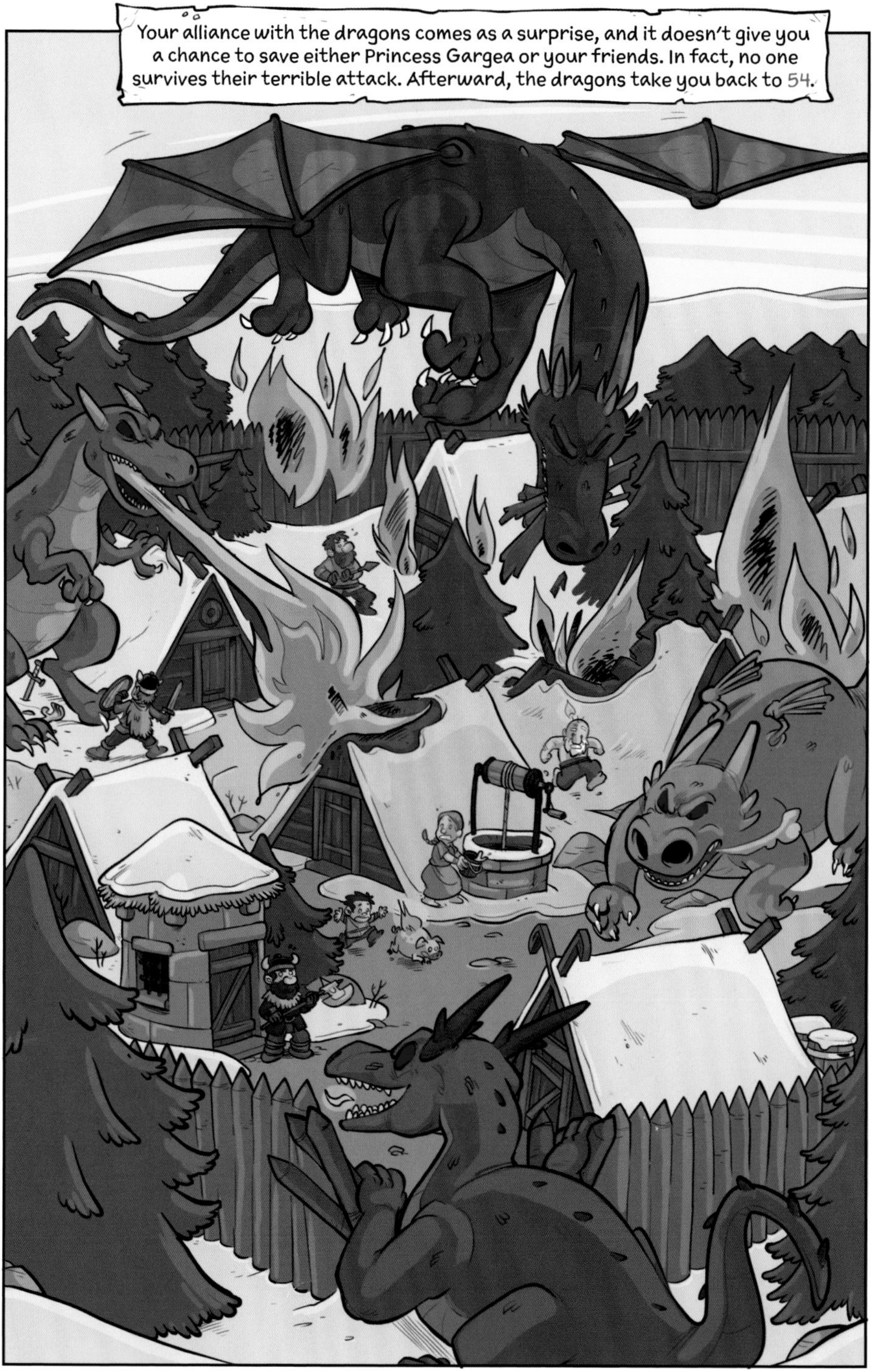
Your alliance with the dragons comes as a surprise, and it doesn't give you a chance to save either Princess Gargea or your friends. In fact, no one survives their terrible attack. Afterward, the dragons take you back to 54.

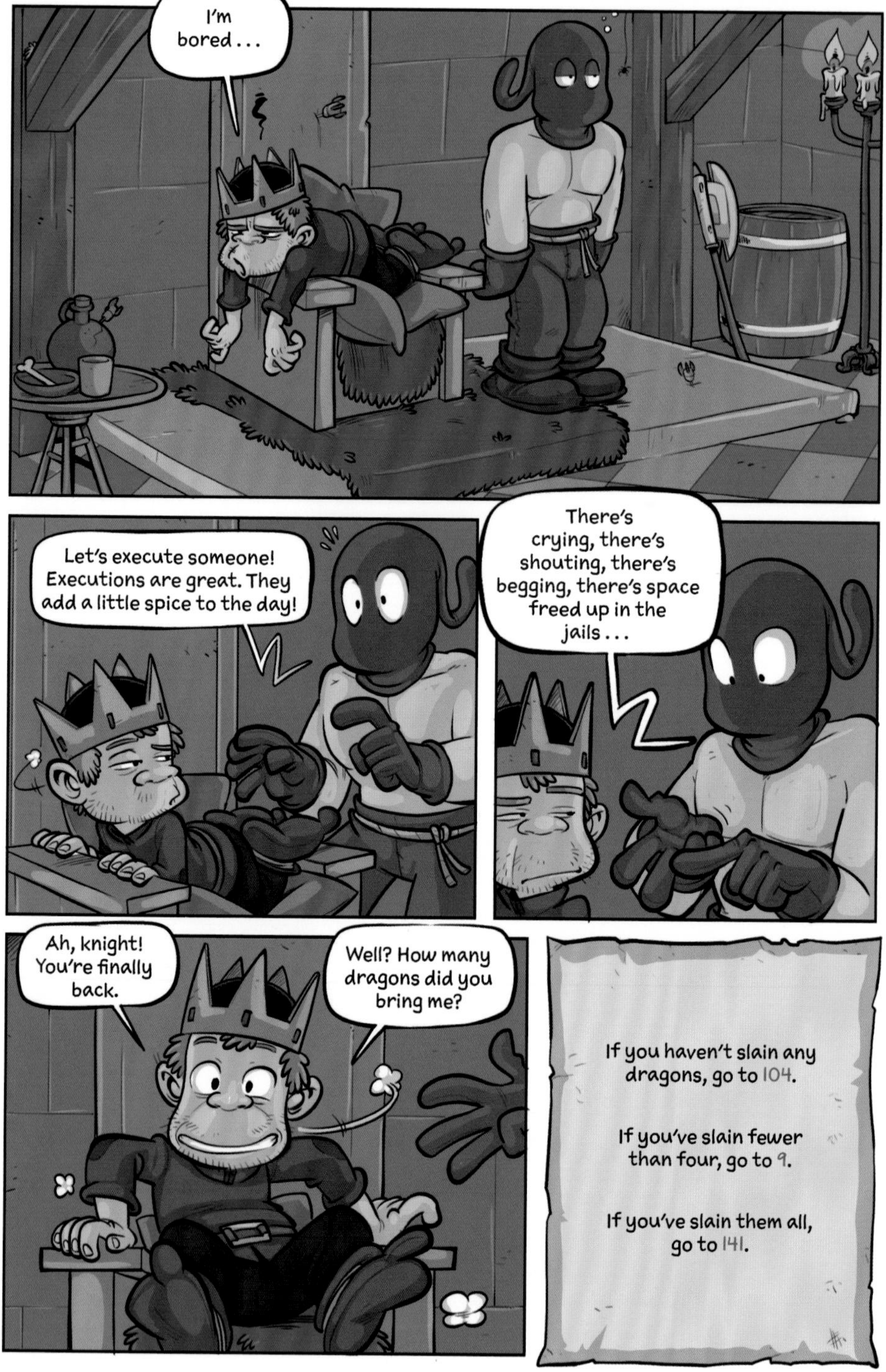
I'm bored...
Let's execute someone! Executions are great. They add a little spice to the day!
There's crying, there's shouting, there's begging, there's space freed up in the jails...
Ah, knight! You're finally back.
Well? How many dragons did you bring me?
If you haven't slain any dragons, go to 104.
If you've slain fewer than four, go to 9.
If you've slain them all, go to 141.

COMBAT WHEEL

Use this disk to fight the enemies you encounter on your adventure. If you are unable (or don't want) to cut it out, you can download one from comicquests.com. Then spin a pencil on top of the disk. Wherever the pencil tip stops is what you play.

No matter what resistances your foe has, your blow makes a total impact.

You do as much damage as a "Hit," but you can spin the wheel to attack again.

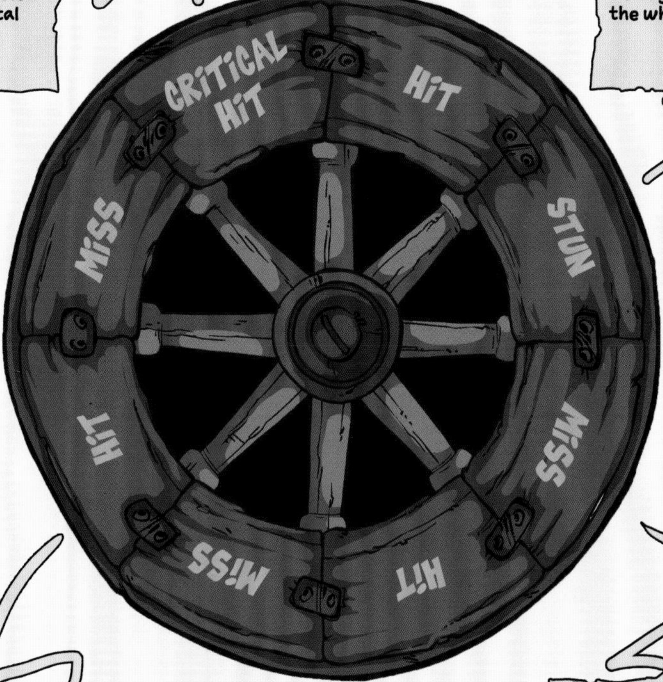
CRITICAL HIT
HIT
STUN
MISS
HIT
MISS
HIT
MISS

You've struck a blow, taking off as many of your foe's Strike points as you have Attack points, unless your enemy has Resistance points. For example:
5 Attack points – 2 Resistance points = 3 Strike points lost.
Also, if your foe has a Special Resistance against you, you must also subtract those Resistance points from the damage. For example: 5 Attack points – 2 Resistance points – 1 point of Resistance to archery = 2 Strike points lost (if you attacked with bow and arrow. If you used something else, the point of Resistance to archery isn't subtracted).

Your turn passes with no damage to your foe.

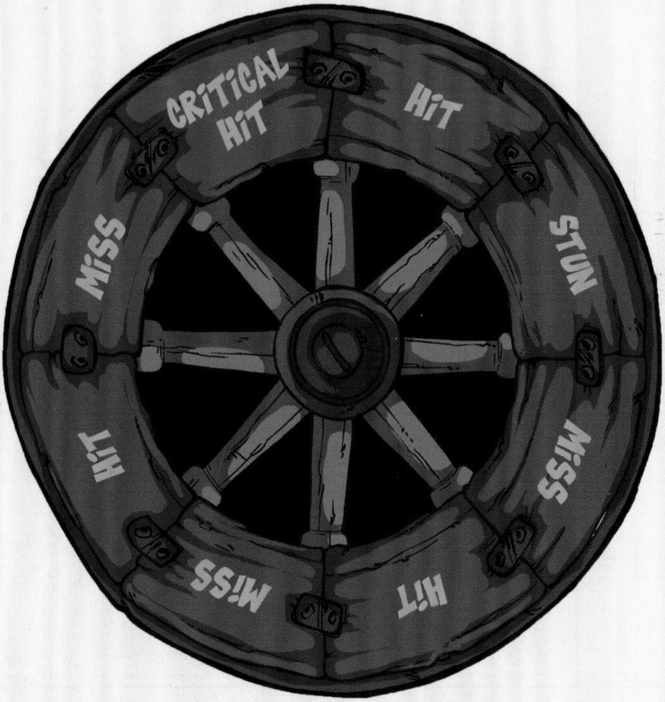
CRITICAL HIT
HIT
STUN
MISS
HIT
MISS
HIT
MISS

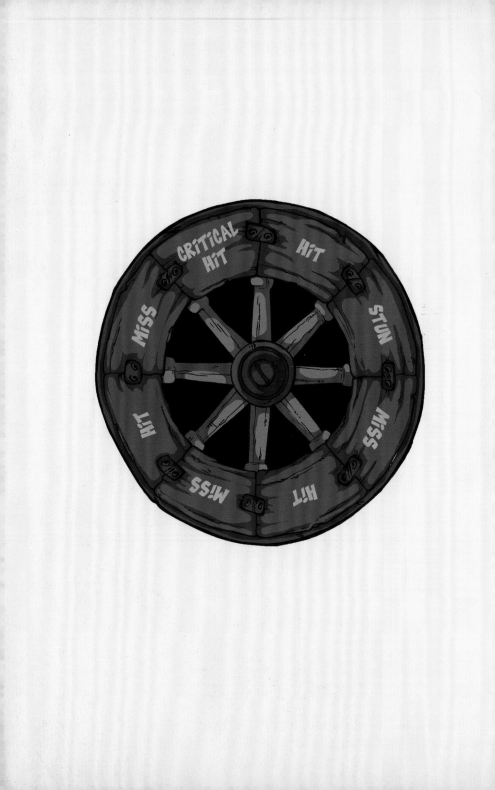